Waves the Color of Onyx

Leah Joanne

Earl Grey Sunday Press

Early Grey Sunday Press

Published by Earl Grey Sunday Press
Waves the Color of Onyx

www.leahjoannewriter.com
Book and Cover design by Reuben Upton.
Edited by Bethany Anderson.
ISBN: 979-8-991-8863-0-7
First Edition: December 2024
10 9 8 7 6 5 4 3 2 1

Waves the Color of Onyx

Book #1 in the "Onyx Series"

By Leah Joanne

To 18-year-old Leah and her mom.
Although years have passed,
thankfully my passion remained.
Now my dreams are finally fulfilled.
I couldn't have done this without you mom.

One

I CAN REMEMBER MELANIE telling me, "Valletta, loneliness kills faster than cigarettes, mi amor." I laughed at her ridiculous statement. Loneliness doesn't kill. Trust does.

Besides, I wasn't lonely. I was just busy, there's a difference. Yeah, sure, let me worry about dating someone when I have to work double shifts as a waitress to pay my bills. I could give in and get a roommate to help manage the rent . . . but my apartment is the one thing that's mine. I've worked hard to get myself through college with no help. My two friends and my apartment, that's all I have; that's all that matters. Sleeping pills are my solace, forcing my memories to remain dormant so I can make it through the night. But hey, I have to do what works, and I'm okay with that.

I would be lying if I didn't admit to that part of me that wonders what that connection feels like . . . you know, the kind that people write songs about? I'm twenty-three and have never really dated anyone. So, I guess that's why I'm here tonight. Of course, Chad's picture didn't hurt, on top of Melanie's endless nagging.

I practically spit out my latte.

"A therapist named Chad?" I laugh. "Oh Mel, that's too good. Oh, and he goes to hot yoga?" Just the thought of him made me cringe. "I'm

not that desperate." I shake my head at her. Then one day, when she finally hadn't mentioned him for an entire week, she gasps.

"¡Ay, Dios Mio!" she squeals, rushing over to me, "this is like, totally fate!" She shoves her phone in my face. "This is Chad! You guys are a match!"

I grab her phone, looking it over quickly, confused about how I'm looking at my profile on Bumble and yet I'm holding her phone.

"Mel, why do you have MY profile on YOUR phone?!" I accuse her, glaring into her big brown eyes.

She waves away my anger as if it's an unpleasant fart, "That's not what's important right now! You are going on a date with him and that's final." She crosses her arms like she means business.

So, here I am. With Chad. The therapist from Melanie's hot yoga class.

The light catches the sparkles on my nails as they hold the stem of the crystal wine glass. It's been ages since I put in the effort to get a proper manicure. I slide my other hand down the uncomfortably tight black dress Melanie shoved me into, tugging it over my knee. My hand settles there for a moment, a smile forcing my Very Berry colored lips apart, a color I'm hoping complements my olive skin tone. I sip my merlot while Chad tells me about his life. I must admit, he has some funny stories. Despite how skeptical I was to go on this date, I notice my smile is lingering, a gesture my muscles are not used to making. Honestly, my best friend Mark has been the only guy to ever make me truly smile. His friendship means more to me than any boyfriend could, anyway. Between Melanie setting me up on dates and Mark constantly cooking for me to ensure I have nutritious food to eat, I think it's safe to say my friends think I'm a train wreck. But I don't resist, because even though I wouldn't dare admit it out loud . . . I need them.

As I take another sip of my merlot, my smile still intact, Chad stops talking, clears his throat, and sits upright.

"I've been talking too much. Please, tell me more about you." He looks at me with anticipation. I shift awkwardly in my chair, removing my hand from the seam of my dress and sliding it over my sandy-brown waves, hoping my hair isn't starting to frizz.

"There's really not much to tell." Sharpness accidentally comes out in my tone.

"I know that can't be true; Melanie's told me some things." He smirks. "I would guess you must be quite flexible and disciplined to hang from those ropes in all those different positions." His face twitches, a smirk appearing despite his attempt to hold a genuine expression.

"I'm sorry?" Oh no, is this guy a creep after all? I knew I couldn't trust a guy named Chad, or Melanie's taste in guys for that matter.

He tilts his head with a hint of confusion. "Aerial dancing? It looks intense. I looked it up because I had no idea what it was. Melanie said how much you love it."

Just kill me now.

I swallow, trying to figure out what on earth he's talking about, then I remember. Melanie, oh Melanie, I am truly going to kill her. She made me go to an aerial class one time because she found a Groupon for it. I was horrendous at it and never did it again. Of course, that didn't stop her from adding it to the list of my non-existent impressive accomplishments so I could bait good old Chad here.

Chad thinks he's on a date with a gorgeous, flexible aerial dancer. I smile, but this time completely fake, an expression my muscles are much more comfortable making.

Grabbing my wine, I take a big gulp, then steady myself, preparing to lie.

"Well, it certainly is a challenge," I smile awkwardly as my eyes drift to my nails again.

"You really don't like talking about yourself, do you?"

"What? Me? Oh, you're mistaken, Chad, I love talking about myself! It's my all-time favorite topic. Really, it is!" I cringe at my shrill, sarcastic voice. As if they have a mind of their own, my fingers stray to one of my curls, dangling at my shoulder. I'm silently imagining myself pulling my hair, almost feeling the burning sensation on my scalp, trying to get relief from this excruciating moment. It's not as satisfying as actually pulling my hair, but I don't want to look any crazier than I already do. Maybe he found my response cute and charming. I look at his face and it's clear he thought it was anything but cute and charming. I can tell he's feeling the awkward tension.

"Valletta, I'm sorry if I offended you. I just want to learn a little about you. That is usually what a date is all about, right? Getting to know each other."

"You're right. Sorry. I guess I'm just not used to talking about myself." I take another gulp of my merlot, then steady myself, sitting upright. "So, what do you want to know?"

He smiles. "We can start simple. Do you have any siblings?"

My palms sweat. "Yes."

He's silent with an expression of encouragement, waiting for me to go on.

"A sister." I pause. "Older sister."

"Are you guys close?"

"I thought you said we were starting simple," I say under my breath.

"I'm sorry?" Chad squints his eyes at me as if that will help him hear better.

"No, Chad, we are not close." I rush to take another sip of merlot, but there's barely any left. My eyes dart around the dimly lit restaurant, frantically looking for the waiter for a refill. I catch the waiter's eye, and I point to my wine glass as if I'm letting him know the restaurant is on fire.

"Wow." Chad chuckles, scratching his head. "Okay, we didn't like the sibling question. How about where you grew up? Was it here in San Diego?" He picks up his IPA and sips it while staring at me uncomfortably. Like he's trying to figure me out.

I despise this.

"Yes, I grew up right here in San Diego." I take a deep breath. I just need to get that merlot, and I can get through this stupid interrogation disguised as a 'date'.

"Where in San Diego?"

"Well, definitely nowhere near Encinitas." I can't hide my sarcastic tone. He tilts his head to the side, like a confused dog, not understanding why being from Encinitas is significant in any way. "Point Loma. Not too far from where I live now." I lie.

"Oh, that's not too far from Encinitas." He smiles. "Hey, maybe I saw you around in the summer. I'm sure we went to the same beaches." It takes all my self-control not to visibly roll my eyes. I'm starting to not like this Chad after all. "So, your parents must still live close by?"

I cough in response, picking up the bread that has been signaling me as a tap-out button.

"Mhm," I nod and stuff the bread in my mouth to avoid talking. He looks defeated.

"Melanie did say you were a tough nut to crack." He sighs.

"Oh, she did, did she?" I aggressively tear off another piece of bread, slowly caring less and less what Chad thinks of me. The waiter finally answers my SOS and comes far too late with a bottle of red.

"So, are we ready to order?" he asks as he pours my relief. We place our orders, and as soon as the waiter leaves, a heavy silence falls over the table. I embrace the silence, looking around the restaurant. The lighting is dim, people are chatting quietly, the music is soft lo-fi beats. Everyone seems to be in their own world. I spot someone who's sitting at a table for one. I can't help but notice how attractive this man is. His curls are dark and they look so soft. I wish I could just go over there and touch them. But what catches my eye more than anything else is the look of concentration on his face as he writes in a small leather journal. He seems completely unaware that he's in a restaurant full of people. I'm fascinated by him. I mean this isn't a café, it's a fine boutique dining restaurant, a place I could never afford. I'm only here because Chad insisted on buying me dinner here. The more I watch this mystery man across the restaurant, the more my heart almost skips a beat . . . There's something about him that's captivating. He looks at his watch; I wonder if he's waiting for a date? Suddenly, I wish more than anything I could drift over from this table to that one. That's the date I want to be on. There's no way that guy is named Chad.

I'm startled by Chad clearing his throat. Oh gosh, how long was I spacing out? I feel myself blush. I smile at Chad as I grab my wine glass, bringing the much-needed red liquid to my lips. Chad also grabs his IPA and takes a long gulp. He slowly puts down his glass.

"Well, clearly this isn't working." My eyes dart to his in confusion. Did he really just say that before our entrées even come out? "You know, I'm a therapist, and I just want you to know that I would be more than happy to help you if you need someone." He looks directly into my eyes. "You know, Valletta, it might be liberating to free yourself of that dark cloud you're living under." He reaches into his pocket and pulls out a small business card.

He continues, oblivious to the daggers shooting from my eyes. "I know I'm new, but I'm legit, and I'm just starting to build a clientele, so I could definitely work with you on your budget."

My mouth falls open, and I stupidly look down at his business card. The nerve. The absolute nerve. I'm too stunned to even reply. I'm afraid if I speak, I'll just scream.

"I'm not trying to offend you. I just think maybe that would be a more fitting relationship between the two of us right now. I'm sorry to be so direct. I've never been one to waste time or beat around the bush. I mean, you agree, right?"

It's official, Chad is a douchebag. My gut is always right.

I look at him, the shock wearing off. "Wow, I am SO thankful we had this dinner—well, this bread and wine." I jab my eyes at him. "I mean, I really can't thank you enough for your intuition and wise words. Are you sure you don't want me to pay you extra for this almost dinner? I mean, how much do you charge per hour anyway?" Chad's face is white.

I stand up from the table. "You know, I think the bread might be bad; I'm suddenly not feeling so well." I grab my glass of merlot and down what's left.

"It was lovely," I continue, on a roll, "You have a lovely night. Oh, and Chad is such a great name for a therapist. I'm sure people open right up to you!" Shaking with adrenaline, I start to walk away. I stop a few feet from the table, then turn around. "Whoops! I almost forgot this." I pick up the business card, shaking my head sarcastically. Walking away, I squeeze the card so tightly the sharp corners pierce my skin. It's ironically symbolic.

As if in slow motion, for just a moment, the dark, curly-haired man with the small leather journal catches my eye, and I'm taken aback by the darkness in his eyes.

Then, before I know it, the fresh San Diego breeze hits me in the face, and my stomach is in my chest, the contents threatening to come up. I steady myself against the stucco wall outside of the restaurant, trying to calm my rapid breathing.

Stumbling into my apartment, the wine from dinner still running through me, I throw my bag onto the floor and flop down on my couch. Feeling anger and frustration starting to build inside, I grab my phone and hit the call button. Mel is huffing on the other line.

"Hey, sweet cheeks!"

I roll my eyes, not able to handle her craziness right now. "Mel, I don't even know where to begin with you. Aerial dancing?! Are you kidding me?!"

"Calm down, you're aggravating my positive vibes."

"Are you doing yoga? It's midnight!"

"Of course I am." She lets out an exaggerated breath, "It's great to relax before bed." She says things so nonchalantly that she seems to convince herself that she's perfectly normal. "Okay, so what's your crisis? Wait, how did the date go? You should still be with him, strolling along the water under the midnight moon, eating gelato."

I can hear the frown in her voice as she realizes her fairy tale evening wasn't happening.

"Oh, it was AMAZING. Literally the best date I've ever been on. In fact, I'm holding his business card right now. He said he might even give me a discount." My voice is like gravel.

"Oh no." I can pretty much hear Melanie fall out of her pose from disappointment. "What did he say?" She's anxious to hear.

"You know Mel, I don't know if I'll be able to tell you. I'm such a tough nut to crack after all." I'm not letting her get away with any of this. "Oh, and apparently I'm living under a cloud of darkness!"

"He said that?" Melanie's voice is surprised.

"That's not all!" I'm fired up.

"Well, good."

Her words hit me like a brick smashing into me.

"Did you just say, well, good?"

"Look, he's honest! You need that! Someone had to say it, Valletta. I knew he was a good match for you." Her 'told you so' tone makes my fist clench.

"This has to be a nightmare right now. There's no way you're taking his side on this."

"I'm only on your side, I always have been. I love you so much it's gross. I wish you could see that. So that's why I'm going to say this out of nothing but pure love. Stop with the self-pity already; you do it every time. I can't just sit back and watch you hide behind yourself anymore. It's just not healthy. Open up for goodness' sake! I wasn't even on that date tonight and I'm sure he put in all the effort and you gave him nothing to work with. Am I wrong?"

There's silence on my phone. I close my eyes, pinching back tears that threaten to escape. The silence lingers because I refuse to talk with a cracked voice. I don't want to give her the satisfaction of knowing she is completely right.

She sighs, "I'm sorry, I know I'm being harsh." Silence.

"I should get to bed. I need to sleep this wine off." I keep my tone pure and even, not a hint of emotion.

"Valletta, wait! Please don't go like this. We can talk this out. I didn't mean-"

I interrupt her, raising my voice suddenly to drown out her thoughts. "Look, forget it, Mel! You're right, okay? Is that what you want to hear?"

"No, I don't care about being right, all I care about is your happiness."

"Melanie, just stop! Okay?" I sigh, needing this conversation to end. "Look, I need to get some sleep."

"Okay." Her voice is soft and dripping with pity. I hate pity.

"Goodnight. I love you." She whispers.

"Night, you too." The words barely come out, but then merciful silence finally comes when I hit that red button and drop my phone on the floor in the dark.

I would give anything to just drift away right here on my couch. But there's no sleeping pill on my couch, and that's the only thing that will bring me any relief tonight. I don't bother turning any lights on. I make my way to the bedroom, feeling my way by sliding my hands along the walls. I crash onto my bed, feeling the rumble of a plane flying overhead through my mattress. The noise mercifully quiets my thoughts. I hold the capsule in the streak of light coming through the slit in my curtains.

I swallow it dry, gladly letting the darkness overtake me.

Two

ONE DAY, I WOULD like to just look at myself in the mirror and feel comfortable in my own skin. Wake up and smile just for the sake of being alive. Meal prep even!

Today, however, is not that day.

Today is the kind of day where I need to ignore the wallet-friendly option of making my coffee in my French press. Instead, I'm sinking into my favorite chair at Catalina's Café and sipping a steaming six-dollar latte. Letting the magic coffee seep into my bloodstream, washing away the date from hell that I lived through just twelve hours ago.

The high industrial ceilings in Catalina's allow for perfect acoustics. You can hear people's chatter flowing through the room without being able to make out a conversation properly. The perfect background of noises lets my brain rest without being too silent. The silence always kills me.

My favorite chair nestles between two palms, perfectly hidden away. Each time the door opens, the breeze carries the scent of fresh coffee beans, making my nostrils flare. My eyes close for a moment, settling into the comforts that are holding me together. The door opens. I breathe in deep. Before opening my eyes, my senses hone in on something different in the air. It's as if a cedar tobacco candle was lit and blended into the coffee beans. I anxiously open my eyes to see where this glorious smell is coming from.

I'm sure my eyes widen in size as I take him in. Jet-black curls softly falling over his forehead. Even with just the side profile, I recognize him. My eyes travel down to his navy-blue button up shirt, the collar grazing his Adam's apple. A dark brown leather bag is draped over his shoulder.

It's him. The man I saw leaving the restaurant last night. The man who was laser focused on writing in his small leather journal as he was waiting for someone. I can't help but wonder if he was stood up last night, or if he was even meeting anyone in the first place. What are the chances I see him the next day? The mystery man with jet-black curls checks his watch while waiting in line. I strain my ear to try and hear his order, for the first time annoyed at how airy this place is.

He turns around, his eyes exploring the café. I freeze like a deer in headlights, holding my breath. As soon as his front profile is fully exposed, there's no mistake. Black eyes pierce outward, demanding attention. I try to pull my gaze away, knowing how creepy I must look, but I can't. I'm drawn to him in a way I've never been drawn to anyone. By pure lust.

I haven't heard one word come out of his mouth and for some strange reason I am yearning to know him, desperate to hear even one syllable escape his lips.

My nervous system explodes, vibration running down my leg followed by a few drips of my steaming latte.

"Ouch!" I whisper to myself, rubbing my jeans, trying to cool the hot liquid. My phone ringing pulls me out of this consuming curiosity and back to reality. I glance at the screen. It's my boss. How does he always call at the worst times?

"Yes, Gregg?"

"Oh, good, I caught you. Hey, I need you to fill in. I got a call out. Could you come in for the last shift?" Working on my one night off this week feels like the last straw, a herald to my looming breakdown. But, unfortunately, I need the money.

"Fine," I groan.

"You are the absolute best Valletta. I owe you one!"

"Yeah, no problem, Gregg." I swallow my annoyance. He owes me a million times over. I guess that's what happens when you are way too willing to say yes all the time. Granted, I will work every shift available if it means I don't need to get a roommate.

As soon as I hang up, my eyes scan the room in desperation, hoping I didn't lose my mystery man.

Then I spot him, sitting near the wall of local artists. His chair is directly facing me. I love looking at that wall, seeing the uninterpretable brush strokes of people's minds. In a room full of headphones and laptops, he is sitting with only a pen and the same leather journal from last night in hand.

What is in that journal?

In my mind, I'm walking right over to him to find out. A small smile forms on my lips at the thought of being that brave.

Instead, I take a long sip of my overpriced latte, promising myself to make coffee at home for the rest of the week. But then again, maybe it's worth the six dollars for another chance to see the mystery man with those intense eyes. As I stand up, I keep my gaze on him, hoping for a bit of rom-com magic. He would glance up at just the right moment, meeting my gaze with a soft smile, suddenly just as desperate to know me. I yearn for the courage to make that moment happen.

Sighing, reality kicks in and my thoughts become clear. Because what would be the point anyway? Why ruin a good fantasy with the sad bite of reality? As I walk away, he doesn't even glance up from concentrating on whatever words he's writing in that small leather journal.

And now I'm off to therapy. The last place I want to go. Although, a twenty-three-year-old waitress who can't even approach a man at a coffee shop, and who has never once put herself out there, should probably be going to therapy.

With a lump of self-pity in my throat, I leave Catalina's, deciding not to look back at him one last time.

"What do you want to talk about today?" Dr. Sage asks, her pen hovering above the notepad, as if to threaten that whatever I say is 'on record'.

I shrug, focusing on her silvery-blonde hair tucked back, only a few strands floating free. Just behind her is a cactus on the windowsill, bathed in sunlight.

"We could start with how your week went?" She tilts her head to the side, in predictable concern. The kind of concern that you know people are trained to show.

"I don't have much to share. The week was fine." I swallow, determined to shove down any mention of last night's horrors. I don't feel like prolonging this appointment today. Or any day really.

"Did you have any nightmares this week or trouble sleeping?"

"I slept well. I think I just might need a refill on the sleeping pills." I try to act casual with my request. My greatest fear is her cutting me off because I'm acting too desperate. Granted, I have no idea how that works.

"We will talk about that at the end of the session. For now, let's focus on what may be making you need those pills." Her smile seems genuine, but I don't trust it.

"Okay," I say softly, not sure what to say, my mental energy drained already.

"Did you ever call your mother back?" Dr. Sage crosses her leg and repositions herself as if she's getting ready to finally write something down.

The word "mother" sends shooting pains into my heart.

"No," I say simply.

"Has that been weighing on your mind this week?"

My finger starts tapping my knee. I'm trying hard not to pick at my nails. I rub my pointer nail, it's smooth from the polish. The feeling gives me the restraint to not start picking so as not to ruin them.

"I can't tell yet. Do you think we can table that for another week? I need more time to process it."

"Sure." She half-heartedly smiles, her pen finally making contact with her notepad. My heart sinks. She can see right through my lies.

"You know Valletta, no medication can do what talking things out can do." Her voice is level, confident even.

I can only imagine what her notes are saying. I exhale, giving in, picking the dry skin around my nails.

For the rest of the session, I focus on the cactus, imagining the warmth of the sun on my skin. Holding out until I get my prescription refill.

"Am I imagining it, or did Melanie get replaced by a far less annoying, beautiful brunette with hazel eyes?" Mark grins as he circles around me.

"You are so bad." I shake my head at Mark's sarcastic way of asking why I'm at work tonight and not Melanie. I seem to be her regular shift filler at this point. I would be more upset if Melanie wasn't working herself to death trying to juggle grad school and work. Mark and Melanie act as if the other is the most annoying person in the world. But I know deep down they care about each other. It's like siblings who constantly bicker but always end up hanging out because they have the same friends. I am that friend.

"So . . . how was your day?" Mark asks slowly, as if I'll have something life-altering to tell him.

"It was fine." I shrug, trying to put my therapy session out of my mind. I focus on putting on my apron, preparing mentally for my shift.

"Wow, sounds thrilling," Mark says sarcastically while sipping his coffee. "Nice blouse by the way. But you know you have a stain on it, right?" He points to a coffee stain I somehow missed. Shows how together I am.

"Perfect, just perfect," I groan.

"Hey, hey now, don't worry Letta. You still look stunning." He grins, flashing his perfect Crest commercial smile. I roll my eyes, such an obvious flirt. At this point his compliments mean nothing.

"Come on, I have a Tide stick." He sips his coffee and tilts his head in the direction of his bag. "Here. Don't cry over spilled coffee." He hands me his Tide stick, his smile softer now, more real.

"Thanks."

"You okay?" His bright green eyes are searching me over, looking for an answer to his question.

"I'm fine. You know I just hate when you call me Letta," I answer playfully, not wanting him to keep searching for answers.

"Oh stop, you totally love it. You're like, obsessed." He smirks, pulling my chin up with his pointer finger, staring into my eyes. "You would tell me if something was wrong, right? I know your mom calling last week was a bit of a shock, and I've been worried-"

"Hey dummy, I'm fine!" The mention of my mom puts a pit in my stomach. "I just want to get through my shift and blow off some steam." I twist my lip as I think of the perfect thing to distract Mark from asking me more questions. "You want to go out tonight?"

Mark's face instantly lights up. I can even see a twinkle in his emerald eyes. "Wait, wait, wait," he pauses, holding my shoulder to keep me in place. "Did I hear you right?" He squints.

"Yes, I want to go out! Don't act so surprised." Except we both know how rare it is for me to suggest we go out. Usually he is the one dragging me places.

"So, you did in fact say you wanted to go out, hmmm." Mark's face gets suspicious.

"Huh, you feel different." He squeezes my shoulders. "Oh no, why didn't I see the signs sooner! I should have known." Mark shakes his head dramatically. "It all makes sense now, why you're here instead of Melanie."

"Are you losing your mind?" I can't help but laugh at his ridiculous performance.

"I need to find The Doctor. He's the only one who could help!" He puts on an English accent while looking around dramatically. I roll my eyes, knowing exactly what he's doing.

"You are actually an alien who body-snatched my best friend Valletta and her annoying friend Melanie! And now you're trying to take me too!"

"You need help." I shake my head, trying to hide my laughter. Mark and I binged Doctor Who episodes during college. We would spend entire weekends watching it and stuffing our faces with junk food. It was my happy place.

"I demand you tell me where the real Valletta Skye is."

"She's probably on her way to kill you for how incredibly annoying you are!" I shove him away. Whenever something is off and unusual, he does a whole bit where he acts like we are in a Doctor Who episode. Sometimes the bit lasts all night. Even though it drives me crazy, I can't help but love it, and it always takes me out of my bad moods.

"Wow, now that's freaky because that sounds like something the real Valletta would actually say."

"How about you go cook the food so there's actually something for me to serve?" I cross my arms.

"Hey, I was on my break. Who's the one who's been here all afternoon?" Just then, as if on cue to create the perfect comedic timing, we hear a pot smash on the floor.

"Well, maybe I should be getting back. Tom's no good today." He smirks at me as he slowly backs away. "You get the real Valletta back for me. I want her there for tonight." He points his finger scoldingly at me, his face full of warmth. I can tell he's trying to cheer me up. He can always see right through the 'I'm fine' line I've mastered.

I smile, feeling more hopeful now that I have something to look forward to. My phone vibrates, and I pull it out of my back pocket.

My stomach drops.

It's my mother.

The second call within a week after not talking to her for over two years. Something is up. My finger instinctively touches the red button. My smile is replaced with a straight line and a feeling of pure determination. Pure determination to fill the growing pit in my stomach.

Three

Sizzling sounds come from the small grills lining the streets, onion fumes burn my eyes.

"How many do you want?" Mark yells over the trumpet coming from the bar next to us.

"Two please." I grin in anticipation, the smell making my stomach rumble.

"Can I have two with the onions extra cooked?" The vendor with the bright red cap nods his head at Mark. Trumpet sounds battle with the club music across the street, both demanding attention from passersby. Neon lights blind me with their sporadic flashing.

Mark hands me my two hot dogs before turning around to pick up his. My stomach is now burning as the steam goes right into my nose.

"Just how I like them." I smile wide.

"Yeah, I keep a cheat sheet with all your meal preferences in my wallet," Mark jokes.

"Oh shush, I'm not even that picky!"

Mark practically spits in laughter, "Oh you're right, I'm sorry! I forgot I was talking with Alien Valletta."

I turn my head to the sky, exasperated, "Are you really gonna keep that bit going all night?"

"Depends." He shrugs.

"Depends on what?" I give him side eye, knowing anything at all could come out of his mouth.

"Depends on how nice you are to me." He winks at me as he bites into his hot dog.

"I guess I can try." I smile softly at him. "I really do appreciate you trying to cheer me up."

"Wow! That's like, an actual 'thank you,' isn't it?" Mark flashes a grin at me.

"Hey, don't get used to it. You still drive me totally nuts." I stick my tongue out playfully as I reach into my pocket to give Mark cash for the hot dogs. He immediately shoves my hand away.

"I don't want your dirty money," he says with his mouthful.

"You always pay. Can you just take it?" I try to shove the cash into the pocket of his jeans, but he quickly jerks his hips back to prevent me.

"You waitresses and your dirty money." He shakes his head.

"Fine, but I'm buying my own drinks," I say, resolute.

"I mean, let me at least buy you one. Otherwise, I'm just going to buy a random girl one, and I'm trying to avoid that tonight."

"HA! You wouldn't last twenty minutes without buying a girl a drink," I say through chews.

"Watch me!" he smiles. "Plus, tonight is about cheering you up. I'm avoiding all damsels in distress." As he bites into his hot dog, a glob of mustard drips down his chin. I burst out laughing. Just then, a loud group of girls in tight black dresses starts chanting near us. I turn to see that one of them is wearing a skimpy white spaghetti strap dress and a bride-to-be sash. Mark looks over at the future bride, clearly checking her out.

"Hope your fiancé knows how lucky he is!" Mark yells over to the girl in white.

"Mark, stop!" I turn bright red, always embarrassed at his candid openness with strangers. To my dismay, his voice carries over the pumping bass that practically vibrates the concrete. The bride's party of girls look over at Mark. You would think a guy with mustard dripping down his face yelling a cheesy, unwelcome compliment would make any girl nauseous, but somehow Mark can pull off anything. Which drives me nuts.

It's so effortless for him, he can just gently brush those dirty blonde waves out of his stunning, bright eyes, and girls swoon.

The bride walks straight up to us, her frizzy curls escaping a tacky Party City crown. As she gets closer to us, her eyes narrow like a predator who has spotted her next meal.

"You have a little something." She gestures to the same spot on her face, where the mustard remains.

"Do I?" Mark wipes his chin with the back of his hand, smiling wide.

"You got it." She looks at him in a way that a person getting married shouldn't be looking at a person who isn't her fiancé.

As if reading my judgmental thoughts, she turns her predatory eyes my way, the girls in black dresses all snickering behind her.

"So, is this your girlfriend?" she asks as she twists a frizzy lock around her finger. This girl is not original when it comes to flirting.

Mark looks over at me with mischief in his eyes. I smile back at him, ready to play.

"Yeah, this is Graceland; we've been together for—" Mark twists his head to the side as if thinking. "How long now, sweetie?"

"Oh, just since we were ten." I gleam at Mark, trying to sell it.

The bride-to-be's face falls, almost with a small amount of disgust.

"You guys have been together since you were ten?" Okay, a full amount of disgust now.

"Oh yeah. He is the love of my life; I would die if he ever left me."
I take another bite of my hot dog because, as fun as this is, I'm not
letting my food get cold.

"Oh, she's just being dramatic." Mark winks at the bride-to-be. The
mixed signals are clearly making her head spin.

Her eyebrows crease as she stumbles backwards, her ankle slightly
rolling.

"Okay, well I'm getting married so . . ." Her posse screams in cel-
ebration at the word married. Clearly the drinking game word of the
night.

"Hey, if it doesn't work out, I live right around Mission Beach, so
maybe you can come find me there." Mark winks at her, full of confidence. I have to cover my mouth to stifle my laugh. The bride-to-be
looks right at me. I return her gaze with a look of sadness. She whips
around, more confused than ever. Mark and I are trembling with
laughter, pinching each other, barely holding it together until the
black dresses surrounding the crown are completely out of sight.

"Well, that was fun." Mark nudges me with a full-blown
post-shenanigans smile. His happy place.

"I can't believe I went along with you on that one." I shake my head
in my own disbelief.

"So, why did you?" he questions.

"I mean, come on, she totally had it coming. I did it for her poor
fiancé," I grin.

"Hey, how do you know he's even a good guy?" Mark says as he
finishes off his first hot dog.

"From what I have observed, in most relationships there's always
one person being thrown under the bus by the other." I shrug.

Mark's taken aback. His eyes widen. "Wow, that's a warm and fuzzy
thought." He shakes his head.

"Yup, and I stand by it." I sigh as I shove a huge bite of my hot dog into my mouth.

The night was going great until I realized I mixed. The different alcohols were flowing through me, giving an uneasy swirling feeling. Mark decided it was time to take me home.

My head bumps against the window as we go over a pothole.

"Oh." I put my hand on my stomach, trying to press away the nausea.

"I told you not to mix like that." Mark shakes his head in disapproval.

The Uber driver anxiously checks his rearview mirror.

"Hey man, she's not going to be sick, right? I can't afford to have someone vomit in this car."

"No worries, dude. She's good, I promise." Mark flashes his smile at the Uber driver. This guy is not Mark's demographic, so the charm falls flat.

I roll my eyes. "Dude?" I whisper. Mark shrugs it off like there's nothing wrong with calling a stranger dude. He rests his hand on my shoulder and makes small circles on my back, trying to calm me. Thankfully, I make it to my street without losing it in the Uber.

"Awesome, just let me walk her up and I'll be right back. Two minutes tops!"

"Hurry up, I have people waiting." This 'dude' is done with us.

"I don't need your help, Mark; just go."

"No way. It's late and I need to make sure you're safe. This isn't exactly a 'Leave it to Beaver' neighborhood," Mark jokes. Ever since he saw my neighbor Tim sitting outside his door on the porch, sipping his coffee and staring at me the entire time without a blink, Mark has been extra paranoid. I personally think the guy is harmless, but I guess you can never really be sure these days.

I run my hand along the stucco, keeping me stable as we head up the stairs. The chirping of crickets fills the silence between the roar of the planes above and the police sirens in the distance. I stop. Suddenly, I'm desperate for a wastebasket.

My stomach starts to swirl. The smell of that perfume is filling the air. Flowers that have been drenched in the rain, almost as if rusty roses were made into a fragrance. Millions of memories are triggered within a millisecond.

"What's wrong? Are you about to lose it?" Mark rubs my back gently as I'm stopped dead in my tracks. Then my brain kicks in and brings some much-needed logic. So many people could own that horrid perfume. Plus, who said my nose was perfect? The alcohol could be throwing my senses way off. I nod my head as if I have solved it and continue up the last two steps.

As soon as I round the corner, the pit in my stomach comes back with a vengeance.

"Mom?"

The woman sitting on the floor, her head resting against my door, turns her head to the side and makes direct eye contact with me. Her blue eyes are sharp and filled with annoyance.

"Oh finally, I've been waiting here for hours." She slowly stands up, her stilettos making her balance uneasy.

My stomach turns. I might hurl right here, outside my door on the cement.

"What the hell are you doing here?"

She stiffens as if I am acting harsh, almost as if I should be kinder. Her hair is colored auburn, her spray tan making her look desperate.

"Is that the way you talk to the woman who carried you for nine months?" she purrs.

When my mom talks about being a mother, the only thing she talks about are her pregnancies. I think she feels that as soon as the baby takes their first breath on their own, she is no longer responsible. She holds so much pride in carrying both her daughters for nine months but ignores the eighteen years that followed.

"Mom, you can't just show up at my apartment. How did you even find out where I live?" I hold my breath, eager for the answer. A part of me can't help but want to hear how much work she went through just to find me and apologize. Apologize for all of it, and then just hug me. Hug me all night until I can finally settle into her hug, settle into what it feels like to have a mother who cares.

Instead, she completely ignores my question as her eyes drift to the spot next to me. I had completely forgotten Mark was still here. His body is stiff, as if he has no idea what to do.

"Hi, I'm Jennifer." My mom puts on the most see-through fake smile. Her eyes drift up and down Mark's body, openly checking him out.

That's it. I'm going to lose it.

I rush over to the side of the railing. I can't stop myself anymore. I blow chunks over the edge.

Mark rushes over to me, holding my hair out of my face. "Valletta, are you okay?" he whispers. I nod my head yes, as I take a deep breath and wipe my face, trying to steady myself. Mark nervously clears his throat. I never see that side of him.

"Uhm, do you think you can just let Valletta rest for tonight? She can call you when she's ready."

Jennifer smiles coldly at Mark.

"You are very gorgeous, I have to say. I didn't know Valletta had such a good catch."

"Mom, stop." I get my breath back, my stomach feeling more stable.

I jump at the loud horn, clearly coming from the impatient Uber driver who is probably ready to take off without Mark. I turn to Mark, placing my hand on his arm.

"Hey, thanks, but I got this, okay?" I look right into his nervous green eyes, trying to give reassurance. "You should go." I nod toward the direction of the Uber.

Mark furrows his eyebrows. "No, I can stay."

"Mark." I lower my voice and speak slowly. "Please just go. I'll text you in the morning."

I can tell Mark really doesn't want to leave, but this is my choice, and he knows to respect it. He nods his head before reluctantly turning around and vanishing down the stairs. Not even a goodbye to my mother. I can only imagine what he wants to say to her, but we both know it will only make it worse.

I turn back to Jennifer, her skin-tight blouse exposing way more than I could care to see, nestled between the lapels of her small leather jacket.

"So . . . do you have peppermint tea?" she asks casually.

"Yes," I stammer. I don't know why I do it, but before I know it, I'm opening the door to my apartment and letting in the woman who carried me for nine months.

"You can hang your coat there," I say as I flick on the lights. I can't help but wonder if she's judging my messy apartment.

Why do I even care what she thinks?

"You kept it," my mom says as she hangs her small leather jacket on the coat rack, running her fingers over the bronze, shaped pineapples.

I nod but don't say anything. I won't give her the satisfaction. My coat rack is the one thing I have left from my grandma. My grandmother was the best person in the world, the opposite of my mother in every possible way, which gives me hope that genes don't always fully carry over in personality traits.

My grandma used to joke with me that she wished a lightning bolt of common sense would strike my mother. I always remember laughing at that visual.

When she passed, I was inconsolable. My mother promised me that when I grew up, she would let me have my grandma's favorite coat rack. She actually kept her word with that one. Next to the nine months of pregnancy, I know giving me that coat rack was a selfless act she remained proud of. Seeing it tricks her brain into thinking she's a good mom.

"I still remember the day I gave that to you. You were so sad until I was able to-"

I cut her off. "Mom, why are you here?"

She huffs, annoyed that I won't feed into her narcissistic speech. "Clearly I'm here to see you. What kind of ridiculous question is that?"

I tighten my grip around the tea kettle's handle as I fill it up with water, anger running through me like electrical currents.

"So, you show up randomly in the middle of the night without any warning?" I glare at her.

"I called you twice, Valletta, but you just refused to call me back. I'm your mother, for goodness' sake." She spits it out. There's the anger I'm so used to hearing in her voice.

She smooths her expression. I think she's trying to be nice. Jennifer clears her throat and sits upright. "Look, Valletta, I wanted to see my baby girl. I mean, it's been a couple of years, not to mention I hardly count the last visit. I mean, it was so ugly." She airs out the space in front of her as if she's wiping away the past.

"Also, there's something you need to know about your father." Now she's getting to the real reason why she's here. "Actually, it's very important that I find him. I know he still lives in San Diego." She looks at me for a moment. I can tell she's waiting to see if I know where he is.

"No." My voice is deep. "I don't want to know anything about any of this," I command. "I have no idea where he is, and honestly, I don't care to."

Silence.

"He's in trouble." Her words make my heart skip a beat. I hold on to the edge of the counter, squeezing as hard as I can.

"Mom, I said I do not care." I glare at her. It takes everything I have to look into her eyes. They're like a portal into my past. A past I don't want anywhere near me. In fact, I want to destroy the portal until there's nothing left but ashes. You can't recreate anything from ashes.

"Fine. You want to be heartless? Well, that's just fine." She snaps, her voice like a viper.

My chest is tightening. I close my eyes, trying to hold myself together. I won't let her do this to me, bring out my demons like this. I know what it leads to. I silently command my body to relax.

I jump at the sound of the tea kettle whistling. I can't move.

"Well, aren't you going to shut that off?" My mom starts to walk over to the stove.

"NO!" I rush ahead of her. I don't want her to touch my stuff, desperate to keep as much control as I can. This is my apartment, after all.

"Valletta, I'm not blind. I know you hate me being here. But you need to put aside your feelings right now. Your father has put me in a very bad situation." She shakes her head in anger. "Listen to me." Her voice demands my attention. "I need to stay here for two days. No more than that, I promise."

"You can't stay here," I say firmly.

"If you don't let me stay here, my life is in jeopardy."

For a brief moment, I hear fear in her voice. Her blue eyes are filling up with desperation. My mother refuses to be vulnerable, but for the first time, I can see vulnerability.

"If you can't do this for me, do it for yourself. I know you. If something happens to me, you will forever blame yourself for turning me away." As sick and twisted as her logic is, deep down inside me, I know she's right.

"So, what, you stay here, and now you're putting me in danger too?"

"No, it's only two days and your father has always hidden your identity from this part of his life. No one knows Derek Skye even has a daughter." My mom says this proudly, as if it's heroic. But her words just sting.

I look at my desperate and afraid mother. I have two options. I can force her out of my apartment, or I can let her stay for two days. Two days of torture. Two days forcing the portal open. Two days of anger boiling inside of me.

I hate myself for what comes out of my mouth next.

"Two days and you're out. No matter what, you're out." My voice is shaking.

My mother smiles at me, satisfied.

As always, Jennifer Skye gets what she wants.

Four

PALM TREES CONTRAST WITH the gray tents against the twilight sky. As I follow the almost intentional path they create, I try not to gag on the smell in the air. I can almost taste it in my mouth. Clashing music assaults my ears from all directions, making it impossible to identify any single melody. A woman jets out from the path with a handwritten sign, hoping to elicit the sympathy of strangers. Out here it's a gamble whether or not to trust people or their stories.

"I need to go to the doctor!" a man screams while lifting his pant leg and showing a wound that looks infected. "I just need five dollars for a bus ticket." He stumbles around, falling from side to side, clearly under the influence. I swallow and keep my eyes on the twilight sky.

When I arrive at my destination, I realize nothing has really changed, besides paint chipping in the doorway and overgrown ivy covering the stucco. Inside, I turn the corner into the all-too-familiar burnt-yellow colored room. A circle of chairs fills the center with new faces.

I see Jessica by the refreshment table, pouring the brown sludge this place calls coffee. She seems amused by the guy next to her. He leans in to whisper something in her ear, and her laughter echoes toward me.

The scene makes my stomach turn. She's too vulnerable to have someone make her smile in that way. At least, she was a couple of years ago.

Something about the guy next to her feels familiar, even from the back. I think it's the hair. There's something about it. Wait. He grabs his plate and turns around slowly, almost in slow motion, like he needed to do a 360 with his eyes before picking a seat.

Oh my gosh. It's him. I stare in disbelief, quickly shifting my gaze as he notices me.

"Valletta?!" Jessica squeals as she rushes towards me.

I force myself to look at her, desperate to look into the mystery man's eyes.

"I can't believe this! You didn't tell me you were coming." She frowns as she pulls me in for a hug. Her skin is cold, and I can smell cigarettes on her hair.

"I thought you quit smoking?" It comes out more judgy than I mean it to.

She pulls away and touches her hair, her cheeks flushed.

"I did, but my roommate didn't." She rolls her eyes playfully. My motherly instincts seem to come out around Jessica.

"Sorry to interrupt. Valletta, was it?" The mystery man with dark curly hair is now standing right next to us, his hand extended towards mine.

"Oh, uhm, yeah." As soon as our hands touch, I swallow. His hand is soft, not even the slightest amount of palm sweat. For a moment I'm able to take him in up close. His skin is smooth, his glasses perfect for his face, giving him a distinguished look. His curls still look soft, but I notice how disheveled they really are, at least compared to how they were at Catalina's.

"Valletta is a poetic name." He smiles. "I'm Owen." The smell of his cedar tobacco cologne alone puts me under a spell.

"Valletta is the absolute best," Jessica says enthusiastically. "She's like my mentor and confidant. Although you have kind of abandoned me lately." She pouts.

I feel like the worst person. I needed to disappear for my sanity. I guess I didn't realize how my disappearing would affect Jessica. I hate the thought that I abandoned her.

"I'm sorry, I can explain-"

"No need!" Jessica puts her hand on my arm. "Look, we all have our issues. I'm not holding it against you, I promise." Her smile is warm and gentle.

I return her smile. No more words are needed. I guess that's the beauty of being with a group of people who get it.

I look back at Owen. I've never seen eyes as dark as his. It's like looking into the ocean on a stormy day, no sign of life under the surface but still breathtaking.

"Nice meeting you, Owen," I manage to say despite my rapid heartbeat.

"We should probably take our seats, we start in a minute." Jessica's words bring me back to reality.

Owen sits directly across from me, pulling out the same small brown leather journal.

Part of me is relieved that Matt is still leading the group. The other part of me is anxious, knowing he was there at my worst. He knows bits of my past I hold close. So does Jessica.

"Well, today we have a returning friend. Nice to have you back." Matt smiles at me warmly. "Why don't we start off with some introductions today since we may not all know each other. Who would like to start? Please let us know your name and how your week went if you're comfortable sharing."

A girl with jet black hair and light eyes sitting next to Matt raises her hand. "Hi, I'm Cherri. I've been coming here for six months now." Everyone smiles at Cherri, greeting her in low, concordant voices. She continues, "My week was great actually; I was finally able to get a job that will support me to move out, so I don't have to live at home anymore." She was proud of this update. "I also applied some of the techniques my therapist gave me to use when things don't go well." Cherri looks at Matt, waiting for a sign of approval to continue.

"Please, go on," Matt nods.

"Well, I woke up in the middle of the night Tuesday from a smash in the kitchen. I'm pretty sure my brother was just getting home. I took deep breaths in, holding back my panic. I knew going out there would only make things worse." She pauses, swallowing. After a moment of gathering herself, she clears her throat. "This is his fight, not mine," she says simply.

I already feel like coming here was a mistake. I close my eyes and imagine myself going underwater. If I go down deep enough, I can drown out their stories, keeping my own flashbacks at bay. I keep myself down there for as long as I can. I open my eyes while keeping the rest of my senses drowning.

To my horror, Owen is staring right at me. I know the polite thing to do is look away, pretend I don't notice, but I'm held completely captive by his stare. It feels like falling into two black holes.

Jessica's elbow into mine forces me to the surface, with no choice but to disconnect from him. Everyone is staring at me. I quickly sit up, realizing it's my turn.

I clear my throat. "Uhm, hi, I'm Valletta." Everyone's mumbled version of 'Hi Valletta' echoes in the room. I smooth out my plain black T-shirt, grasping onto my favorite gold pendant. It's the one Mark gave me when he brought me here the first time two years ago, his way of supporting me while I sit here. I grasp it whenever I'm overwhelmed to keep me from pulling my hair.

I try my best to smile in response to their welcome. "I am twenty-three and I, uhm-" Why did I just say my age? I'm starting to panic. "So, my mom came to my door last night and asked to stay with me." I keep my eyes on the floor. "Her being here, at my place . . ." I pause, trying to find my words. "Well, I shouldn't have said yes, and I'm- well, it's just not good." It's as if at this moment I forgot how to use words, how to put sentences together.

I take a deep breath. "I came here tonight because-" My jeans suddenly feel too tight, like they are sucking all the oxygen out of my body.

I give in. I grab a chunk of my hair and pull.

Pull hard.

Pull until the burning sensation takes over my senses.

"Why did you come here tonight?" Matt asks. I can tell by his tone that he's trying to be soft and encouraging, to help me continue on. But instead, it makes me panic more.

"Well, I don't know why." I completely choke. "Can I just listen for now?"

"Of course. We are here for whatever you need, Valletta." Matt's voice is dripping with pity, and I hate it. Why did I think this would help? Why didn't I just say no to my mother? Scream it! It's her fault I'm back here, back to this place, desperate for help. The air is too thick. I'm not able to breathe. My vision blurs from the lack of oxygen. I need to get out of here.

The circle of chairs makes me dizzy as I stand up. Jessica grabs my hand.

"Are you okay?" she whispers.

I put on the fakest smile I can manage, nodding yes.

"I just really need some water, I'll be back," I whisper in response. She nods, half-convinced.

I bolt to freedom.

I struggle to catch my breath outside, running over to a bench to sit down. I put my head in my hands, letting myself fall apart. My body is trembling for so long, I feel like if I lift my head I'll pass out.

I need to get home.

Home. Crap. My mother is there.

The only thing that's bringing me hope is knowing I have some sleeping pills with me. I can call Melanie and crash at her place, avoiding my mother on the last day I granted her. I can let the darkness take me away tonight, embracing the easy passage of time.

My peripheral senses alert me that a body just sat next to me. I can't even have a bench for five minutes to have a meltdown.

"Make sure your breaths out are longer than your breaths in."

My panic skyrockets.

It's Owen.

"Here." Owen's arms grazes mine. I slowly sit up, removing my hands from my hot, sticky, tear-drenched face, and realize Owen is handing me an actual handkerchief.

"Is that even clean?" I say before thinking.

He smirks, amused by my question. "That is not what I was expecting you to say after you just had a panic attack."

"I'm fine. It wasn't a panic attack. Trust me, I've had those," I say as I take the handkerchief from his hand, examining it.

"It's clean, I promise," Owen says, still amused.

"I've never seen one of these in real life." I take my chances and use the foreign cloth, turning myself away from him. We sit for a moment, distracted by the sight of a grizzled man with a salt-and-pepper beard sporting a magician's hat. He's dancing as if he's a princess stuck in an old man's body. He lets the San Diego breeze flow through his shirt and spreads his arms as if he had wings. Owen and I both chuckle at the sight.

"Hey, come for a walk with me." Owen stands up and extends his hand toward mine for the second time.

The moon has almost fully replaced the sun, the time of day when everything transforms. Downtown releases the working professionals and welcomes those of them willing to cough up eighteen dollars for a cocktail. It attracts with its blinking lights and catchy music, luring in the people anxious to wipe away the stress of the day.

I look upwards, focusing on the California palms swaying in the breeze. Owen guides me, and for whatever reason, I follow silently. There's something about him that makes me feel like any corner he takes, I want to follow.

The smell of salt water fills the air. The sight of the boats on the water ahead lifts my mood. Being near the salt water always gives me clarity.

I look over at the Coronado Bridge as we step onto the pier. This bridge hosts precious memories for me. Depending on the angle, you can see San Diego in a new light every time you're here. The healing sounds of waves crashing into the sides of the boats soothe my frayed nerves.

"I figured, if you're going to sit on a bench, you might as well be looking out over the bay." Owen's voice makes me realize we didn't talk during that entire walk.

I just met this stranger, and he already helped me out of a dark moment. He brought me to the water without a single word between us.

"I love this bay," I say, smiling as I watch the boat lights on the water.

"Why?" he asks, following my gaze.

"I guess there's just a lot of action, always something to watch. Especially all the planes and helicopters. I try to guess where they are coming from and going to."

Owen chimes in. "One time, I couldn't take it anymore. I went right over to the airport and hopped on the next available flight."

"Are you serious?" I turn to him in shock, wondering if I can believe his story.

"It was going to JFK, which I guess isn't surprising considering it's a major airport." He chuckles. "I love New York, though. The people out there are tough, and the streets are filled with chaos, but not the kind of chaos we have in Diego or LA. It feels more authentic. I don't know if that makes sense."

"Well, I've never been, so I'll take your word for it." I tilt my head to the side, imagining the streets of New York, the chaos.

Silence falls between us again. It's a comfortable quiet. It feels so good to just sit here with him and not say a word.

There's laughter coming from behind. I look over at the bridge and zone out on the cars going over it.

"Can I ask you a question?" Owen breaks the silence.

"Sure." My response is timid. I hate questions.

"Why did you tell your mom she could stay with you if you knew how hard it would be?"

His question jolts me, reminding me that despite this magical moment, looking out over the San Diego Bay with a guy I already feel so comfortable with, I am only here because of what transpired with my mother.

"You would have to know my mother." My response is simple, but anyone who can relate would understand.

"She sounds like my father," Owen responds, and then I realize . . . he gets it.

I look over at him, my eyes centering. Who is this guy? An overwhelming feeling overtakes me. This is too good to be true.

"Don't run away from her, Valletta. Face this head-on, trust me."

Confusion takes over my face as I try to process what he just said. "I think I'm fine with just running out the clock until I get my apartment back again."

"What happens if she comes back? If you don't put your foot down, she will always rely on your fear."

I shift uncomfortably at his overstepping. I think he notices, because it's as if his body relaxes, dropping his intensity.

"Sorry if I'm making you uncomfortable," he says.

I don't respond because, truthfully, he is making me uncomfortable. I look over at him, unprepared for the intensity of his eyes. I can't help but feel that maybe he's right.

"So, what? I just go home and demand that she leaves? Throw her stuff outside?" Despite my sarcastic tone, I'm actually considering it.

Owen reaches into his pocket, pulling out a pack of cigarettes. My stomach turns. He gently places one in his mouth and carefully lights it. As he lets out a puff of smoke, he leans forward, facing me.

"Yeah, why not?" He makes direct eye contact as he inhales. The smell makes me want to gag.

"Why would you fill your lungs with those toxic chemicals?" I cough away the smoke.

"Valletta, stress is far more deadly than smoking." He sputters, "So, what are you going to do about your mom?" He leans back, as if leaving the options dangling in front of me. I sigh, looking back at my favorite bridge, thinking about what this woman I call my mother is doing to me.

Owen's right, stress will kill me before anything else has a chance to.

"I'm going to kick her out," I say softly.

I look over at Owen. He nods his head in approval but doesn't say another word. His silence is no longer a comfort. I lean back, facing the bay lights, as the smoke from Owen's cigarette makes my eyes water.

Five

DETERMINATION BRINGS ME TO my doorway. Owen is right. This is my apartment, my mother has no right to come in and tear my world apart. I swing the door open, switching on the lights. My eyes search all corners of my apartment. She is nowhere in sight.

"Jennifer!" I holler. This is not a moment I feel comfortable calling her mom. My ears buzz with nothing but silence. If she's not in this room, the only other place she could be is my bedroom. I storm around my apartment, which takes all of two minutes because I practically live in a closet.

The pull-out couch is put back together with the sheets and blanket folded on top. Out of the corner of my eye, I spot a tiny piece of paper on the counter.

It's a note.

Valletta. Since it's such a problem for you to have me here, I figured I'd be better off sleeping on the streets. It's probably warmer out there than here, anyway. Just in case there's any part of you that still cares, I found your stupid father. He's in big trouble. Goodbye.

-Mom

Anger rages through me as I crumple the note. My mother knows exactly what she's doing. She's not sleeping on the streets. She found what she needed. She used me up and left me out to dry.

It's better this way, anyway. She's gone. That's what's important. I shove down the hurt and abandonment that creep up when she's around me.

Then I smell it, fumes lingering. I lean my head down into the sink, breathing in. My nostrils burn with anger. She was drinking. In my apartment.

I open the trash, and a clear, empty bottle of vodka is buried underneath some Kleenex.

I'm shaking, holding back the waterfall of anger flowing through me. I won't let her control me anymore. Pressure is building deep inside, it's rushing to the surface. I need to release it.

I grab the empty vodka bottle, smashing it into the sink. My ears ring from the explosion. I refuse to let a sound escape my mouth. Not a swear or a scream, or even a sigh. I don't lend her a single breath.

Warm liquid runs down my arm.

Blood.

I didn't even feel the cut. That's the trouble with shattered glass. Sometimes you can't feel it cut until it's too late.

MELANIE SWIRLS A VENTI iced latte in my face.

"So, are we, like, good?" She bats her eyelashes.

"I told you, Mel; we're fine." I grab the coffee and chug it, welcoming the caffeine hit into my bloodstream. Last night was full of tossing and turning, the smell of vodka haunting me.

"Oh geez, you look like hell! Also, what happened to your hand?" Melanie's eyes are fixed on the bandage covering the shattered glass cuts.

"Thanks for telling me how beautiful I look! I really needed that this morning." I flash her an irritated smile.

"Ugh, I just mean your beautiful self is a bit disheveled today. But for real, what happened to your poor hand?" She tilts her head to the side in concern.

"Oh, that's nothing." I shrug it off.

"I can tell you don't want to talk about it, so I'm going to respect that today." I think Melanie is still trying to make up for the horrid date with Chad from hot yoga. She says she sticks by her attempt to get me out there, which I just have to accept. Thankfully, we have talked it out and moved on.

"The fair will help you blow off some steam so you can sleep well and get rid of those bags under your eyes." She winks.

"Oh, crap. I totally forgot about the fair." I bite my lip, knowing she won't take this well. "Mel, I'm so exhausted, I don't think I can go tonight." I place my sunglasses over my eyes, leaning back against the bench.

"What? You have to! We go every year, it's our tradition!" Her voice is desperate. "Plus, it's the only way we know it's summer. The weather is always the same here. But when we are driving to Del Mar, it's when I know I can truly put on my summer playlist and break out my sundresses." I'm not facing her, but I know she's planning out all her summer outfits in her mind as she's talking.

I just lay my head back, keeping my eyes on the blue sky, watching pelicans fly overhead. The last thing I am in the mood for is a county fair. I always love going, but today I just want to sleep.

But what if I can't sleep again? I've gone through my sleeping pills too fast this week. I can't run out. As much as I don't want to be at a fair, being alone in my apartment, tossing and turning, is a much scarier thought.

"Fine. I'll go."

Melanie squeals in excitement.

"I know just what you're wearing!"

I groan at the sky above, thinking of Owen as a plane flies overhead, wondering what it would be like to take the next available flight.

The light coming in through the window has the shape of the California palm outside, casting a shadow between the bright strands. I'm zoning out as a plane flies by, the sound drowning out Melanie's questions. She's going on and on about what we should wear to the county fair, her lip twisting as she puts different pieces of clothing against me, trying to figure out what looks best against my skin.

My eyes are following the plane, almost out of sight now. It's so close, I want to reach out and hold on to it.

"Valletta! Are you even listening to me?" Melanie's voice cuts through the roar of the aircraft, coming in clear as my mind refocuses on the present moment.

I jump as she snaps her fingers an inch in front of my face. I slap her hand away.

"My goodness, what?" I glare at her, giving her the direct eye contact she needs to know that I'm paying attention to her.

"Ugh, whatever! You are clearly not listening to me at all. Just put this on." She slams a blue sundress into my chest, then has the nerve to shake her head at me.

"What's wrong with what I'm wearing?"

"You are wearing one of the five black T-shirts you rotate through every week!" she snorts in disgust.

I look down at my outfit, my hand drifting to the gold pendant hanging over my favorite black tee, not wanting to admit she's right. "But this one is my Passenger T-shirt," I reply softly, knowing she couldn't care less.

"Even more of a reason to change; his music is depressing. Tonight is about fun, fun, fun!" she exclaims.

My mouth falls open, instantly offended. "His music is beautiful, not depressing! You don't even-"

"*¡Me choca!*" Melanie groans, "I am not getting into this with you right now! Just put the blue dress on, you stubborn, stubborn girl."

I huff and look down at the blue sundress. I have two options. I can stand my ground and have Melanie complain all night about my outfit, or I can suck it up and put on the dress, leading to a peaceful evening.

By now, I'm used to Melanie yelling at me in Spanish, I've learned it's her love language. You needed to be boisterous and dominating if you were in the Martinez household. Going over to Mel's family abode growing up was like stepping into an alternate universe. At first glance, (or, I should say, at first sound) it seemed like a family full of hot-tempered shouters. I was stunned by their bold speech.

At home, my mother and sister were soft-spoken, yet their words cut deeper than Melanie's mother's words ever could. The amazing thing was that the Martinez family's love was just as bold and in your face as their voices. Melanie was one of six siblings; all of them were within two years of each other. It was true chaos, but in the best way.

The first time I got yelled at by Melanie's mom was at a sleepover when we were thirteen. It was a big misunderstanding and I was completely mortified. She caught me giving Melanie bangs over the bathroom sink. I cried for an hour afterwards. I thought I lost my second home, my favorite home.

Later that night, I got some curse words in Spanish followed by a bear hug and a, "Welcome to the family!" while Mel snickered behind her mom. She found the whole thing amusing and it didn't seem to bother her at all that she was now grounded for a month. She was just thrilled that she got her dream bangs to cover over her acne-prone forehead. Her silky black hair went all the way down her back and laying on the very top were her thick, poorly cut, straight-across bangs. I smile at the thought as I look over at Melanie now with her fancy salon-layered cut and honeycomb highlights.

Melanie's phone dings. She rushes over to it, "Mark's here, we gotta go."

"Who's here?"

"Mark. You know, the guy lurking in my shadow, trying to take my title as your ultimate confidant." She's talking as she changes into her cherry-red spaghetti strap jumpsuit. "Of course, he's dreaming if he thinks he's closer to you than I am," she scoffs.

I roll my eyes. Melanie always gets jealous of Mark and me. It was just the two of us until freshman year of college. She was thrilled I met someone, thinking he was going to be my boyfriend, and we could go on double dates and vent to each other about our relationships. When she realized we were just close friends, her excitement turned to jealousy.

Melanie holds tight to me. We've survived a lot together. She is the most loyal friend I could ask for, but I would be lying if I didn't admit how much she drives me crazy. I can't help but perk up a little remembering Mark is coming.

I pick up the blue sundress, examining the color, it's a beautiful shade of blue. It reminds me of the blue sky on a perfect summer day. I feel a stabbing pain in my throat, suddenly realizing why this color feels so special.

Mark is headbanging in his Volkswagen Golf GTI. He's so lost in his music that he doesn't realize we are there until I'm pretty much sitting in the front seat. Melanie gets in the back and sprawls out before taking out her small mirror and makeup bag.

Mark looks over at me while turning down the music. His face lights up.

"Whoa! Look at you. How did you get her out of those jeans, Melanie?" Mark laughs, looking in the rearview.

"It's her color, isn't it?"

I look back at Melanie and she's gleaming proudly at me. You'd think I'm her creation the world is finally seeing. I bang my head against the headrest in frustration, "You guys are literally the worst."

Mark reaches out to graze the sheer, embroidered waistline of my dress, interested in the texture of the floral material.

"I haven't seen you in a dress since your graduation. I like this, whatever this is." He has no idea what sheer or embroidered is, and I can't help but burst out laughing.

I can never take them too seriously. Even though they can both be annoying in their own way, it is always so easy to laugh when they are around. They are my comfort zone.

Mark grows silent for a moment. When I look over at him, he's staring at my bandaged hand that I've been trying to keep hidden by my side.

"What in the world happened?" His face is full of concern. He reaches out to grab my hand, but I pull it away sharply.

"It's nothing, I tried chopping some onions and you know how I can't handle the sting in my eyes, so I closed them for a second and BAM! Small flesh wound is all." I speak quickly trying to act as nonchalant as possible. Mark can always see through my lies, but I was not about to get into this right now.

He shakes his head in frustration, "You shouldn't be allowed to own knives, I swear."

I grab Mark's phone quickly to get us off this subject. "Yeah, I never learn my lesson." I shrug.

"Hey! I didn't say you could change this song!" Mark knows exactly what I'm thinking.

"I'm just creating a playlist, chill." I point to the road, while looking down at his phone. "Drive!"

"Yeah, *¡Vámonos!*" Melanie exclaims from the backseat.

"I'm sorry, who owns this car?" Mark grabs the phone back from me playfully, looking me in the eyes, waiting for an answer.

"You do, captain my captain," I reply sarcastically.

Mark smiles at me, satisfied, then twists back to Melanie, "If you even get a puff of that powdery eye stuff on my seats, I swear."

"*¡Ay Dios mío!* Chill! It's just a stinking old GTI. Never mind the fact I'm a pro at doing my makeup in the car." She winks. "Now, drive, before I smear my most glittery eyeshadow all over this headrest."

I chuckle and grab the phone back from Mark, throwing on Noah Kahan.

"Nooo!" Melanie groans from the back seat. Mark grins, turning up the volume.

"Ohhhh there was heaven in your eyes!" Mark and I sing in unison at the top of our lungs as he puts the car in first gear, taking off. We have a little bit of a Noah Kahan obsession. I think part of it may be how much it annoys Melanie.

"SHE CALLS ME BACK, SHE CALLS ME BACK!" We scream as we head toward "the 5" to Del Mar.

I roll down my window, singing along as the wind whips my face and the sun warms my skin. It's one of my favorite feelings in the world.

"I can't believe you're meeting a girl you met online at a county fair." I scoff at Mark as he anxiously scans the crowd.

"Don't listen to her, she's like, super judgy." Melanie rolls her eyes while plopping a spoonful of soft serve into her mouth.

"Hey, one of the few things we agree on." He sticks out his tongue at me playfully.

"I hate you both!" I shake my head. "Not to mention the fact that you guys are totally abandoning me!" Melanie is anxiously waiting for her new obsession, Jayce, to text her where to meet him. At this point, I might as well have come alone.

"You're so dramatic, Letta. Lighten up! We are going to have a blast tonight!" Mark picks up a chunk of my hair and playfully whips it in my face.

"Grow up!" I shoot back at him. A strand of hair gets stuck on my lip gloss. I try to wipe it away, but it gets in my mouth. I sputter, trying to blow it off my lips. I look like an idiot just in time for Mark's date to pop up out of nowhere.

"Mark?" Blinding highlights rest on the top of this girl's unusually small head. Her legs are long for someone so petite.

"Trisha, right?"

It's like seeing Ken and Barbie meet for the first time, but in real life.

"Yeah, totally!" she gleams. Her voice is like nails on a chalkboard to me, as Valley Girl as you can get.

I look over at Melanie, and she's one step ahead of me. Eyes wide, she's mouthing the word 'wow.' I have to turn away to hide my laughter. I guess we can both see why Mark was anxious to find this one. He's a simple man when it comes to dating. If they are gorgeous, he will date them. It's sad, really.

Melanie's phone buzzes, "It's Jayce! I'm gonna go find him and we will meet up soon, K?" She turns to Mark, "Have fun with Barbie!" She runs off, laughing.

Mark's face is bright red at Melanie's jab. The funny thing is Trisha just smiles and waves at Melanie. I don't think she even noticed.

"Hi, I'm Trisha!" She leans in for a hug before I have a second to respond.

"I'm Valletta." I smile as she pulls away.

"It's so great to meet you!" she gleams at me.

"Yeah, Valletta is one of my good friends, she's also a waitress at the restaurant I cook at."

I interrupt Mark, "Well, sometimes we're friends, when he's not being obnoxious." I smile at Mark sarcastically.

"Oh, that's so great! I could, like, never waitress. It looks way too hard." Trisha lets out a long breath, as if the thought alone is exhausting.

I have no clue how to respond to or communicate with this real-life Barbie in front of me, so I just smile and nod awkwardly.

"So . . . Should we start with a big salty pretzel?" Mark smiles at Trisha and me as if we are all on a date together. It feels very uncomfortable.

"You guys go enjoy! I think I'll take a lap around and grab some cotton candy. It was great to meet you, Trisha."

"You sure? I mean we can get that nasty sugary goop after." Mark always prefers salty over sugary.

"Yeah, totally!" Trisha smiles wide at me. Personally, if I showed up on a date and he was with a girl, I would be desperate for her to leave, but Trisha doesn't seem to care one bit. Just Mark's type, easy-going and carefree.

Seven

I MANAGED TO FREE myself from the awkward Ken and Barbie date. Salty mist rests on my arm now, as it's carried in by the warm breeze. I'm surrounded by laughter, balloons, and the smell of fried dough. Everything is telling me I should be having fun. I fight the sweaty bodies to get closer to the edge of the fair where the crowd is thinning out. A man with a top hat is riding a unicycle. Great, a tacky danger act. At least it's something to pass the time. I join the circle of chanters watching this man put himself in danger. A woman emerges holding three knives. Next, the performer lights the knives on fire. The crowd gasps as he circles around her, juggling the flaming knives. I hate the feeling these performances give me, but I also can't look away. Logically, I know the performers have practiced this act a million times, but my body reacts to the suggestion of danger. I shift uneasily.

I scan the crowd, ready to make my way back into the fair, seeking to satisfy my sugar craving. Just before I turn around, I see him.

How is this even possible? Three times in one week? My body freezes, ignoring my brain's urgent warning to hide. Should I walk casually by, pretending I don't see him and pray he notices me instead? Or should I just turn around and go get some cotton candy, continuing my low-risk night? But then again, I am here alone because both my friends have dates.

It's time to be brave. I close my eyes and grab a chunk of hair at the nape of my neck, giving it a quick pull. Just enough of a burn to get me out of my head. I march over to Owen.

As soon as he sees me his face lights up, and my knees almost buckle. Act normal. I can do this.

"I definitely didn't take you for a fair guy," I say casually. I give him a quick glance, trying to flirt a little but play it cool at the same time. For a millisecond, I swear I see Owen's face light up a little but he plays it cool, which leaves me second guessing.

"Oh, I'm not. I'm here for this guy." Owen turns slightly, revealing the boy that I saw in my peripheral. The young boy is watching the end of the performance, his eyes fixed.

"Oh, I didn't realize you were with someone." A young boy with coffee skin looks over at me. I'm struck by his eyes. They are so dark and familiar.

"This is Josh," Owen nudges the young boy. "This is my friend, Valletta." My heart swells. Owen considers me a friend.

"Hey." Josh is uninterested. "When are we getting cotton candy?"

Owen rolls his eyes. "He's addicted to sugary chemicals."

"Hey, those sugary chemicals are better than smoking." I shrug at him, proud of my composure.

Owen looks at me, his eyes squinting. "Touché," he smirks.

"Plus, I was about to go get some sugary chemicals for myself."

"Well, that's perfect. We can grab some together." Owen smiles at me, and once again I follow him without another word.

The line for the cotton candy was insane. Owen insisted on buying mine. He shocked me when he then bought a ball of blue cotton candy for himself. Although, he still hasn't touched it. I pull out a large puff of pink clouds and let it slowly melt into my mouth, my tongue buzzing from the sugary beads. I figured out what gets Josh talking . . . skateboarding. The kid's obsessed. He's taught me more than I would ever need to know about skateboarding, just standing in line for cotton candy.

"Why do you have a bandage on your wrist?" Josh points to my hand while stuffing his face.

"Shark attack." I hold up my wrist nonchalantly, while I grab another chunk of pink clouds.

"Liar!" Josh yells. I laugh, taken by surprise at how comfortable I feel with Josh and Owen.

Above, yellows and oranges slowly take over the sky, creating a golden glow around us. We walk around, watching Josh play games, losing prizes he so desperately wants. I'm seeing a whole different side of Owen come alive with Josh. His lone wolf persona has transformed into a caring big brother, with even a slight sense of humor. I like this more carefree, witty version of him.

The full moon rises above the concession stands. It has been a perfect evening.

"Hey, Sue just texted me. It's time to meet her at the entrance," Owen says softly, looking over at Josh.

All the playfulness in Josh's face vanishes, replaced with irritation. "No. I don't want to go."

Who is Sue? I wonder.

"Come on, Josh, today was great. You must be exhausted."

"Why can't I just stay with you tonight?" Josh's irritation quickly turns to desperation.

"You don't live with me. Are things okay at home?" Owen's voice is laced with concern.

"It's not my freaking home!" Josh's anger rises. I swallow uncomfortably. I feel like I shouldn't be listening to this. I tap Owen on the shoulder, gesturing that I'm going to wait a little further away.

"Here, take this." Owen hands me his untouched blue cotton candy stick. "I'll be right back." He takes Josh's hand. Defeated, Josh allows himself to be led to the entrance. As they walk away, questions flood my brain along with an uneasy pit forming in my stomach. All I can see is the look on Josh's face when Owen said he had to go home. It was familiar, and not in a good way.

As ridiculous as I feel waiting here with Owen's cotton candy stick, a part of me feels a swell. I love holding something that belongs to him, a reassurance of his return. The moon is high and bright in the sky now, leading the way for parents as they bring their sugar-high kids home. I close my eyes to take in this moment of peace.

"Thanks for waiting for me." Owen's voice jolts me, my eyes fluttering open. For a brief moment, there's a hint of sadness in his eyes. He erases it quickly as if he senses my thoughts. I want so badly to reach out and touch his soft curls, partly for him and partly for me.

Instead, I just smile.

"No problem." I hand him back his cotton candy stick. He doesn't take it back.

"You know why I grabbed blue?"

"I think I'm more confused by it being completely untouched. Do you just like walking around with it?"

Owen laughs. "I don't plan on eating it, it's not really my thing."

I look at him confused, my eyes narrowing.

"I wanted to see you holding it. That dress is incredible on you. You are truly a vision in blue. I have to get a picture with you holding the cotton candy, it's the perfect accessory." He grins with anticipation.

"What?" My cheeks burn with heat, my stomach fluttering. "I really hate pictures of myself." I look away, embarrassed.

"Well, that's just sad." Owen steps back as I awkwardly stand in front of his lens. "Stand over there, under the palm tree, beneath the full moon."

I groan. "I really hate this."

"Just trust me." He smiles warmly. His smile is deadly.

I think he knows the power of his charm because he pushes me into making all these different poses. I obey his instructions and put on the best smile I can manage. He stops and looks at his phone, and a mile-wide grin emerges.

"Come look." He proudly holds up his phone at me. I almost don't recognize the girl staring back.

She looks . . . beautiful. The blue cotton candy cloud is a perfect complement to her sky blue sundress, her hand holding up the stick gently, as it floats above the sheer embroidery around her waist. The one thing that looks most familiar is the gold pendant. It takes on a sparkle as it hangs from her neck softly. Smooth dark waves frame her face, highlighting the color in her cheeks. Nothing like the girl I see in the mirror every day.

"Wow," I say, stunned as my gaze remains on the picture. "Are you, like, a photographer?" I look at Owen, realizing I don't even know what he does for work.

"No, just a passion I've always had. It got me through some darkness." His eyes sharpen.

"Well, the passion shows. That's the first picture I can tolerate of myself."

"You made it easy. I was right, that cotton candy gives you a certain irresistible look." His dark eyes burn into mine. He pulls away, looking at his watch,

"We have just enough time for one more thing before they close down. Come with me." He grabs my hand as if that were normal. Electricity runs through me again, but this time I feel it travel up my arm and into my chest. I run with him, my dress flowing in the wind. I feel so free.

"Here we are." We look up at the Ferris wheel towering above.

"Oh, no, no, no," I stammer. "I don't do heights."

"You've never been on a Ferris wheel?"

"Nope, not interested." I release my hand from his and back away.

"Sorry, but I don't think you have a choice with this one. It's happening." He grabs my hand again, pulling me forward. I stand still, holding my stance.

"Valletta, life is too short for fears and regrets. I am offering to take you on your first Ferris wheel ride on this most magical night. There's even a full moon. I promise that you will be safe. Trust me." His words, along with the look on his face, make my body hot, chills flooding through me. He pulls my hand forward, his grip strong. As afraid as I am of getting on that Ferris wheel, I stop resisting and let his hand pull me along.

My thigh feels the cold metal bench below as the ride operator pulls the safety bar down in front of me. My heartbeat rises in perfect sync with the Ferris wheel. I close my eyes, gripping the bar. Owen rests his hand on mine.

"You're okay, I promise." His gentle voice tickles my ear.

I open my eyes to my feet dangling. It seems like I could take my foot and crush someone below. Owen's hands gently guide my face closer to his, "Look at me."

I can't tell if it's nerves or butterflies now, but the feeling is so intense, my entire body is on fire.

"The worst thing is to look down," he says.

I swallow in response.

"How about I ask you a question? Distract you a bit?" His eyes are locked onto mine. I nod, too nervous to speak. "If you had the opportunity to be a kid again, would you?"

I furrow my brows. "That's your question?"

"Mhm." He acts like he just asked me tomorrow's forecast.

"No, never."

"Why not?" His curiosity exceeds the question.

"Would you?" I counter.

"No, I asked you first." I'm learning how stubborn this guy is.

"I wouldn't want to go back to having no control over my life." The Ferris wheel creaks, coming to a stop at the highest point. "Why did we stop?" I sit up anxiously, forgetting not to look down.

"Look at the moon, it's like we could touch it." Owen looks so comfortable, a soft smile on his face as he takes in the sky above. I follow his gaze. The breeze is cooler up here. I wipe away the goosebumps on my arms. He's right, the moon looks like a short plane ride away. I can even see the craters, little specks of darkness against the light.

"Your turn," I say, as I keep my eyes above.

Owen sighs. "I would never want to be a kid again, but I would jump at the opportunity to go back and warn myself of some things . . . or some people," he mutters. It feels like his mind was gone for a moment.

"So, you want to be Marty McFly?" I joke, trying to lighten the mood.

"Precisely."

"That could be very useful, but in *Back to the Future*, things didn't turn out so well. I mean, how can you talk to your younger self if it would just cause a catastrophic mess?"

"I'll take my chances," he says softly. Despite it all being a joke, his tone makes it seem real. For a moment, my fear of heights leaves me. I rest my hand on his leg, meeting his eyes with mine.

"So how do you know Josh?" I blurt out the question without thinking. I guess it was sitting in the back of my mind, eager to be asked. Owen takes a deep breath, breaking our eye contact to stare at the moon.

"He's my little brother."

"Oh, wow," I say softly, slightly surprised. "There was something so familiar about him. I think it's his eyes. They remind me of yours." I smile.

"No, my little brother through the Big Brother program." His Adam's apple bulges, as if he's swallowing a deep emotion that I can't figure out.

"Ohh, I didn't realize-"

"It's okay. He's a great kid." Owen's words come out sharp. "Okay, next question." He grins, pulling his thoughts out of the darkness he seemed to sink into. I can tell I hit a nerve, so I don't pester.

"Ugh!" I groan. "I really hate questions."

He ignores me, continuing on.

"What's something you've always wanted to do, but haven't had the chance to yet?"

"That's easy. I want to go sailing."

Owen's face seems to light up at my response. "Why?"

"I work right near the docks, and on my breaks, I sit there and watch people sail off. As corny as it sounds, I'd love to just sail off into the sunset." I take a deep breath in, imagining myself escaping by boat. I can smell the salt water, bringing the fantasy to life.

"That's not corny," Owen replies. His eyes are so dark, so intense, they intimidate me. Yet, at this moment they feel soft, almost caring. It hits me. I just opened up to someone, however small. I did it.

This was real. I could feel it in my chest . . .

It almost felt like a connection.

Nine

I SAVOR EVERY STEP as Owen and I stroll toward the parking lot, not wanting this night to end.

"Oh, crap." I look at my phone for the first time since seeing Owen. There are several missed calls from Mark and Melanie.

Mark

> Hey, where are you?

Melanie

> Let's meet up! I want you to meet Jayce!

Mark

> Okay, it's been an hour since you ran off, where are you?

> Just let me know you're safe…

Melanie

> Ok, are you like, purposely ignoring me?!

Melanie

> I guess not... Mark said he hasn't heard from you either.

> Where the heck are you?!

Mark

> Hey, I'm starting to get nervous; I'm with Mel, we are ready to go...

> Do I need to have a security guard looking for you??

> Answer your phone Letta geez.

Melanie

> Ok, we are literally looking for you everywhere. You better be off with the love of your life or something. That is the only excuse I will accept after this stress. You know the posters we see in public bathrooms!

Owen is peeping over my shoulder at my phone as I scroll through all the notifications. I turn my phone away, embarrassed.

"Geez, you have some worried friends."

"Yeah, they're panicking. I should call them."

"Hey, you know it's a good night when you don't even check your phone," Owen winks. A rush flows through me. I think I just died.

Right before I go to call Melanie, Owen puts his hand on mine to stop me.

"Let me take you home." He smiles.

"What? No, that's crazy. I live in Point Loma."

"That's not far from me at all. Please, I want to." I am completely captivated by his dark eyes.

"Are you sure?" I bite my lip. I can't believe I'm considering this.

"Beyond sure," he gleams.

Blinding siren lights swerve around Owen's car as he pulls over, letting them pass. On the car ride home, the inevitable subject of my mother came up. I updated him on her sudden disappearance.

"She leaves as quickly as she comes." I shrugged. "The solution is to just wait a day. I guess I should have learned my lesson by now."

"I wish you could have had the satisfaction of kicking her out," Owen said bluntly.

His words keep ringing in my ears as we drive, a sting in my eyes as the memories come up without permission.

Thankfully, we got off that subject soon enough, before too many emotions bubbled over. One thing I can't get over is how nice this car is. It's the smoothest ride I've ever been in. If this car is any indication of his financial situation, Owen is rich. Which only adds to his intimidation factor.

I can't help but feel a thrill riding shotgun with him. I love the silences that fall over us. I've never felt so comfortable not talking with someone. And when we do talk, it feels meaningful. None of the clunky small talk I always feel the need to make when there's silence. The only other people I've felt this connection with are Mark and Melanie. But Owen, I mean, I've only known him for a matter of hours. This is the fastest I've ever felt a rush to be around someone.

My heart starts racing. The two cop cars pull up right in front of my apartment building.

"Right here." I direct Owen with my finger. My voice unsteady.

"Where the police are?" Owen looks over at me concerned. Two cops emerge and head up my staircase. This is not good.

"I'll walk you up." Owen unbuttons his seatbelt while staring at the flashing lights.

"No need. I'm sure it has nothing to do with me," I manage. Owen doesn't look convinced.

"It's okay, I want to make sure you get in okay." I know there's no use fighting with him. Any person with even basic manners would walk me to my door at this point. My heartbeat increases with every footstep I take.

As we walk up the stairs, muffled talking comes in over a radio along with pounding on a door. We round the corner, coming face to face with two cops right at the door of my apartment.

"Hi, excuse me, I live here." My voice shakes.

"Hello Ma'am, are you associated with Jennifer Skye?" I grip the railing, my eyes bouncing between the male and female cop. I look beside me at Owen. His face is stone cold. Just another thing my mother is about to ruin for me.

I swallow. "She's my mother."

"Is she staying here?" the male cop questioned me.

I shake my head, "No."

"Do you know where she is staying?"

"No."

"This is serious, Ma'am." The male cop looks at me with intensity. He turns to his female partner. She cuts in as if they are playing good cop, bad cop.

"Ma'am, can we speak privately for a moment?" Her eyes are softer than those of her male counterpart.

"I really don't know where she is. I have nothing to do with her."

"She's telling the truth." Owen speaks up, taking me by surprise.

"What's your name, sir?" The male cop has a pen and paper out.

"Owen Belmont." I think this may be the worst way ever to hear Owen's full name.

The cop stops writing and looks at Owen. "You don't happen to be related to Mr. Lance Belmont?"

"That's my uncle." Suddenly, all emotion from Owen's face has vanished.

"Oh, wow. He's a good man, a pillar of his community, that's for sure." Owen remains expressionless.

I speak up. "Look, Owen has absolutely nothing to do with whatever this is. He just brought me home from the fair."

The female cop chimes in, "We understand. We don't want to scare you. You aren't in any trouble. We would just like to ask you a couple of questions."

"Okay." I nod, turning to Owen. "I've got it from here, thanks."

"I can wait for you."

My heart sinks as Owen looks at me. I can't imagine what he's thinking.

"I really appreciate the ride home, but I'd rather do this alone." I mouth the word sorry. It's all I can manage without falling apart.

"It's not your fault." Owen keeps his poker face as he leaves.

I follow the cops back down the stairs, getting out of the cramped hallway and standing in front of the cop cars. Thankfully it's late, so there aren't many people walking around.

I take in a shaky breath. "What is this about?"

"Your mother, Jennifer Skye, is currently under investigation. She needs to come in for questioning. We have reports that she was staying at this address, but the resident came up under Valletta Skye. That's you, we presume?"

"Yes, that's me."

"And just to clarify, your mother is not staying with you?" the male cop asks as he studies my face.

"She showed up two days ago. I avoided her, and then when I came home yesterday, she was already gone. I have absolutely no idea where she went. That was the first time I've seen her in years." I cross my arms, angry that I feel guilty, as if I did something wrong.

"If you hear from her, we need you to report it to us." The female cop hands me a card. "Our main suspect, we believe, is your father, Derek Skye. Have you heard from him?" Her question makes me feel like I'm free-falling down an elevator shaft. My surroundings blur, the name Derek Skye buried in a deep void.

"Ma'am? Are you okay?"

I manage to pull myself out of the void to answer, "I have no idea where he is." The words barely come out.

I turn my head to face the street, the familiar engine sound coming closer. My stomach drops to my feet. Mark's car is pulling up to the side with none other than Trisha in shotgun.

"If you do hear anything at all from either of them, we would appreciate your cooperation." The male cop speaks as his partner follows my gaze to Mark's car. I snap back, anxious to get them far away before Mark runs over.

"I understand. I will call you guys if I hear anything at all. What I've told you is all I know. Now can you please leave?" I hold my breath.

I can't even listen to their final words. I'm just thankful they are finally walking away, leaving me overflowing with anger. As soon as the cops are in their cars, Mark bolts towards me. I shake my head, not ready to deal with him, especially as Blinding Highlights watches from the front seat like she's on safari.

"What in the world is going on? Are you okay? What happened?" Mark's questions come out panicked, with no separation.

"Mark, why are you here?" I hiss as he approaches.

"What am I doing here?" He seems shocked that I would have the nerve to ask. "Uhm, I don't know, Valletta, just making sure you haven't been freaking sold and sent across the border," he hisses back. "Why were you just talking to the cops?" I've pissed him off, which takes a lot to do. Even so, his anger could never match mine at this moment.

"I cannot deal with this right now. You're not my freaking bodyguard. Just go take Barbie home." I swat my hand toward Trisha and turn to walk away.

"Oh, hell no." Mark reaches out to grab my arm trying to stop me. I yank my arm away. "Valletta, I swear to God, do you have any idea what you put Melanie and me through tonight? And now you won't even talk to me?" His voice is rising by the vowel. I turn to see if anyone is around. "You completely ghosted us, and then after we walked around that fair all night looking for you, you finally called Melanie saying you're getting a ride home with some guy?!" I'm taken aback by the emotion in Mark's face. The emerald in his eyes is screaming with rare anger.

"Mark, I'm a twenty-three-year-old woman. I am not your responsibility."

"Oh, wow, okay." Mark laughs angrily, shaking his head. "Wake up, dammit! It's 2023, we are literally hours from the border. You know how insane kidnappings are right now. What is wrong with you?" Mark's eyes sharpen on mine. "If you drive with me to the fair, you can't just vanish like that! Without even meeting up with us so we can know if you're safe. And then I get here and there are literal cops. And what? I'm the bad guy for checking on you? Geez." He backs up from me, shaking his head.

"Is everything okay, Valletta?" Owen's voice comes from behind me.

Crap. Crap. Crap. I cover my face with my hands, needing to escape this moment.

"Oh my God," I whisper into my hands.

"Who the hell is this guy?" Mark's about to fully lose it.

"Valletta, are you okay?" Owen's hand rests on my shoulder.

I uncover my eyes, "Owen, what are you doing?"

"Owen?" Mark furrows his angry brow. "Oh, what, so this is the guy who drove you home?"

Owen keeps ignoring Mark, his focus on me.

"I came back to check on you. I was seeing if the cops left yet."

"I'm fine, Owen, really. I just need to get to sleep. You should go home," I plead.

He ignores my plea, now looking at Mark. "Clearly you're upsetting her. Maybe you should leave."

Mark puts both hands on his hips, closes his eyes, and takes a deep breath, letting his head fall back.

"Hey, Mark!" Trisha's high-pitched voice carries over to us. "Is everything okay over there?" She has the door open as she yells over.

"Yup. One minute," Mark says, slowly composing himself. He opens his eyes, looking directly at Owen. "Look, I don't know you and this is not a good first impression. You don't just drive someone home like that. I mean it's common courtesy to meet the friends she came with. Be a gentleman." He glares at Owen. Mark doesn't even glance in my direction. He just shakes his head as he walks off, Barbie anxiously waiting in the front seat.

"Is he your friend or your protector?" Owen glares off at Mark.

"I'm so sorry about that. He's just worried. Honestly, I don't normally run off like that and I'm usually good at communicating with my friends, so I think I really freaked them out." I swallow, realizing slowly why Mark's so upset.

"Well, you should be free to do what you want. It's not healthy to have someone breathing down your neck." Owen's eyes rest on mine. I suddenly feel guilty that this is his first impression of Mark. I shake it off. I have bigger things to worry about.

"Hey, so what happened with the cops?" Owen's looking at me for answers. Answers I don't have the energy to give.

Answers I don't even have.

Ten

I was 8 years old, two years before my dad left. Two years before I had to become an adult overnight.

I stood proudly in front of my sandcastle. I was gleaming from ear to ear as I admired the details, like the small seashells for windows and the big white pearl shell that created the front door. My nostrils filled with the perfect aroma of the beach.

My happy place.

"Here, put this around the top. They can be like carvings on a fancy castle." My dad hands me two broken shells in cool shapes with different colored pebbles. He winks at me, and my face lights up in appreciation.

I can't remember what my father was like before he was sober. It's days like these that I remember. Sandcastle contests with Abby, my dad cheering me on from the sidelines.

"Hey! That's cheating!" Abby cried. "Mom! Derek just helped Valletta!"

Our mom was sunbathing with her sunglasses on, always half-asleep at the beach.

"Abby, your sister is only eight; be a big girl," she mumbled, never opening her eyes.

Abby glared at me, "Cheater! You're just a little kid; you can't do anything on your own!"

Those words stuck with me; Abby always made me feel guilty when my dad helped me.

My sister remembered Dad before he sobered up; she remembers the horrors. Him and my mom met when Abby was two. She survived four years, living with two addicts.

Apparently, I was the reason he changed. I don't remember, but my sister said I was constantly crying and yelling, "Daddy, NO!" when he was drunk. I either blocked it out or simply couldn't remember that long ago.

I was naive and happy.

Cold water washed over my feet, a huge wave sending a tsunami over our castles. Abby and I both stared wide-eyed, anxious to see which would survive.

"Way to go, Blue Sky! Abby, your little sister just showed you up." My dad smiled playfully at Abby, who crossed her arms at him, clearly upset. She was a very, very sore loser. My dad always called me Blue Sky. He said I was his clear blue sky after a hurricane.

I ran over to my dad, feeling proud. The tsunami had formed a moat around my castle, making it fancy. He picked me up, cradling me in his arms, kissing my cheek with pride.

"Okay, enough gloating you two." My mom peered at us over her sunglasses. I always had a gut feeling my mother was jealous of me; she hated the way his love for me made him a better person. She wanted him to stay on her level because she was intimidated by people whom she felt were better than her. And for many years, my father was in fact better than her.

Until he wasn't.

Eleven

LIGHT WAS PEEKING THROUGH the curtains, a sign it was officially dawn. I had spent the entire night trying to force myself into sleep, fighting a losing battle because of the memories flooding my brain. The image of my dad was in the back of my mind like an etch-a-sketch, refusing to be completely erased. Hearing his name was like using a key to unlock a hidden vault.

All I want to do is sleep. I turn to my nightstand, picking up the bottle of sleeping pills, shaking it. A few bounce around. I don't know if they will get me through the rest of the week. I open the bottle and pour them into my hand, counting them. If I take one more now, I'll be one day short. This week has been an uphill climb during a hurricane.

I pour the pills back into the bottle except for one. As I roll it around in my hand, a knock at the door startles me, sending the pill flying into the sheets.

"No!" I search my sheets desperately. As I stand up smoothing out my shirt, I see the small capsule fall gently onto my mattress.

I sigh in relief.

"Letta!! Open up!" Mark's voice carries into the bedroom.

I stumble out of the bedroom in my oversized Rolling Stones T-shirt, feeling like a puffy, exhausted mess. I rest my forehead on the door in frustration, peering into the peephole. I see Mark on the other side, holding two cups of coffee.

"Valletta?"

I swing the door open. Mark is standing there in a white T-shirt and jeans, his hair a ruffled mess. It was clearly a sleepless night for him too, judging by the red in his eyes.

"Wow, you look almost as bad as I do," I say as I look him up and down.

He holds out one of the cups in his hands. "It's your favorite."

I accept his peace offering, standing aside for him to come in. He walks in cautiously and looks around.

"Wow, you need to clean this place up."

I roll my eyes while I savor the first sip of my latte, the taste instantly giving me comfort.

"Not everyone is a clean freak. Leave my mess alone."

Mark's tired green eyes rest on mine, and I can see that all the fight and fire from yesterday is gone.

"How are you holding up?" he says. "You know, after last night?"

I look down at my furry gray slippers. "I'm okay. Didn't sleep."

"Me neither."

I look up expecting to see pity, but instead I see vulnerability.

My heart sinks, realizing how cruel I was to him. This isn't us. I need to break the tension. I step closer, sucker punching him.

"Ow!" He rubs his arm and slowly I get my smile. Mark has one of the most infectious smiles that anyone could have. You can actually see his eyes dance and sparkle as he looks at you.

"So, I see we're resorting to violence to solve our problems?" he says, as a mischievous look comes over him, one I don't trust, and for good reason. He lunges forward, coming at me with mock hunter's eyes. I squeal while dodging him, trying to hold my coffee upright.

"STOP! I'm gonna spill my latte!"

It was too late. He tackled me, forcing laughter out of my mouth by doing the thing I hate the most . . . tickling. Oh, and he knows how much I despise it.

"Okay, TRUCE! Please!" I beg, out of breath, not able to handle any more.

I spin around to glare at him. "Not fair at all! You know I'm not strong enough to fight back, you gym rat!"

He beams, proud of himself, flexing his muscles. I try so hard not to smile, I don't want to give him the satisfaction. But like I said, his smile is infectious.

"You are the worst." I shake my head.

"Hey, you started it with that killer punch." He rubs his arm again.

I leaned forward to smooth his greasy, dirty-blonde hair. "You need a shower."

"So do you." He looks at my messy bird's nest bun.

"Eh, there's always time to shower. Let's enjoy our filth." I grin.

Mark laughs, "Well, if anyone can pull off filth, it's definitely you."

"I really can't tell if that's a compliment." I look sideways at him.

He doesn't reply. Instead, his eyes settle on me. "Hey, did you eat?" he asks.

"Considering I literally rolled out of bed to answer the door, what do you think?"

Mark walks past me into the kitchen, opening the fridge.

"Geez, there's nothing but pickles and whatever the heck this is." He picks up an unused jar of hot sauce that has probably been in my fridge for a year.

"Yeah, it's been a while since I went to the store." I bite my lip.

"What have you been eating?" Mark looks concerned.

"I don't know, just stuff out I guess." It hits me that I can't remember my last meal. I had cotton candy last night and some coffee yesterday morning, but besides that, I couldn't think of anything. Had I been eating? The thought makes my body feel weak, like suddenly I realize I have nothing to run on.

I really needed to get myself together.

"Okay, well, I need to get you some food. This is crazy, Letta. Why don't you shower, and I'll run to the store? I don't have to be at work till later."

I can't help but find comfort in him calling me Letta. As much as I say I hate it, today I need it. I need familiarity, knowing someone cares.

"Okay." I run over to him, giving him a hug, holding on to his strong arms. "Sometimes you're not so bad." I playfully stick out my tongue as he holds me.

"This thing is crazy." Mark grabs my bird's nest bun, tugging gently at it. He looks way too amused.

"Okay I get it, I'm filthy!" I smack his chest as we part, laughing. Glad he saved me from using my sleeping pill.

I breathe in the steam, letting it relax my muscles, the water practically scalding me. I could stay in here forever, the sound of the water drowning out my thoughts. I keep my eyes open because whenever I close them, flashing lights appear, the two cops standing at my door. Worse yet, I see my dad's face.

I hear the clashing of pans in the other room and I realize I have been in here way too long. Why does taking a shower feel like the biggest burden until you're under the water and surrounded by steam, and then you never want to leave?

When I clear off the foggy mirror, I realize that the shower has done wonders for me. Hints of green are in my hazel eyes again. I wrap myself in one of my big, fluffy white bath towels, feeling invigorated.

The smell of butter, toast, and bacon fills the air. It's so strange to have someone here making me breakfast. I could get used to waking up like this every day.

Mark is in full chef mode. He's humming as he multitasks, completely focused on not letting anything burn. I love watching him work.

I clear my throat to get his attention. "Please tell me you didn't buy the whole store."

Mark looks at me and smiles innocently, "You know how I get around food." He continues whisking some eggs while looking me over. "Wow, you look like a new person, no more messy bun of hidden wonders." He points his whisk at me.

"Ahh, yes." I walk up to him and swing my soaking wet hair around like a dog.

"Hey! Watch it! Not in this kitchen, no hair allowed."

"Uhm, last I checked this was my kitchen, so I make the rules." I shake my hair against his arm laughing.

"Okay, that is like, a major health code violation." He grimaces.

"Wow, am I making carefree Mark nervous?" I shake my head more, holding on to my towel with both hands.

"Hey, why don't you get dressed, you crazy health code viola-tor?" He shakes his head as he picks up his bowl away from me. For a moment, I swear I saw him blush.

"I'm sorry, am I making you uncomfortable?" I'm having way too much fun finally being the one to make Mark feel out of his comfort zone.

"Hey, you'll be the one with burnt food if you don't get dressed. Most chefs don't work with, you know, all this going on." He circles his whisk at me.

"I like my toast a little burnt!" I gleam. "But fine, I'll go get dressed, Mr. Serious Chef Sir." I salute him before walking away to the bedroom.

Just then, there's a knock on the door. I turn to look at Mark, confused.

"Did you hear that?" I ask. Mark shakes his head.

"No more distracting me with imaginary noises," he replies, rolling his eyes at me playfully.

I walk over to the peephole to see if I was hearing imaginary noises. Sure enough, I wasn't.

It's Owen.

Twelve

PANIC FLOODS ME. OWEN is at my door while I'm in a towel with sopping wet hair. Not only that, but Mark is in my kitchen cooking me breakfast. This could not look worse.

"Who is it?" Mark says while pouring the whipped eggs into the hot pan. I freeze, not knowing how to handle this situation.

"Uhm, one minute please!" I bite my bottom lip, thinking.

"Valletta? Hey, it's Owen. Sorry to come by unannounced. I wanted to check on you." Owen's voice comes through the door.

Mark slams down the bowl, running over to the door.

"Owen?!" he whispers, pushing me out of the way to look through the peephole.

"Hey! Stop!" I whisper-yell at Mark while shoving him back.

Mark looks at me. "How well do you actually know this guy?"

"Valletta?" Owen spoke again from the other side of the door.

"Hey man, it's not a great time, try again later." Mark rolls his eyes at me as if we were both annoyed at Owen being there.

"You're dead! Get back over there!" I whisper, mortified. I use all my strength to shove Mark into the kitchen, just in time for the timer to go off.

"Uhm, who are you?" Owen sounds confused.

I swing the door open and hide my body behind it, my head popping out.

"Hi Owen, I am so sorry, I really wasn't expecting anyone. Uhm-" I awkwardly tuck my wet hair behind my ear with the hand not holding my towel up.

"Is there a guy here?" He twists his body to try and look around me and into the apartment.

"Oh, no, there isn't," I stammer.

"Then what am I?" Mark yells from the kitchen.

I close my eyes for a second, trying to compose myself.

"Owen, can you give me like two minutes to get something else on?" I close the door before he has a chance to respond.

"Just give me two minutes!" I yell as I run toward my bedroom.

With no time to think about what to wear, I throw on a gray tank top and jeans. When I open my door, I collide with Mark. He's standing in front of me with his arms crossed.

"How do I know this guy isn't a serial killer?" Mark's face is somehow serious while asking me this absurd question.

"I promise you. I know him." I look directly into Mark's suspicious eyes. "Mark, I really appreciate your concern, but I am not a child, and I can choose who I want to hang out with. Now please, just stop worrying."

Mark holds my glare for another couple of seconds before uncrossing his arms and walking back to the kitchen.

I carefully open the door, stepping outside, the sun blinding me. Owen is leaning against the railing with his hands in his pockets, looking over his shoulder.

"So sorry about that. I was just getting out of the shower." I give him a hesitant smile.

"No worries, I'm the one who stopped by so early, unannounced. I realized I didn't have your phone number, so I had no way of getting in touch with you. I wanted to make sure you were okay after last night.

"Thanks for checking on me. Last night was a little intense."

Owen looks past me at my front door, "So, uh, did I interrupt something?"

I blush, realizing what the situation looked like.

"You didn't. It's actually Mark, my friend from last night."

Owen's face is tight. "I thought I recognized his voice."

"Yeah," I say, wanting to move past this as quickly as possible. "He was also just checking on me, and he's a, uhm, chef, and well-" Why was I being a stuttering idiot? I clear my throat. "He is cooking me breakfast because I had such a full-on week that I never went grocery shopping."

Keep it simple Valletta.

Owen's eyes narrow. "I guess that makes sense. I have to ask, is there something going on between you guys?"

"Oh no. Not at all. Just really good friends." I flash an uncomfortable smile.

"Well, I can't say that's not a relief."

I swallow, suddenly aware of my heightened heartbeat. "I don't really know what to say to that."

Owen smiles self-assuredly. I envy his confidence.

"I just want to be upfront with you. Last night was memorable, even before the cops showed up." Owen winks. "I like you, Valletta, but I'm not trying to make enemies here. Mark seems very protective of you."

"We're just friends, we have been for years. He just wants me to be safe. If you know Mark, you know, well . . . you would know that's just how he is." I'm starting to stumble over my words. "I mean, his mom was like, well... he had to take care of her, and now he does that with me. At least, that's my opinion, but..." I pause my rambling to breathe. "I have no clue why I am telling you all this." I laugh in the most awkward way, my face fully blushed.

"Go out with me Friday night." Owen's directness is startling.

"I work late on Friday," I say, disappointed.

"Call out," Owen says plainly.

"Call out?" I laugh. "You make it sound so easy."

"Well, isn't it?" he smiles.

"Definitely not for me." I shake my head, looking down.

Owen pulls away from the railing and steps toward me, "Valletta."

He continues commandingly, "You are going to call out because you had a really awful week. I mean, the police were involved. Also, you just admitted that you haven't even gone grocery shopping, which is a sure sign of personal neglect. That is cause for concern in itself." He grabs my attention with his stormy eyes. "Just say yes. I promise it will be just what you need."

I want nothing more than to say yes.

I take a deep breath in, and on my exhale, I say, "Yes."

Owen's face lights up, which in itself is a reward for my decision.

Just then, my door swings open, almost making me fall backward into my apartment. Mark looks at Owen and then me, and then back at Owen with suspicion and a hint of anger in his eyes.

"Breakfast is ready. You don't want it to get cold." He pauses, "Owen, right?"

Owen nods without saying anything.

I'm stuck in the tension between them. Mark looks at me, I'm shooting over a warning look.

"Sorry for last night," Mark says, "I hope you can understand what it seemed like, as Valletta's friends. I mean, crazy things happen, you never know who to trust." He clears his throat, extending his hand. My heart is pounding, praying Owen will reach out.

"Sure. It's in the past." Owen extends his hand, and they shake. I smile at the small victory.

"Well, I guess there's enough food if you want some." Mark's invitation is flat, delivered with a poker face.

"I appreciate the offer, but I'm going to head out." Owen puts all his attention back on me as if Mark isn't there. "See you Friday at five sharp." He winks and turns to walk away before casually raising his hand at Mark. "Enjoy your breakfast."

Mark's patience for him has already been used up, so he doesn't reply.

Thirteen

"**THANKS AGAIN** FOR BREAKFAST. It was delicious." I smile over at Mark as we pull into a parking spot near the visitor's center.

"Of course," Marks says, opening the door quickly. He had insisted on taking me on a small hike. His motto is to get outside and enjoy the sun as often as possible.

"Which trail do we want to take today?" Mark stretches as he asks me, his eyes shielded by his Ray-Bans. He was so quiet during breakfast. I can tell Owen showing up really threw him off. I wanted to know what he was thinking, but I didn't want to push him. Between last night and this morning, I think we both need a break from drama.

"Let's go to our spot," I say, as I walk over to peek at the view. The marine layer is lifting, slowly revealing the panorama of mountains, city, and ocean. "It seems like by the time we get there, we will have a clear view."

My body is already soothed from the warmth of the sun. I breathe in the calming feeling. We pass the Monterey Cypress trees. The fronds drape over themselves so beautifully, I've always been partial to them. It feels like, if you sit underneath one, you will hear a story from long ago. Mark's favorite is the Shaw's Agave, its pointy yellow flowers explode from the stalk. It's like a hummingbird feeder from an alien planet. A crazy-looking plant, the stalk shoots up so high from the prickly bottom. This canyon on the tip of Point Loma surrounds us with the best plants, and birdsong competes with the roar of passing helicopters. As we walk the dusty trail, I look above at the bright blue sky, an aerial freeway for millions of migrating birds. They stop here when they are tired and need some food. Mark and I try to show each other up with our bird and plant knowledge. It's like a competition at this point. Our rule is no phones on a hike, in case one of us cheats and uses Google while walking.

It's kind of perfect actually.

"I can already smell the sage," I say excitedly as we round the canyon. The temperature drops because we are walking on the shady side. Whiffs of the pungent, earthy smell carry on the breeze.

"You and your hound nose." Mark shakes his head, breathing in, trying to catch the scent.

I grin happily, looking out for lizards crossing our paths. Nature never fails me. Right when I'm about to fall apart, all the life surrounding me gives me the shot of energy I need.

"Remember when I jumped on your back, when the snake crossed in front of us?

I smile at Mark, enjoying the memory flooding my brain.

Mark chuckles, "Oh yeah, how could I forget? You practically attacked me, and Melanie ran screaming all the way back to the car." Mark shakes his head. "You guys are so city."

I laugh, "Melanie is way more city than me! I've come a long way!"

"This is true. I guess you have me to thank for that." He smiles softly at me instead of his usual big grin.

It was true, Mark was the one who was constantly pushing me out of my comfort zone, especially with anything related to nature. I didn't grow up going into national parks or hiking in canyons. My dad's favorite things all had to do with the water; spending time at the beach, surfing, and swimming. I followed in his footsteps. Except for surfing, but there are reasons for that.

The marine layer fully lifted, revealing the pure turquoise water. Mark and I sit on the bench overlooking the city with the mountains towering behind like protective walls. It was our favorite spot. I anxiously scanned the water for seals. No matter how many times I see them, I still get giddy when I spot one.

"Hey, look, I betcha that's Rosa." Mark points to a seal plopping up on a rock below.

"Oh yeah!" I smile wide. We've named a few of the seals we see regularly here. Of course, there's no way to actually track them, but we look out for little characteristics that feel familiar. I settle into the warmth of the sun as it soaks into the top of my head. A wave of exhaustion flows through me. I lean my head against Mark's shoulder, giving in to the rare feeling.

Mark's voice pulls me out of the blurry sensation of sleep overtaking me.

"So, are you ever going to tell me why the cops were at your house?" he whispers.

I sigh, wanting nothing more than to peacefully drift off. "Why do you think, Mark?"

He shifts, making my head bounce slightly. "Jennifer Skye?" His question is half rhetorical, he knows the answer. What he doesn't know is that my dad is even more involved, something I have no interest in revealing.

"I just want to move on, pretend the past week was a bad dream," I say, my eyes fixed on Rosa, basking in the sun.

"You know that I'm here for you, no matter what," Marks says as he leans his head against mine. "Ouch, your hair is like, burning!"

I chuckle, despite the heaviness that has come up into my chest.

"So, I have to ask . . ." Mark's breathing changes. I can almost feel his heartbeat rise as I lean into him. "How well do you know this Owen guy? I mean, when did you even meet him?"

I slide down, so I can lean the back of my head on the bench. "I met him a few days ago, he was at the support group." I try to get a glimpse of Mark's reaction, his sunglasses preventing me from reading his eyes.

He turns to look at me, "So, you're going to meetings again?"

"Nope, it was just reassurance that I made the right decision to stop going..."

"Are you sure? Maybe it was just a bad first-"

I interrupt Mark, raising my hand to stop him. "Mark, don't go there, ok?"

He silently obliges, nodding his head.

"Anyways, I met Owen there, and we saw each other again at the fair. He is honestly a nice guy who understands what I'm going through." I swallow as my eyes follow a helicopter.

"Look, I can respect that. I guess it just seems a little soon for him to be so, you know, like, involved in your personal business. Not to mention his reaction when I was rightfully worried about him driving you home." Mark crosses his arms, still bitter. "I mean, two days is not a lot of time to get to know someone, and then to show up at your apartment unannounced, asking about what happened with the cops."

"Don't forget where we met, Mark. He knows my family life isn't great, otherwise I wouldn't have been at that meeting. Don't take this the wrong way, but he actually gets it, more than you ever could."

Mark shifts uncomfortably, his silence lingering an extra moment.

"You may be right," he eventually says. "But you have known me for longer than a few days. We've had time to, you know, build trust and stuff. This isn't the movies, it's not actually that romantic when a guy acts so fast. You need time to get to know someone before showing up at their apartment early in the morning with no warning. I don't know. It just seems off."

I tried to brush off Mark's warning, but his words hit me more than I would like to admit.

A few moments of silence pass, a blast from the horn on the Navy ship filling the air. Mark looks over at me, lifting his Ray-bans to show me his emerald eyes. "Look, I'm sorry if I'm making you upset. I know at the end of the day it's not my business. You are an incredibly smart, independent woman. I just had to voice my concerns as your best friend." He winks, allowing his usual big grin to overtake his face.

I return his grin with a smile. "Melanie would be yelling at you right now for assuming you took her position."

Mark smirks, putting his sunglasses back on. "Oh, please, I've had her beat for years now." He nudges me playfully.

I breathe in the salty air, trying to find the scent of sage in the breeze. I lean my head against Mark's shoulder again. Enough time passes in silence for the blurry feeling of sleep to settle back over me. I daydream of sailing away as I watch the sailboats in the distance, drifting off for a moment to the sound of the waves crashing against the rocks below.

Fourteen

I was SHAKING SO much I needed to redo my eyeliner three times.
An equal mixture of excitement and nerves, the kind of nerves that
keep you from being able to hold any food down.

I hear a ding, it's a text from Melanie.

> You called out??!! What's happening?

I take a few deep breaths to calm my shaking, one of Dr. Sage's
strategies. I laugh at the thought. How can deep breathing be the solution? I get my head together and shake off the tension while texting
Melanie back.

> I have a date. I'll explain it all soon.

> WHAT!

> A DATE?! STOPPPP!

I manage a smile, despite everything, Melanie can always rally. She
is my cheerleader, my support.

> Don't say anything. I'm out with a sore
> throat.

I laugh, putting my phone away with newfound confidence, ready to conquer this date.

Owen is a vision in blue, contrasting with his deep coal eyes and jet-black curls; it's enough to make my chest tight.

"I think it's safe to say this is my new favorite color," he says, noticing how my face lights up while I examine his outfit.

"It looks like the color of the dress I wore to the fair," I say, surprised.

"Like I said, it's my new favorite color." Owen winks at me.

Seeing him is way better than imagining him. He has on a gorgeous sky-blue fitted button-down with white buttons like the clouds that dress the sky. They lead down to fitted white jeans.

"You look stunning." Owen examines me. He steps closer, picking up the gold pendant that's dangling down my chest, leading to my

V-neck maxi dress. "You wear this as if it's a part of you, it's beautiful." He smiles, gently releasing it.

My face goes hot realizing he's noticed my necklace, a sign he's been examining me, maybe almost as much as I've been examining him. Of course, now would not be the time to tell him who it's from.

"You look great as well. I think that may be your color more than mine." I smile at him. "Also, good job matching the shoes." I point to the sky-blue cotton boating shoes holding up his whole outfit.

"We must find you some sunflowers to hold. I can't end the night without a picture of you in that dress with yellow flowers in hand." He grins, "I will have to start a collection."

I blush. This yellow floral maxi has been in my closet for way too long. I've never felt brave enough to wear it. But tonight is about finally putting myself out there.

"Where are we going?" I ask.

"You'll see. Enjoy the journey." He winks, reaching out his hand for me to hold. I stop for a moment, my anxiety causing hesitation. I've always been a people watcher when it comes to love. I enjoy love objectively from the sidelines, never wanting to get close enough to someone for them to hold my hand.

But with Owen I can't help but want it all. I reach out letting Owen's hand slide into mine. I get such a rush as I follow him out to his car.

When I get into the car, I smile to myself. I'm on a date I'm excited about for the first time.

I waited in the car while Owen made two mysterious stops, both times coming out with paper bags. Although, I'm pretty sure one of the stops was a taco truck that he parked just far enough away from to keep me guessing.

"You know I can smell the tacos," I laugh, looking over at Owen as he drives.

"Patience, Valletta, patience." He smirks.

Owen parks at the small beach on Shelter Island. As we walk past the fire pits, a soft smile comes over my face as I think about the many nights that Mark, Melanie, and I have spent here. When we get to the dock, we keep walking out toward the water. I pull Owen's hand back, forcing him to look at me.

"Wait, what are we doing?" I look anxiously at him.

"Just trust me, come on." He turns around, leading me to a beautiful sailboat swaying in the gentle waves.

"Here we are." He turns to me. "This is the lovely *Frisson Merveilles*." He steps aboard the stunning white sailboat. The side bear the words *Frisson Merveilles* in golden calligraphy.

"You own a sailboat?" I stand there stunned, taking in the vision of this beautiful vessel. Owen extends his hand to help me on board. "I cannot believe this!" I'm still dazed as I make my way onto the boat.

"Pretty soon we will be sailing off into the sunset," he says, as he quickly disappears in the cabin below with the brown paper bags. A lump forms in my throat. He remembered my dream.

I take in the cockpit. It has a gorgeous bronze steering wheel in the center. There's a bench on both sides with decorative white and gold throw pillows.

Owen emerges from the cabin with a bottle of champagne and two glasses in his hand. "So, what do you think?"

"I am speechless right now," I say truthfully. I never expected this.

There's a loud POP as Owen opens the champagne, carefully pouring and handing me a glass.

"Did you name this boat?" I ask as I take a sip.

"Yes, she's all mine. This is my escape, I guess you could say, the one thing I have that I truly feel is my own. I bought her for cheap and I spent two years getting her seaworthy."

"Wow. I would have never guessed you were the type to restore a boat, or a sailor for that matter."

"To be fair, Valletta, we really don't know much about each other, do we?" He looks at me earnestly while sipping his champagne. "I'm hoping today is the first step to changing that, though."

I swallow, suddenly feeling a rush of nerves. "So, what does Fri-san Mer-vel-eess, or whatever, mean?" I completely butcher the pronunciation, of course.

Owen chuckles, correcting me. "Frisson Merveilles."

"Yes, that." I laugh, embarrassed.

"Well, Frisson is a French term that describes some goosebumps, or chills you might say. The kind of chills you get after experiencing a form of art so beautiful or even haunting, that your body can't help but respond." Owen's voice is soft, and as he draws closer to me, my entire body gets covered in exactly what he's describing.

"And Merveilles is French for wonders. So, when you put the two words together, I feel that's when you know you're alive. Seeing wonders so amazing that your body is electrified."

"Wow. I feel frisson after hearing that explanation," I say, blushing.

Owen looks over at me, reaching his hand out, and gently grazing my arm. His hand goes over my goosebumps, which just makes more.

"So you do." He smiles, pulling away and taking another sip of his champagne.

Okay, sailing is hard. I never knew there were so many technical terms to remember. Owen had me doing everything as he explained it. I was able to put the mainsail up and get it into the wind, which is the most important thing if you actually want to sail away. He guided my hand as I pulled the halyard around the winch. There was a bit of a thrill that came over me as I got the mainsail up. It felt like freedom as I watched the dock slowly disappear.

The boom can be the most dangerous. It's a big pole that controls the angle of the sail. If you get hit in the head with it... well, good luck.

"When can I use the beautiful steering wheel?" I ask anxiously.

"Lots of sailboats don't even have steering wheels. The most important thing to learn is how to work the sails." Owen's passion comes out on the sea. I can tell that this is his happy place. Wind and sun hit my face, my hair tangling all around me. Owen has timed this perfectly. Soon we will be officially sailing off into the sunset.

He listened to me. He remembered. I light up from within at the thought. My life doesn't even feel real, it's like I'm dreaming and I'm afraid I'll wake up.

After a while of navigating, I finally get to use the fancy steering wheel.

I love it.

Owen directs me close to a cove where we drop anchor. There are other sailboats sprinkled around us, bouncing around like jellyfish.

"Okay, now for the best part," Owen says as he disappears into the cabin, reemerging with the two mysterious brown paper bags.

He reaches in and pulls out a few tacos, handing them to me.

"Oh, I would have never guessed that's what was in the bag." I smile sarcastically.

"Hey, they're worth the wait, trust me. I can guarantee you haven't had tacos like this yet. She makes them special for me."

"Is that why we had to go to Guam to get them?" I joke as I unravel the aluminum. A glorious smell rises into my nostrils, my stomach making me very aware that this will be my first meal of the day. That first bite infuses pleasure into my mouth.

"Oh my gosh, these are insane," I say with a mouth full of taco, my manners leaving me. Tacos are around every corner in San Diego, and yet I never get sick of them.

"Told you." Owen grins as he slowly unravels his first taco, making me aware of how fast I was eating. I put it down to breathe.

"I could watch you devour tacos all day," Owen says. I cover my mouth, feeling self-conscious.

"So, how did you learn how to sail?"

"My uncle taught me when I was a kid."

"The same uncle who is apparently a pillar of the community?" I ask.

Owen's face turns white.

"You remembered that, huh?" I can tell this is not his favorite topic. I nod as I finish off my first taco, anxious to get to the next one.

"I have a question for you," Owen says, clearly wanting to change the subject. "What's the story with your dad?"

The question completely throws me off, making me choke.

"Are you okay?" Owen draws closer to me, rubbing his hand along my back as I try to stop choking.

"I-I-I'm fi-fine." I sigh, finally swallowing properly, grabbing my champagne to clear my throat. "Just went down the wrong pipe."

"That's good. I was afraid it was the question," Owen says as he bites into his food. I awkwardly take another sip of the bubbly.

"My dad isn't my favorite topic, to be honest." I avoid eye contact. A moment of silence passes, causing me to look at Owen.

"I have screwed-up parents, Valletta, trust me. I don't want you to try and cover your past." As his words pass through me, I feel completely naked.

His eyes change as I peer into them. They almost become stonelike. It's as if I'm looking into pure, glimmering onyx.

Fifteen

"WHY DO YOU HAVE to go this weekend? You said we could go to the beach to see the sunset." My eyes were puffy and red from crying. I sniffled, and my dad reached over to dry my tears.

"I know, but I have to work. I promise to bring you home a new stuffed animal." He smiled gently at me. "I bet you can't guess what kind I'll find."

As sad as I was, I couldn't help but get excited about the possibility of a new stuffed animal. "I really want a turkey."

My dad laughed, "A turkey? You're a weird kid." He reached over and ruffled my hair, "Why a turkey?"

"They aren't appreciated enough. Too many people just view them as food."

He laughed, "Fair point!"

"Why can't I just come with you to work?"

"You have school, sweetie."

"I don't need to go to school if I just help you work."

"You're too smart for my work."

"What do you do?" I perk up, excited to hear his answer.

"Oh, I could never tell you that."

"But, Dad! Please!"

"You really want to know?" he asks, lowering his voice and getting close to me. "If I told you, you would be sworn to secrecy for the rest of your life, and if you ever told anyone at all you would turn into a stuffed animal and be put on a shelf for eternity."

Even though I didn't believe him, there was a small part of me that was still frightened by the thought. "Liar!"

"I've seen it happen to someone. In fact, that's who Poke is!" He points to the bear on my bed, "I could never tell you till now. It's top secret. He was a little boy once, until he told a secret he wasn't supposed to." My dad picked up the bear on the bed and put it in front of his face, imitating a little boy's voice and moving the bear around as if Poke was really the one talking.

"Help me, I'm trapped!" Poke squealed.

"Dad, I'm too old for this. I'm seven!"

"He's telling the truth! Help me, help me!"

I laughed, pushing Poke out of my dad's face. He smiled at me, grazing my cheek. "You are my Blue Sky. I don't want you to have to carry any secrets. I want you to stay happy and young forever. I can't come home to my baby girl turning into a stuffed animal."

I reached over and squeezed my dad. He kissed the top of my head and said, "I'll be back in three days with a new stuffed animal, I promise. We will go to the beach the day I come back and see the sunset."

In my dreamlike state, I start to hear water lapping against the sailboat underneath me, and I open my eyes to soft moonlight. How was my dad's voice so real? The dream was so vivid, I feel like I'm still seven years old. Why did I have that dream? I turn my head over to see Owen, who remains sleeping, remembering how he had been asking about my dad. I guess the champagne and deep conversation got to both of us. I mean, I opened up to him about my family. Like, I actually told him about my dad, and honestly, it felt good. It felt good to open up to someone who might actually get it.

I stand up, my legs stiff. I walk to the front of the boat and sit down. The water is sparkling in the moonlight. There is an eerie sense of serenity, a soft swooshing from the gentle waves. I bring my knees to my chest, hugging them. Thinking about when I came home from school three days later, I found none other than a beautiful stuffed turkey on my bed. I named her Greta.

My mother thought it was the most disgusting, ridiculous, hideous waste of money. I held Greta so close, ignoring my mother's negative energy. That night, just as promised, my dad took Greta and me to the beach to watch the sunset.

I wish I hadn't found out what my dad was doing for those three days, but I can't help wanting to squeeze Greta in my arms again.

The ocean is so still. For all I know, it's the middle of the night. I can hear Owen snoring, a surprisingly comforting sound, as he sleeps on the bench toward the back of the boat.

As dawn approaches, I watch pelicans fly overhead, the light above changing.

"Valletta?" Owens' groggy voice comes from behind me.

"Hi," I say softly. Owen's curls are all over the place, his sky-blue button-down covered in wrinkles.

"Can't believe I fell asleep. How long have you been up?"

"Not sure." I look at the sky again, remembering how bright the moon was when I first woke up. Owen comes to join me, plopping down beside me while yawning. He looks completely disheveled.

"If I had known we would fall asleep, we could have slept on an actual mattress in the cabin." Owen winces, touching his lower back.

"That's okay. I like the fresh air."

"I would kill for a coffee," Owen says, rubbing his temples. I'm sure he's also feeling the champagne's revenge. He reaches into his pocket, pulling out a pack of cigarettes. I watch him close his eyes as he lights one. A large puff of smoke floats away from us.

"What do you write in your small leather journal?" It's a question I've been dying to ask him.

Owen chokes on his next puff, gently smacking his chest. "Wow, are you getting me back for all my questions?"

I shrug. "I'm just curious. I saw you writing in it at the meeting." I leave out the other two instances, not wanting to come off as a stalker.

"We all need our outlets," Owen says softly as he turns his face away. He stretches out, knocking the ashes from his cigarette off the side of the boat and into the water.

"Hey, there's one more thing we need to do before I bring you back." Owen gets up without another word about his journal, which only makes me even more curious. When he comes back, he's holding a sunflower.

"Mysterious stop number two." He smiles, handing me the flower that perfectly matches my dress. He takes his phone and snaps a photo before I have the chance to object.

"Perfect," he gleams. As he takes his last puff, he nods for me to follow him toward the cockpit.

"Come on, we should get you back."

I sigh, not feeling ready to return to reality.

I wave goodbye, climbing the stairs one by one, arriving at my apartment door exhausted. I look at my bedroom, thinking of my dream. For years I have kept that shoebox untouched. Right now, the urge is almost unbearably strong to look inside it. However, my fear keeps me at a distance.

I get some water and just stare off toward my bedroom, finally telling myself I'm being ridiculous.

I observe the dust swimming in the air within the sunbeams streaming into my bedroom, and then I look over at my closet. I reach under the hanging clothes until I feel a large shoebox. I pull it out carefully, as if an explosive were inside. Finally, I take off the cover and pull out an adorable stuffed turkey. Under Greta was a note.

I open the worn-out paper . . .

For my Bluest Sky, who makes my day sunny and bright. This turkey looked like she could use someone to give her a new home.

Love, Dad.

I run my fingers over my dad's handwriting, pressure coming into my chest until the box falls from my grasp. The note crinkles in my hand as I squeeze Greta to my chest. I can't breathe. I can't stop. I can't stop.

Sixteen

GRETA WAS DAMP WITH my tears as I placed her back into her shoe-box with the crumpled note, and yet I woke up this morning feeling like a newborn baby. It was a long-overdue cry that had mercifully let me sleep.

Since I have two hours before work, I decide to walk instead of getting behind the wheel in my current state. I leave my apartment with enough time to stop and treat myself to a much-needed latte at Catalina's.

The trees rustle in the gentle breeze, a few clouds scattered across the blue. My first sip immerses my mouth in vanilla and espresso. As I lounge in the sun, I observe a family on the grass. They almost look like actors, paid to shoot a commercial for some antidepressant medication. The daughters dance around on the grass, while the mother blows glistening bubbles, and the father assembles a kite. On Saturdays, I love getting to work early so I can spend time people-watching at the parks around Liberty Station. My sunglasses are my shield, hiding my puffy red eyes.

Melanie tackles me with a hug as soon as I walk into work.

"Tell. Me. Everything. NOW!" She squeals.

"Can you give me a minute to settle into work?" I laugh, walking past her and into the kitchen. I'm waiting until the last possible moment to take off my sunglasses. Melanie anxiously follows behind me as we walk into the kitchen.

"So, how did it go?" she asks eagerly.

"How did what go?" Mark asks as he preps potatoes for the dinner rush.

"She had a date! Can you believe our sweet Valletta called out for a date?" Melanie yells over to Mark.

"Shhh!" I hiss. "Let's not announce it, please."

"Whoops, sorry! Guess that's what happens when you leave me in the dark and ignore me for literal days. I explode!" She waves her hands expansively.

Mark puts his head down and starts chopping again, "So, you went out with Owen last night?"

"Owen?! Mark knows your date's name but not me? What the-"

I interrupt Melanie before she spirals, "Calm down! He was there when I was with him."

"Whatever, but someone better tell me who this Owen is before I lose it!"

"Why don't you get your own life, so you're not so obsessed with Valletta's?" Mark snaps at Melanie.

"Shut up and go chop some onions," she growls at him.

Mark makes a face at her but doesn't reply.

Thankfully, our boss walks into the kitchen, which shuts Melanie up, and we scatter into our separate sections. I wait until Melanie runs off before removing my sunglasses. I can probably fool the customers, but I definitely can't fool her.

The first half of my shift was flying by, we were slammed.

"ORDER UP!"

I rush to get table nine's order, "You made sure this is gluten-free?"

Mark pauses, making brief eye contact with me. "Yeah, all set," he says, quickly returning to his station.

The restaurant has the typical Saturday night roar. My table is filled with picky eaters and food intolerances, causing me to double-check a bunch of orders before putting them through. Halfway through the shift, I get into a flow state. My mind focuses on each order, each request, each complaint. Hot plates burning my forearm, my pen running dry, sweat beading on my forehead. No time to think about anything other than the task at hand. It's honestly the best part of waitressing.

I have five minutes to scarf down a grilled cheese Mark forced on me. He's always making sure I'm fed. In between chews, Mark rushes over and grabs my arm, pulling me towards the back door underneath the exit sign.

"Are you ok?" Mark's face is full of concern.

I return his question with a look of confusion. "Yeah, I'm fine, why?"

"Your eyes." He pauses, clearly trying to find the words. "Well, you look like you've been crying." He swallows. "What happened last night?"

I feel my cheeks get hot, "Why do you assume something bad happened on my date?"

"Look, I'm sorry if I'm crossing a line, but I just want to make sure you're okay, I can't bear the thought of something happening to you on that date and-"

I hold my hand up to stop Mark, "Woah, slow down. Nothing bad happened. He was a perfect gentleman for your information." I take another bite of my grilled cheese.

"He was?" Mark's eyes narrow, as he searches my face.

"He was."

"MARK! Get back here man!" Carlos yells from the kitchen.

"Crap, I gotta get back there. But, you're okay?"

I nod, "I'm okay. The red eyes have nothing to do with Owen."

Mark nods his head like he understands. He knows by now that it's probably family stuff and I won't talk about it.

"I didn't see your car. Do you need a ride home?" Mark asks as he begins to walk backward away from me.

"Actually, yeah, that would be great." I swallow my grilled cheese, needing to get back to work.

Seventeen

Pain radiates through my feet, sweat making my baby hairs stick to my face, and my back feels like cement. I'm beat. I slump into Mark's car and push my head back against the headrest. Mark looks exhausted too, but way better than me. I have no idea how he manages to still look like the city's hottest chef after being in a hundred-degree kitchen all night without a break. It drives me nuts.

"Did you even eat today?" I turn my head to look at him.

"Yeah, I had a protein shake."

"You only have protein shakes after the gym."

"Yup." He grinned at me.

"Are you seriously telling me that you went to the gym before work?"

"Maybe." He shrugs and starts the car.

I aggressively roll my eyes, "You are psychotic."

"Hey, how else am I supposed to keep this body up?" He flexes jokingly. I shake my head. "Going to the gym is the only way I can feel good mentally throughout the day. The body is just a bonus." He smirks.

"Hey, you're the one who's always on me for not eating." I shrug, looking out the window.

"There's nothing like smelling food for twelve hours straight to make me lose my appetite. I'll eat tomorrow." He yawns.

I will never forget the first day I met Mark. It was the first semester of my freshman year of college and Melanie forced me to go to a frat party with her. It was pretty much like every frat party on TV, just less romanticized. Essentially, unless you were drunk, it was a nightmare. As soon as I stepped foot through the door, I regretted it. Melanie ran off with that week's boy toy and I was left to fend for myself. As I was walking around the loud, dimly lit, smelly house, I saw this maniac trying to skateboard down the stairs with no shirt on. Everyone was cheering for him. He looked fearless at the top of the stairs, like he was doing the smartest thing in the world. Despite his incredible stupidity, I couldn't help but notice how gorgeous this guy was. I mean, picture-perfect abs, commercial-worthy, flowy, dirty blonde hair, perfect cheekbones, and eyes so vibrant and green you could even see them in the dimly lit room.

It might have been because I was the only sober one at the party, but apparently, I was the only one who thought this trick he was about to do was a horrible idea. I had two options. I could keep my mouth shut and stay out of everyone's way or I could try to be a voice of reason to this moron. I chose option two.

"Hey, frat boy! Maybe you should sober up a little before doing that!" I yelled up the stairs.

He had one foot on the top of the stairs and the other on the skateboard. He looked up at me and grinned. "I am sober, but thanks for your concern!" he yelled back, then added, "You should stay there and watch me." He winked.

"You're seriously going to hurt yourself." I crossed my arms.

"You wanna be my nurse if I do?" He and his frat brothers around him all broke out into laughter.

"Excuse me? This guy was a pervy jerk.

"Relax, it's just a joke."

"DUDE LETS GOOOO ALREADY! STOP TALKING TO THE DEBBIE DOWNER!" A guy screamed, then started chanting, "GO! GO! GO! GO!" He got the whole room going.

The jerk on the skateboard shook out his nerves, put the foot on the front of the skateboard down, and jumped his back leg up, making him fly into the air.

He landed on the side of the stairs trying to keep momentum but instead, his skateboard caught, unable to slide down. He flew forward, slamming onto the floor right near my foot. I heard a crunch, and my stomach clenched. I closed my eyes, unwilling to see him hurt.

I was expecting a deafening scream but all I heard was some low cusses and "OW!" I opened one eye first to see him. He was holding his arm but already sitting up straight. What was this guy made of?

Everyone was cheering, and he held the arm he didn't land on up in the air in victory. I was mortified. No one came over to ask if he was okay. He was acting like he didn't just fly off the stairs and land on his arm.

I crouched near him, "Are you ok?"

He turned to look at me, his face full of adrenaline. "Never better," he grinned.

"Are you sure? You fell really hard. I mean, I heard a crunch." I bit my lip. "Can you try moving your arm at least?"

"You're really worried about me, huh?" he smiled, almost pleased. "And yet, I don't even know your name."

"My name is not important. Do you want me to get you some ice?"
Although this guy was the biggest moron alive, I didn't have the heart to
just leave him there.

He tried moving his arm, wincing. "If you're gonna get me ice, I need
to know your name first," he smiled through the pain.

I rolled my eyes, "Your priorities really need adjusting." I paused,
looking at this crazy frat guy in front of me, who was clearly hurting
but didn't seem fazed by it. "I'm Valletta."

"Valletta?" He repeated it back carefully. "Can I call you Letta for
short?"

"No, it's Valletta, no nicknames." I stood up, reaching my hand out
to help him up. "Come on, let's go find you some ice."

He held onto my hand to get up but didn't let go when he stood up.
Instead, he moved his hand up and down, giving me a firm handshake.
"I'm Mark. Nice to meet you Valletta, not Letta."

His smile reminded me of a puppy who just found a new friend.

He did break his arm that night but somehow powered through. I
ended up staying with him all night at the hospital. Don't ask me why.
We became close friends that year. I came to learn that he was in fact a
harmless, hyper puppy who just needed a good influence. He was also the
most caring, loyal friend I could ask for, and he came just in time.

I smiled in the car, thinking about that memory, then I looked to the
side at Mark, "You know you're not actually invincible. You're capable
of breaking too, don't forget."

"Oh, I know, but I always have you to help me if I do break, so
I'm not too worried." He smiles through another yawn, then clears

his throat and glances at me. "So, what's going on? You know, with everything?"

There's no energy in my body to possibly explain anything to Mark, and I honestly don't want to. Which shouldn't come as a surprise to him anyway.

"I'm so tired, Mark."

Mark taps his thumb on his steering wheel, taking a moment before responding. "I want to be there for you. I want to know what's going on with your parents and the cops. I want to know why you've been crying so much."

All I can do is sigh in reply and rest my head on the window, looking at the streetlights and dark houses, no lights left on.

"Okay, fine. No family talk. Can you at least tell me more about Owen?" Mark's hand clenches the steering wheel on "Owen".

"I'm still getting to know him, but all I can say is, I want to keep getting to know him." I smile to myself.

"That says a lot." Mark sounds surprised.

Mark and I have been friends for over five years, but he was always the one introducing me to his girlfriends, never the other way around. This was a new dynamic and I could tell Mark was thrown off.

When we pull in front of my apartment building Mark is quiet, and it feels like he wants to say something but doesn't know how.

"Valletta-" He's using my full name which means this is serious. "I don't want to push you, but you need to know I'm here. I'm always here for you. I don't know why the cops were here, but just be careful. I can't bear to see a repeat of two years ago." Mark's staring down at his lap.

"I'm not getting involved," I say with resolve.

Mark lifts his head and looks at me for an uncomfortably long moment. I can't tell what he's thinking, which is rare.

"Thanks for the ride home," I say softly.

He seems to come out of his daze. "Goodnight, Letta," he smirks, his green puppy eyes back to their usual shine.

Eighteen

"**I have** a surprise for you today!"

"Oh?" I balance my phone while trying to wash the dishes that have been sitting in my sink for a couple of days. "Owen, I don't know how I feel about surprises."

"You will like this surprise, I promise."

"You know we've only had like, one date. How could you possibly know what I like?"

"You mean one epic date, plus, I'm pretty sure we've talked on the phone for a week straight at this point."

I smile, drying my hands, thinking about our daily phone calls.

Just then, there's a knock on my door. "Oh, hold on a second."

I swing open the door to see Owen standing there with his phone to his ear and right next to him is Josh, his little brother from the foster program. "Oh my gosh." I shake my head, smiling, "You're too much."

He comes in for a hug then gently releases me, and places a soft kiss on my cheek, leaving my insides screaming.

"Josh kept asking me about you." Owen nods toward the young boy dressed head to toe like a skateboarder.

I smile at Josh, "What's up?"

"Nothing," Josh shrugs, trying to act uninterested, "I was promised pancakes." It's then I notice he's holding his skateboard, it's fitting.

"Nice board," I wink at him.

"You like skateboarding?" Josh lights up a little.

"Uhm, not really, if I'm being honest. I had a friend who broke his arm trying to do a trick down a flight of stairs. Learn from him." I give Josh a warning look.

"Amateur." Josh shakes his head like he's a forty-year-old man. "I would never do something so stupid. I could show you some basic stuff." He shrugs as if it's no biggie.

"I'd love that. As long as you can promise I won't fall and twist an ankle."

"No pain, no gain," Josh says plainly.

I can't help but laugh, "Well said."

"Ready to go?" Owen asks. I nod, "Let me grab my purse."

Josh spends the whole car ride talking about skateboarding, enthusiasm pouring out of him. It's nice seeing him like this. I can tell how much this kid means to Owen, and it warms my heart so much I almost want to burst.

"Are we going to La Jolla?" I ask as we take the familiar route.

"Yeah, there's a great farm-to-table breakfast spot, and then I figured we could go see the seals before taking Josh to the skate park."

"Awesome!" Josh says excitedly from the back seat. "I can show you the new trick I've been working on!"

"Can't wait." Owen looks behind him at Josh, giving him a quick smile.

Watching Josh bopping along to the music in the rearview mirror, I can't help but wonder what his foster home is like.

"You know, you could have told me you were kidnapping me for the day. I would have been a little more prepared," I say, realizing I'm in my old, basic jeans and black tee. I can't help but wonder if he is judging my lazy day look, bare-faced and all.

"What's the fun in that? Plus, I remember you saying you had the day off."

"Well, how do you know I didn't have plans?" I ask, testing his answer.

"I figured you could always cancel them." Owen shrugs playfully. I almost feel that he knows he's right. I probably would cancel any plans to spend time with him.

"So, La Jolla huh? I have to say, I never had you down as a tourist area kinda guy."

Owen looks at me. "Oh I'm not. But It's one of Josh's favorite spots, so, you know." Owen winks at me. I never expected this side of Owen. He really acts like Josh's big brother. I didn't think anyone could convince him to go anywhere he wasn't crazy about. But then again, it's hard to say no to a ten-year-old in foster care.

There's one major reason why I avoid La Jolla. It's so dang expensive. I mean, all of San Diego burns a hole in your wallet, but La Jolla is posh. The view from our table is insane. Waves crash on the rocks in the distance, and you can even make out the seals basking in the sun. Multi-million-dollar villas lay scattered on the rugged cliff coastline. Five-star dining and valet-service hotels fill in the rest of the gaps between the tall palm trees swaying in the ocean breeze. We sit outside, taking in the salt air as we dine. I devour my chocolate strawberry crepes, savoring every bite. Owen and I finish with a cappuccino, giving me the buzz I need for the rest of the day. As much as I hate people paying for me, I was grateful that Owen picked up the check for this place. By this point, I can tell Owen has some money. I still don't know how I feel about it. I'm not used to being around people who own sailboats, smooth eclectic cars and take me casually out to eat in La Jolla.

After brunch, we take a walk along the beach. I love seeing the flocks of cormorants scattered on the rugged rocks, their blue necks peeking out when they move. I breathe through my shirt. The smell coming from the beach is far from pleasant.

"I can never really get used to that smell. I guess that's the price you pay for being this close to hundreds of seals," Owen says as he brings the back of his hand to his nose. Once we get close enough, their cute blubbery faces make up for the stench.

"Awesome! Those two big ones are about to throw down!" Josh points to the pair of males wobbling on their flippers as they reach their long thick necks over to try and bite each other.

"That's some clumsy choreography," I chuckle, as I watch them continue to fight. Josh starts belly laughing, which only makes the experience that much better.

"What made you want to join the Big Brother program?" I ask Owen as we watch Josh cruise a ramp at the skatepark.

Owen looks like he's pondering the best way to answer me. "Josh is very special. He deserves someone in his life who can give him the attention he needs. I know firsthand how hard it can be when you don't have an adult to look up to." His words come out full of sincerity.

"So, I'm guessing the adults in your life let you down pretty badly too," I speak to the ground as I slide my sandal along the cement.

"I would say, let me down, is the nicest way you could possibly frame it." He softens his expression as if to make up for the sudden harsh tone.

"I get it, trust me. I lost all my faith in adults at ten years old." I gulp. I can't believe those words just came out of my mouth.

"Why ten?"

Crap.

"Let's just say it was a bad year." I let out a small nervous laugh.

"Can I ask why?"

"I think you learned all you needed to learn about my family on your sailboat. It even made you fall asleep." I chuckle.

"We both fell asleep, and it wasn't while you were talking about your family. I still only know the basics."

"Honestly, you know more than most people. I'm not one to relive my past through stories."

"Running from your demons just creates more demons," Owen replies flatly.

"I also don't like telling the world my business."

"The world? It's just me, Valletta. Someone who totally gets it. Plus, who would I tell? We don't exactly run in the same circles, outside of a meeting of course." He nudges me playfully, forcing me to look up at him. As soon as I do, I regret it. He overtakes me. His eyes are piercing with determination. Determination to know me, to listen to me. It makes me feel special in a way I have never experienced before. The crazy thing is how quickly he came into my life. I have to answer him, I have to keep this connection.

"Well, you know my dad left. I was ten when he did. He was my best friend. Him leaving is why I lost faith in adults. He was just, poof, gone." I push down the lump coming up.

"Have you talked to him since?"

I nod, "He tried to contact me two years ago, but it didn't end well." I swallow.

"I will never understand how anyone could leave you." Owen says this so softly, I can feel myself melt. I want to kiss him, just escape this moment by falling into him. Anxious to know if his lips are as rigid as they appear. His jaw always seems so tight. I want to loosen it. This is only our third time together in person. I wonder if either of us would go for it. Maybe he doesn't want to kiss me. Is this something you have to ask permission for?

"Have you ever tried confronting him?" he asks.

"My dad?"

He nods.

"No. There's no point. He can't change the past. He messed up my life in ways that can't be undone. Confronting him wouldn't help anyone."

"What do you mean messed up? Do you go to those meetings for more than just your mom's alcoholism?" Owen's eyes narrow as he asks. It's like he's searching for a specific answer. I wonder if he can see the truth.

I spring up from the bench as my phone vibrates. Melanie is calling me. "Oh, crap. I forgot I was supposed to call her about hanging out. Do you mind?"

"No, go ahead. I'm going to go check on Josh." Owen gets up from the bench and heads into the skatepark, dodging kids on wheels.

"Hey Mel, I'm sorry. I forgot about our plans, I'm actually with Owen."

"What?! Oh my gosh, this is like, legit! I've never seen you talk to a guy this much."

"Calm down." I roll my eyes at her dramatic response.

"So, when do I get to meet this Owen, anyway?"

"I don't know, it's still so new."

"You're not embarrassed of me, are you?" Melanie's voice is shrill.

"Actually, yes. Yes, I am," I smile.

"You brat. Ask him if he wants to hang out soon! Your friends would like to know who you are spending all this time with, plus, I want you to meet Jayce. We should double!" The thought of doubling makes my stomach churn. A part of me does want Owen to get to know my friends, though, especially since he and Mark got off on the wrong foot.

Melanie and I chat for a couple of minutes as she updates me on the last few days of her life. This past week has been so busy, I've barely seen my friends, just in passing at work. When we hang up, I sit back for a moment to watch Owen talk to Josh. It almost looks like Josh's shoulders fall, his excitement leaving him. When Owen returns to sit next to me, there's pain in his eyes. He must have told Josh we have to leave soon.

"He's lucky to have you, you know." I smile softly at Owen, trying to soften the blow of letting Josh down. "I mean, you give him these incredible days to live for."

"Glad you see it that way," Owen smiles back.

I clear my throat, sitting upright, ready to make a request. "So, how would you feel about doing something with my friends? Just like, a dinner, or whatever." My heart races as I wait for a response.

"Your friends, huh?" My heart sinks at his tone. He continues, "I'm assuming Mark would be one of these friends?" Owens keeps his eyes on Josh as he talks.

"Once you get to know him and Melanie, you will love them. You just need to get used to their high energy." I smile anxiously.

"I don't think Mark cares to get to know me, and I'm not up for any drama."

"Owen, you're getting it all wrong. Things were just intense because of how you guys met. Mark is literally the chillest person."

"I believe you. I just don't think I'll have much to talk about with your friends from what you've told me about them. Don't get me wrong, they sound like really great people, but the kind of people I would need to make small talk with, you know? I am not one for small talk and dull silences."

This is the first time anger has risen in my chest from something Owen has said. He's pried, smoked, and shown up with no notice at my house. Those things were a little bit irritating, but for him to essentially call my friends simple-minded or dull is actually making me angry.

"I'm sorry, are you assuming you're too smart or worldly for my friends?" My defenses are high.

Owen turns to me. He looks over my face. "Valletta, I really didn't mean to upset you. I have nothing against your friends and I definitely don't feel too smart for them. I just don't think we would have a lot in common."

"I'm sorry, I guess I didn't realize how closed-minded you are." I sit back on the bench crossing my arms.

Owen chuckles, which only makes my anger grow. "Okay, okay. I have clearly hit a nerve. I'm sorry, Valletta. I promise, I don't mean it the way you're taking it. If anything, I'm just nervous that it won't go well, and you will be disappointed. They truly do sound like wonderful people."

I look at Owen, his expression carries an intensity that makes me believe him. I slowly uncross my arms and sit upright again.

He continues, "If it means this much to you, then I would love to spend some time with them, get to know them more." He smiles gently at me. His smile is like a defroster on my anger. It slowly melts away the longer I look at him.

Nineteen

A HAND REACHES AROUND me, stealing a few chips from my bag. I'm propped up on the break table facing the window. I turn around, glaring at Mark, "Get your own bag, you thief!"

"You know I would, but stealing tastes so much better," Mark says with his mouth full and a twinkle in his eyes. I respond by pelting a chip at his head.

"Okay, well, that's just wasteful, Letta." He shakes his head in disapproval. I ignore him and look out of the window, watching passers-by.

"Why do you seem like you're actually in a good mood today?" I can tell he's asking me from inside the fridge, his voice is all muffled.

"Hey, I'm always in a good mood," I say.

Mark laughs in response which I find rather insulting.

"Things have been pretty peaceful this past week for a change."

"Oh? What made it so good?"

I can smell the sandalwood spice cologne that Mark always wears, his attempt to override the smell of the food he's been cooking. He's leaning down near my shoulder, looking out the window with me.

"Don't ask questions you don't want the answers to," I reply.

"Why wouldn't I?" Mark stops and exhales, "Let me guess—Owen?"

I look over and smile at him.

"I'm sorry, but I don't trust the guy. He came out of nowhere and he has some weird vibes."

"That is the most superficial reasoning I've ever heard to not trust someone."

"It's called intuition, Letta, and mine is always right."

Now it's my turn to laugh, "You are so full of it."

"Full of knowledge, yes," he says proudly.

I can't handle his arrogance right now, but at the end of the day, Mark is very important to me, and I want him and Owen to get along. I'm sure they will once they get over their prejudices.

"Actually, Mark, I do have a favor to ask." I spin around, making direct contact with his bright green eyes. He's still leaning down towards me, our eyes level.

"A favor? Well, that's gonna cost you." He smirks, not taking me seriously.

"For this favor, I'm prepared to pay fairly."

I can tell he's intrigued, then he holds out his hand and I rest the chip bag on it. He grabs them before sitting in the chair near my legs and looking up at me.

"I'm listening," he says.

I wipe the chip dust off my fingers and sit up straight, clearing my throat. "I want you to give Owen a chance. A fair, unbiased, genuine chance."

Mark doesn't respond, he just pops another chip in his mouth.

"Look," I continue, "he's a really good guy. He's passionate, extremely smart, and really listens to me. He's even in the big brother program. His little brother is very important to him. He cares about the important stuff."

"You know, you don't have to sell me on him. I'm not interested in dating him." Mark looks at me with a smirk.

I roll my eyes, "I know I don't need to sell you on him. It's my business who I date, of course, but I want you to like him." I reach out and grab the chip bag back from Mark, getting close to his face. "Despite your obnoxious ways, you're kinda important to me, you know."

Mark smiles. I already know he's not going to let this go. "How important?"

"Let's just say if a car was coming around the bend while you're crossing the street, I might actually yell and warn ya." I pop a chip in my mouth, not giving him what he wants.

"I guess for you, that's a big deal." He smiles softly at me and despite myself, I soften. He has the golden retriever effect on me sometimes. I just can't help but adore him.

"So, you'll give him a chance? One evening in the same building, all ammunition away?"

"If it means that much to you, you know I'll be there. But you'll owe me, of course." He grabs the chip bag back and leans into the chair, "I just need to figure out what I want." He smiles at me mischievously.

Twenty

As I STROLL TO therapy, I take the time to notice the Birds of Paradise scattered here and there, a beautiful flower I sometimes overlook. There's a sweet smell in the air, making the horrors of a couple of weeks ago slowly fade into the back of my mind, leaving me hopeful. Things are truly looking up. It's the first time in a long time that I'm not dreading therapy.

"So, Valletta, I want you to try and take a break from the sleeping pills. It's a good opportunity to work on the exercises we talked about doing before bed."

I shift my eyes from the cactus on the windowsill and look directly at Dr. Sage, her words sinking in. I'm stunned. I was doing so well today, cooperating with all her seemingly pointless questions.

"I'm sorry?" I ask innocently as if I must have heard her wrong.

"You have been depending on them for a while since your initial incident, and I think it's time we try other methods. We don't want your body becoming too dependent on them." She was speaking carefully, as if she was dancing around something. She said 'incident' like it was a dirty secret and 'depending' as if I were a full-blown addict.

"Look, I know it seems like I've been taking a lot of them, but I have been careful. It was just very stressful a couple of weeks ago."

She does not react.

My panic increases. "Look, Dr. Sage, it's way worse for my health if I don't sleep at all, right?" My eyes are wide, staring into hers for mercy. "I just need a couple more for emergencies. I promise, I'm being careful."

I can tell she is closed off to my pleading. The room begins to feel stuffy. My chest is tightening and my mind is racing to find a way to convince her to give me a refill.

"Valletta, I'm sure you're being careful." She sighs, "But it's time we start to learn how to deal with stress in healthier ways. It's good to know how to calm yourself independently." She says this as if we are in this together, which couldn't be further from the truth.

I was the one who had to lay my head down at night, pushing away the disquieting thoughts and haunted memories constantly trying to break into my brain. I was the one who had to toss and turn all night, going to work with bags under my eyes. This was my problem, not hers.

"So, what do you wanna make for the dinner party?" Melanie asks as we leave In-n-Out.

"I was thinking of curry, perhaps."

"Curry? You sure you can manage to cook a curry?" Melanie snatches one of my fries, smirking at me as she blows on it.

"I can watch a YouTube video, or whatever." I shrug, "I want to do something with a little international feel. Owen has been to so many places around the world, and he always raves about the food in India."

Melanie and I get in her car, our bodies going limp from the ten-hour workday. Our plan was to take our burgers back to my place so we could dust off a bottle of red, like the cheap yet classy girls we are, and then lay on my sofa watching The Great British Baking Show until one of us has the energy to move again. Instead, we sit back in her leather car seats and dig into our grub.

"Is it really wise to cook an Indian dish for the first time for a guy that has eaten in India?" Melanie says.

"I guess, if anything, it shows I care," I reply with a mouth full of burger.

"Wow. I have never ever heard you say anything that cheesy about a guy before. Actually, I've never even seen you care about a guy this much." She winks as she pops in another fry. She always eats her fries before touching her burger, because if a fry is even slightly cooled off, she claims it's like eating rubber.

"As cheesy as it sounds, I've never felt this way about anyone before," I say, even surprising myself at the words leaving my lips.

"Have you guys even kissed? I thought I would have heard about it by now."

"Why would I tell you that?"

"Uhm, because I'm your number one best friend and you're supposed to tell me everything, duh."

I laugh, almost spitting out my food. "You are too much. People don't make a big deal out of kissing someone. We aren't in middle school."

"I mean, no offense, love, but you've barely dated enough to even be at a middle school level." She nudges me playfully, "But come on, I wanna know, have you?"

I sigh, "No, and honestly, I have no idea why. I know I could make the first move, but this guy just puts me under a spell or something."

"Hmm." Melanie is quiet, suddenly looking like she's in deep thought, as she slowly unravels her burger wrapping.

"What?"

"Nothing," she says softly. I can tell she's thinking something.

"Mel, come on, what?"

"Okay, like, don't get mad at me. I'm sure it's nothing, but I just find that a little weird."

"What, that we haven't kissed yet? Seriously? Not everyone has to move as fast as you." I instantly regretted how that came out. Her face turned red and twisted for a second.

"Valletta, that's not at all what I mean. It's totally fine if you haven't kissed because you both want to take it slow, but you should feel comfortable around him. I mean, butterflies is one thing, but if he's making you so nervous that you feel like you are under his spell, or whatever . . ." She pauses, "I don't know, I guess, just be careful. Being under a guy's spell isn't as charming as the movies make it seem."

My face must clearly show how irritated I am becoming. I don't like that Melanie is assuming bad things about Owen.

"Please, don't take that the wrong way, babe. I just don't really know this guy yet, and when you talk about him, you don't seem to know him either. But you are falling faster than I've ever seen you fall. I don't want him to just string you along without any control."

"Oh my gosh," I groan. "You and Mark are so suspicious and judgmental of him. Also, I am twenty-three years old! Just because I don't have as much experience as you guys doesn't mean I'm a total naive idiot."

"Of course not. We just care is all, I promise. Well, Mark more than cares." She smirks.

"Would you stop it with the whole Mark thing!" I roll my eyes.

"Hey, I just say it as I see it. I'm sure he wouldn't make you feel nervous to kiss him."

"Okay, we are moving on from this topic." I sigh, "Also, sorry about what I said."

Melanie instantly waves her last fry in the air, "Forgotten."

I smile at my best friend. She never holds things against me. We dust the In-n-Out from our clothes and head back to my apartment to open a bottle of wine. Having Melanie there makes it so my first night without sleeping pills won't be a complete nightmare.

Twenty-one

I'M HAVING A BIT of an out-of-body experience. Owen is sitting next to me on the pale peach sofa at Catalina's as he writes in his small brown leather journal. All I can think about is when I saw him in here for the first time but was too afraid to make a move. I smile at the memory because look at us now. It takes all the self-control in the world not to try and sneak a peek at the page he's writing on.

I nudge him, "So, are you ever going to share anything you write in that precious journal?" As soon as I ask him, his hand slowly closes the journal, turning it even farther away than it already was. He smiles at me, the expression in his eyes slowly brightening.

"Curiosity suits you," he whispers as he leans towards me, "You know, it's actually been pretty hard to concentrate with you sitting right next to me."

I try to ignore the fluttering in my stomach, thinking about what Melanie said. I hate to admit that she's right, but it's true that I don't know a lot about Owen. I know he went to school for journalism and he's in between jobs. But he won't tell me what this mysterious job he's after is. He said it's bad luck to tell me before he gets it, which is either really endearing that he's that nervous, or he just doesn't trust me with any of his personal information. Of course, the second option would be a major red flag considering I've opened up to him about something pretty much every time I see him.

Owen looks at me with an earnest smile. "What's in that busy head of yours, Valletta Skye?" The way he says my full name could make me literally swoon.

"Honestly?" I say biting my lip.

"Nothing but honesty." His finger grazes my cheek.

"I feel like I don't know a lot about you."

"What do you want to know?"

His casualness throws me off, making me go blank. What did I want to know? I ponder for a moment, until finally it comes to me, a very risky question, but one I think by now I deserve to know the answer to.

"Why were you at that meeting?"

He takes a deep breath in, nodding his head as if he understands why I'm asking. "That's fair." He pauses a moment, sitting upright, "My father is a closet user. He hides it so well. Everyone thinks he is the greatest." He shakes his head angrily, "People have no idea what he put his family through."

"I'm so sorry, Owen," I whisper.

He shrugs, "It's something everyone in that meeting can relate to in one way or another."

"And your mom?" I venture.

Owen's face twists. He stays silent for a moment before turning his gaze on me. I look into his face wondering if I'm seeing pain, anger, or sadness. Then my phone rings with a blocked number. I swipe the red button, and Owen asks if everything is okay.

"Yeah, just a scammer most likely." My phone rings again, the number is still blocked. I sigh, annoyed.

"You sure you don't want to answer it?" Owen asks.

"Nah, it's blocked." I shrug it off, but there's a small part of me that can't help but wonder. After all, it's not the first time I've gotten a call from a blocked number that I shouldn't have answered.

When my phone rings for a third time, my mind starts to race. Owen reaches over and grabs my phone.

"Geez, who has the nerve to call three times like that?" he mutters angrily. I try to protest, causing a few heads in Catalina's to turn, but it's too late.

"Who the hell is this?" Owen whispers fiercely into the phone. I stay still, unable to make out the voice on the other end.

"Never mind who I am. Who are you?" Owen's face is twisted and confused, then suddenly he looks over at me with a blank expression and I already know who it is. Who else would call me three times from a blocked number?

"It's your dad," he whispers as he holds the phone toward me. I furiously shake my head no, as I remain frozen on the sofa.

"She doesn't want to talk to you." He waits. "Okay, I'll let her know." Owen hangs up the phone and turns to me, his eyes deep in reflection. "He gave me an address and time. He wants to meet up."

Fear. I'm frozen with fear.

Twenty-two

I'm graduating college. Wow, I'm actually graduating. I can't believe this day has come. The last four years have been a mixture of failings, winnings, tears, and most of all, exhaustion.

I'm staring at myself in the mirror wearing my dark blue cap and gown, with my white sundress peeking through. I never thought I'd see myself in this outfit. I take a moment and think about how this is real. It's not a dream, it's real.

There's a knock on the door and I hear Mark's voice, "Hey Letta, get your butt out here. We're waiting!"

Then I hear Melanie yelling from farther away, probably lying on my couch, "Let her get perfect, Mark! These pics are super important."

I can hear Mark's groan from behind the door. I smile and take a final look as I smooth my gown and secure my cap.

When I open the door, Mark is sitting on the couch with Melanie. He looks up, and his face becomes a full-blown grin.

"Wow. You look incredible." He takes out his phone and snaps a photo.

"Mark, no!" I put my hand up, but it was too late. He's grinning and turns his phone toward me to show the picture, "This is never getting deleted."

Melanie rushes over to me full of energy, her gown swinging around, "We are going to be the hottest grads this school has ever seen!" She gives me a big hug and then slumps back onto my sofa, picking up the pile of junk mail on my coffee table. "Can you, like, go through your mail already? There's always this big, ugly pile."

I roll my eyes at Melanie as I snatch the mail from her hands and quickly rifle through it. Junk-Junk-Junk . . . I suddenly stop, gripping a blue envelope. My body remains paralyzed.

"You okay?" Mark asks.

"Valletta, why are you like, frozen?" Melanie laughs, then looks at the blue envelope.

"Who's Blue Sky?" She asks, clearly confused. Silence lingers. I feel the edges of the light blue envelope as if feeling the corners would give me an answer, so I wouldn't have to open it. Or, should I? Mark gets up to move closer to me, asking what's wrong.

Almost inaudibly, "It's me," escapes my lips.

"What's you?" Melanie asks.

"Blue Sky." I stare, "Blue Sky is me."

I continue, "My dad-" my voice breaks, "My dad called me Blue Sky." I don't need to look up to see the confusion on their faces.

"Wait." Melanie's voice is slow, "So, this is from your dad?"

I nod and Mark exhales, "Damn."

"I can open it for you," Melanie eagerly offers.

"Melanie, just give her like, a second to think before offering your help." Mark cautions. "This is big."

"Obviously," Melanie replies, hitting Mark's arm. "She's my best friend. I know what she needs, Mark."

"Well then, you should know to let her breathe for-"

"Guys! Stop!" I yell, "This is not helping."

"Sorry," they say in quiet unison.

"Look, it's not a big deal. I'll just open it and then throw it away." I sound so sure of myself, I'm even taken aback, *"I mean, it's just a letter, or whatever, from my dad."*

I start opening it, my heart accelerating as the paper tears. The paper inside is sky blue with clouds. I carefully unfold it. Melanie and Mark are so quiet that I forget they are both inches from me. As I unfold the paper, a check flutters slowly to the floor.

"Oh, my word," I say, shocked.

"What? What is it?" Melanie says anxiously.

"It's a check," I stammer. *"It's a check from my dad,"* I pause, feeling too shy to say the amount. Then I look up at them, my eyes wide, *"It's a check for twenty-thousand dollars."*

"WHAT?!" Melanie squeals

"Holy crap," Mark mutters.

"I know." I am still in shock.

"What does the letter say?!" Melanie asks.

I stare at the page, numb. After what seems like an eternity, I begin to read.

"To my Blue Sky,

I am well aware that you may not feel like my special girl anymore. I know it's all my fault. But you are still and will always be, the bluest sky I've ever seen. I know this doesn't make up for what I've done. Nothing ever could. But I hope it gets you to your next chapter. Your mother told me you were graduating. I guess Abby told her. I am so proud of you. I know you're probably wondering where this money came from. I don't want to make this letter about me, but I want you to know that I'm sober and I have a steady job. I want more than anything to see you, but I understand if you don't want me in your life. Use this money for something great. Don't be like your old man and waste your life away until it's too late. I love you more than you could ever know. Valletta, you are the reason I even try. If you ever want to contact me, I'm at the return address.

Love, Dad."

Somehow my voice stays intact for the whole letter. I can't feel anything. My brain won't process what I just read. It might as well have been read by a stranger in another room.

"Wow," Melanie says softly.

Twenty-three

"ARE YOU OKAY?" I hear Owen's voice, catching myself staring at people in Catalina's Cafe as I snap out of my graduation memories.

"Yes, I'm fine. We should get going."

"You heard me, right? About your dad?"

I nod. "So anyway, Saturday, Melanie and I are going to do a small dinner party at my house and-"

"Valletta, stop for a moment. Your dad just called. That's a huge deal. It's okay to be confused or upset, but we should talk."

"No, and I don't want to talk about this anymore." I get up off the sofa and walk outside, desperate to change the scenery. I stand outside Catalina's taking full breaths of fresh air. A hand rests on the small of my back.

"What happened between you and your dad?" I swing around and look at Owen in disgust.

"Do you really think that's a question I am willing to answer right now?" I growl. "Why do you always do that? You completely ignore the words that come out of my mouth, and you insist on trying to get me to talk about my family. Can't you see that I do not want to talk about my father, period!" I yell, becoming completely breathless.

Owen puts his hands up in surrender, "I'm sorry, Valletta."

I steady myself, embarrassed by my outburst, letting a few moments of silence pass. The roar of the traffic acts as a buffer for my thoughts, observing passersby who seem to be juggling their coffee with their phones as they rush off. After regaining control, I turn to Owen.

"Honestly, Owen, the worst part is, I'm just not strong enough to handle facing any of it. I wish I could go give him a piece of my mind and put this all behind me, but I just can't. I hate to admit that because I don't want to seem weak, especially to you."

Owen steps closer, "Valletta, you are so incredibly strong. Hell, you inspire me." His face carries so much emotion, that he's slowly casting his spell again.

I close my eyes, pushing back tears that threaten to appear, a skill I have mastered. I feel Owen's soft lips gently press into my cheek, his breath like a warm blanket covering my scars. It's like having a wound torn open and then quickly covered in one fell swoop.

"I want to go with you," he says, "To the address. Let's visit your dad." His voice is full of conviction. For whatever reason he seems confident that I will just go along with this crazy plan.

"Owen, no. This is not something I want to do. I especially don't want you to be a part of my family drama. Nothing good ever comes from getting involved with my family, trust me."

Owen takes a deep breath in, then grabs my hand and starts walking without one more word. I probably should ask where he's taking me, but I remain silent. He guides me around a few corners towards the water. As we get out of the building's shadows, I start to feel the warmth from the sun as we approach the docks. Owen gently releases my hand. Without one word I follow his lead, closing my eyes as I focus on the warmth of the sun on my skin and the sounds of the swooshing docks.

For a moment I feel peace.

A shadow casts its chill over me, and when I look up, Owen is inches from my face. His onyx eyes are vibrant for the first time. He gently strokes my cheek with his finger, keeping his gaze locked on mine while using his other hand to carefully pull me closer to him.

My heart is still. He leans in closer, and I don't stop him. His lips gently press into mine. They are cold, like ice.

Just like that, I am completely swept away. It's as if I have become one with the swishing docks, losing all control. His lips are moving mine without any hesitation now, keeping me alive. Kissing him is everything I thought it would be. It's as intense as his eyes. I push even more into his lips, wanting to get completely lost in the dark stormy ocean I see when I look at him. As scary as it is.

As soon as his lips leave mine, I take an anxious breath. Owen is staring at me with a look of contentment, a smile slowly taking over the lips that were just on mine. As he tucks a loose wave behind my ear he whispers, "I would say that was worth the wait."

I still can't respond. I have experienced so many mixed emotions within the last ten minutes. My brain is lost at sea.

"This is real, Valletta. I know you feel it too. I want to be there for you in every way I can. Please, let me. Let's face your dad together. I will be right by your side the entire time. Then we can move on, together."

My dad? As I repeat his words in my head it's like being pulled out of the ocean and forced to stand on land again. My stomach sinks.

"Owen, I can't just-" For whatever reason I fall silent. I feel trapped.

"You can." Owen smiles reassuringly while grazing my hair.

Could I? I mean, I do want to move on. Maybe seeing my father again is the only way. And right now, I have someone in front of me who is willing to face my demons with me, someone who cares. Isn't that what I always wanted?

I take a deep breath before replying, "This is something I am definitely going to regret later."

"So, that means you'll do it?" he asks, narrowing his eyes.

I look at Owen, who seems so invested. Maybe he had to do the same thing before moving on from whatever drama he's been through.

"I'll go." I swallow.

"We'll go," he corrects, drawing me close and pressing his lips on mine again. But this time all I feel is anxiety and fear.

Twenty-four

"**I HAVE** ALWAYS WANTED to co-host a dinner party with you! This is majorly epic, we are like legit grown-ups!" Melanie squeals.

"I don't know why I agreed to this. I don't even know how to cook!" I am frantically cross-checking my recipe for chicken curry. "Oh no, did I forget the ginger?" I go over the pile of ingredients laid out on my counter, which are not leaving any room to actually cook.

"It's right here." Mel picks up the brown aromatic. "Valletta chill, this is gonna be great. That's what YouTube is for, duh."

"You're right, why am I panicking? I just wish Mark was here. He could probably cook this in twenty minutes, and it would taste like heaven."

"Yeah, that man sure does know his way around a kitchen." Melanie winks at me.

"Well, obviously. It's literally his job, Mel."

"Mmhmm."

There's a knock on the door, startling Melanie and me. We both give each other a confused look and then look at the clock on the stove in unison. It's only six pm. No one should be arriving for another hour. Melanie rushes over to the door and squints through the peephole. She laughs, "You got your wish."

"What?"

Melanie swings the door open, "Well, hello boys." Mark and Owen both appear through my doorway an entire hour early. Owen is carrying a bouquet of flowers, and Mark looks like he's holding a lunch box and his knife case.

"Did I accidentally tell you to come at 6pm? I thought I said 7pm." I am in a bit of shock, and completely unprepared for the weird sight of them standing there together.

"Well, first of all," Mark says, "You said you were cooking, never mind the fact you want to cook curry. I pictured you in the kitchen with all your ingredients spread out, but no clue what to do next. Plus, I couldn't let you use any cheap spices." He holds up his lunch box and walks towards me. "Oh, and Owen was right behind me. We had a nice chat on our way up." He raises his eyebrows at me and gives me a little wink. The awkward tension in the room is nearly making me choke. Mark has to move to the side so Owen can hand me the flowers.

"Just wanted to see if you needed anything, plus I wanted to see you before everyone else got here, but I guess that wasn't to be," Owen says, glancing at Mark.

"Thanks," I say quickly, grabbing the flowers. He leans in to kiss me, but I quickly move my face to the side, so he misses my lips and gets my cheek instead.

"Hi," Owen whispers in my ear. I dread PDA, especially in front of my friends. I can see Mark in my peripheral vision, looking over, which doubles my discomfort.

"So, are we gonna cook this curry or what?" Mark asks, pulling out the good Indian spices from his bag. I look over at Melanie. Her face is full of amusement.

"Hi Owen. I'm Melanie, Valletta's number-one best friend. Don't let the scary guy in the kitchen with the sharp knives tell you otherwise."

Owen smirks and reaches his hand out to shake hers, "It's so great to finally meet the famous Melanie. You are my favorite person to hear stories about."

"Likewise." She smirks, "Well, I hope you know Valletta is very important to me, and I won't hold back from asking you any questions I might feel are necessary."

"I'm not afraid." Owen smiles at her, then looks at me and raises both eyebrows. "Do you need any help getting anything ready?"

"No, no, I got it. You just sit back and have some wine. Mel, can you grab him some?" I shoot Melanie a desperate look, hoping she will read my mind and keep him occupied till dinner is ready. She complies.

I look over to see Mark already chopping an onion. As much as I wanted to do this on my own, I am so grateful he came. Now I don't have to stress about dinner.

"Thanks, Mark," I whisper.

"I know you too well." He shakes his head with a smirk, "But just because I'm here doesn't mean you're not helping. Go peel and chop the garlic and ginger." He uses his knife to point to the other cutting board.

Mark and I are in a rhythm, cooking in unison, and not stumbling over each other in my tiny kitchen. I pretty much just follow whatever he instructs me to do. Owen and Melanie are laughing, which eases my tension. This is going okay. Just have to get Mark and Owen talking.

"What are you guys laughing about?" I yell over to Mel and Owen on the sofa.

"Just telling Owen about freshman year of college, and the incident at the spring formal," Melanie yells over proudly. I wince and make a mental note to pummel Melanie later.

"Oh man, I remember that night." Mark flashes me a grin, "The image of you in complete shock and horror when you saw the spotlights hitting your dress is permanently burnt into my brain." Mark starts belly laughing while stirring the curry.

Melanie snorts in laughter, "Valletta isn't the type to actually go out and buy a slip, so it was bound to happen at some point."

"Hey! Enough! Let's not talk about that very unfortunate dress, okay?" I say, flushed.

"Geez, I wish you guys had a picture of that." Owen laughs.

"Oh, so do I," Mark gleams.

I shoot daggers at Melanie, and she has no shame. She just sticks her tongue out at me. I shake my head and ignore the conversation, turning my attention to the curry.

"Is it almost done?" I ask, anxiously looking at it.

"Yeah, just about. Can you check the rice? I'm going to put the Naan on the frying pan."

"I cannot believe you insisted on making homemade Naan. This is crazy, they sell it right there at the supermarket."

"You did not just say that." Mark shakes his head disapprovingly at me.

"Looks perfect," I say, as I stick a fork in the rice.

"It smells amazing in here." Owen is suddenly at the kitchen island sitting on a barstool. "It almost smells as good as one of my favorite restaurants in New Delhi. I spent the winter break of my sophomore year of college there. The food was unreal."

"I've always wanted to go to India to learn how to cook from a local." Mark chimes in.

"Well, from what I can smell, I think they would be really impressed with what you can already do."

"You haven't tasted it yet, so, maybe hold that compliment, but thanks, man." Mark just said 'thanks man' to Owen. I have to turn my head to hide my smile.

"Okay, but I'm cooking too," I say, "It's not just Mark's dish."

"Of course. I'm even more excited to try it because you have been cooking." Owen smiles warmly at me, and for a moment it feels like we are the only two people in the room before Mark speaks up.

"So, what made you want to go to India?"

"I went for my journalism program, which was a dream because I love to travel. The downside was all the injustice. That was very hard to see, and I'll never forget it. It was very eye-opening."

"I can imagine," Mark says genuinely.

"Is it wrong that the main reason I want to go to India is so I can see how good I look in a Sari?" Melanie questions.

"Yes Mel, that is wrong on so many levels," I say, shaking my head as we all laugh, always astonished at her freeness of speech.

"Sorry, but they are just so beautiful!" There's another knock at the door, and Melanie pipes up, "Oh! Must be Jayce." She rushes over to see who it is.

"You sure I can't help?" Owen asks.

"Uhm, sure . . ." I reply, "Do you want to get out the plates and utensils?"

"Of course." He looks around the kitchen.

"Over here." Mark points to a drawer.

"Thanks. You really know your way around here." Owen's tone is flat with a little edge. Mark looks over at me quickly.

"Well, if this girl of ours is ever going to eat a proper meal, I need to cook her some actual food sometimes." Mark says it with a little chuckle, but Owen doesn't laugh.

"I guess I'll have to get to know this kitchen too, so I can cook for you sometime."

"Hey, I'll never say no to a home-cooked meal," I smile at Owen. Mark remains quiet but I catch him rolling his eyes, I look over to make sure Owen didn't see.

"We'll need six plates, Letta." Mark points to the five plates I just placed on the counter.

"Six? Why?"

"I have a date coming."

"Did you just say 'Letta'? Is that your nickname?" Owen's looking at me confused.

I shake my head quickly. "It's definitely not my nickname. Mark just knows how to get under my skin." I turn my attention to Mark, "What do you mean you have a date coming?"

Mark looks at me sharply, "This is a dinner party, is it not? Did I miss the part where everyone could have a date but me?"

"No, of course you can have a date, but you didn't mention anything about bringing one. Would have been nice to know . . . I hope there's enough food." I say passively.

"You know what?" Owen breaks in, "I think I'll have whatever you're drinking, Mark." His tone is tight.

"Yeah, sure, man. Beers' in the fridge. I keep the good stuff in the back because Letta usually buys the cheap crap." Mark nudges Owen towards the fridge.

Owen looks at Mark and raises the beer he's holding, "Bottle opener? I'd ask Letta here, but clearly you know her place just as well."

I am completely mortified at the sudden edge and sarcasm dripping off of Owen, not to mention he just called me Letta after I said I hated it. Before I get a chance to respond, there's another knock on the door.

"I'll get it," I say quickly.

I swing the door open, not bothering to open the peephole. Boy, do I wish I had, because standing in front of me is the worst possible person Mark could have invited. It's Trisha. Blinding Highlights herself. I hate to judge, but why, Mark, why? I take a deep breath, calming myself. "Oh wow, Trisha! Welcome."

A loud piercing squeal hits my ears like a bullet. "Lettaaa! Oh my goodness, hiii!" It's like getting hugged by Barbie herself.

"Actually, Trisha, my name is Valletta, not Letta."

"Oh no! I am so sorry! Mark told me it was Letta, not Valletta. I am so stupid. I must have gotten it backwards." She puts her teeth together and grins in a way to show she's sorry, like an emoji that has come to life. I look over at Mark and glare at him. He's stifling a laugh while finishing off frying the Naan.

For a moment, I completely forgot Jayce was here. I didn't even greet him. He and Melanie are cuddling and laughing quietly on the sofa.

"Hi Jayce. Welcome," I say.

He returns my smile with a small hand wave. He and Melanie have been dating for a while now, and I have yet to have a real conversation with him. He's an interesting choice for Melanie to say the least. He's kind of a wallflower, which is a total contrast to Melanie's outgoing personality.

"Food is ready!" Mark shouts.

I look over at Owen sitting on a barstool at the counter, already halfway through his beer with an irritated look on his face.

What have I gotten myself into? I take a deep breath, putting on the best party face I can manage.

Twenty-five

THE SIX OF US sit in a circle in my living room with our plates balancing on our laps as we carefully place our beverages on the floor. I have no business throwing a dinner party when I don't even have a dining room table, but we are making it work.

"I will say, this tastes as good as it smells. Well done." Owen picks up his beer and cheers towards Mark in appreciation.

"I agree. It's delicious!" Melanie exclaims. "Mark's one talent." She smirks.

"Yeah, one more talent than you have," Mark snaps back playfully.

"Okay, but let's not forget that I was working hard in the kitchen as well, so you're welcome." I hold up my wine glass in appreciation of myself.

"Oh, right, yes, you were in there too. I almost forgot." Mark smiles at me.

I return his smile with an eye roll, "Hey, I was the best assistant you've ever had."

"Well, you're no Sous Chef yet, but you got the job done." He winks at me.

"What's a Sous Chef?" Trisha pipes up, she's taking exaggerated breaths, clearly not able to handle the spice.

"How do you not know what a Sous Chef is when you're literally dating someone who is so close to being one?" I laugh.

Melanie looks at me, her eyes wide as if I just kicked a puppy.

"Oh right, I knew that." Trisha's face turns bright red, and she takes another bite of rice with no curry on it.

"It's fine, Trish. I don't expect us to know everything about each other." Mark smiles at Trisha but I can tell he's hurt.

"I mean, she should probably know your job. That's kind of the basics," I shrug, looking down at my food.

"Why do you care so much?" Owen is glaring at me.

"I don't care. I just find it funny is all," I say, blushing.

Melanie interrupts, clearly trying to break up this conversation. "So, Owen, what is the one thing you've always wanted to do but haven't been able to yet?" She gleams, "Mine's skydiving naked."

I see Jayce choke a little on his Naan at that comment.

"That is not an image I need while I'm eating Mel," I say, even though I am grateful for the ease in tension.

"But what if the wind permanently wrinkled your skin? That would be terrifying." The look on Trisha's face is one of horror. "You know, like in those videos of people skydiving and their faces are full of wrinkles and being all pushed around by the wind. I would be terrified of my skin staying all wrinkly and weird."

We all burst out laughing.

Trisha looks around at us, "Oh, come on, guys! That is a legitimate concern!" She thinks about it for a moment but starts laughing as well. I think I'm grateful Mark brought her after all.

"Well, your body would probably freeze up there anyway," Owen says to Melanie.

"No! Loads of people do it!"

"Loads? Really, Mel?" I snicker.

"Yes, I swear! We should totally go this summer!"

"Aerial dancing was enough for at least the next decade for me." I smile down at my food, amused at all the things Melanie ropes me into . . . literally.

"I still need that video!" Mark says with a mouthful of curry.

"Of course you want that video," Melanie gleams at Mark teasingly.

"What does that mean?" Mark looks at her in annoyance, still chewing his food.

Melanie just shrugs while smirking at me. I realize what she's trying to imply and shift awkwardly, feeling a few nervous butterflies fly into my stomach.

"I think anyone here would want to see Letta fall on her face trying to hang from those ropes. I mean that's just good comedy." Mark snickers, but I can tell he's starting to feel uncomfortable.

I feel Owen's body tighten beside me.

"So, Mark, just curious, why are you the only person who calls Valletta, Letta? Also, just curious, how often are you actually here at this apartment?"

"Owen?" I glare. Where is all this attitude coming from? I can't help but wonder if he's feeling his drinks too much.

Owen looks back at me and gives me a dark smile, "What? I can't be let in on you and Mark's little secrets?"

"Hey man, how much have you had to drink?" Marks snaps back at Owen.

"Why can't you just answer the question, Mark?" Owen spits. I am mortified, I have never seen Owen act like this.

"Look, I just call her Letta to mess with her. It's a joke. No need to take it so seriously."

"Maybe we should talk about something other than Valletta's boring nickname. It's not even cute. If it was, I would use it. Right, babe?"

Melanie looks at me trying to lighten the mood. She throws her arm around Jayce. "We should play truth or dare!"

I quickly shake my head at Melanie, "Let's not. Why don't we just talk about common interests? Mark, did you know that Owen has been to a proper Rugby game in England?"

"That's cool. Must be nice to be able to jet off to all these different countries," Mark says bitterly.

"I have always wanted to go to Paris! We should totally go to Paris together!" Trisha looks hopefully at Mark, snuggling up close to him. I can't help but be repulsed by the sight of them snuggled up. Mark looks over at me and I look away, suddenly feeling like I was doing something wrong. Why am I so bothered by seeing him with her? Is it because Trisha is sticking around and coming to dinner parties that I am hosting? I'm not used to Mark bringing girls to something so intimate. I guess I'm used to having him to myself. Wow. Am I that selfish?

"Traveling opens your mind. Otherwise, people tend to get stuck in a box, only concerned about what's going on in their little bubble . . ." Based on Owen's tone alone, he sounds like he's far into the tipsy stage. He looks at me, "I know that Valletta would agree with me. She wants more out of life than just staying here in San Diego and working at a restaurant with her friends. Isn't that right, Valletta? At least, that's what you told me the other night." He takes another swig of beer while directing his stare at Mark.

"Owen! Stop!" I hiss in his ear, officially done with his evil alter ego.

"You said that?" Both Mark and Melanie speak at the same time, staring at me.

My stomach drops.

"That was said completely out of context." I'm exasperated.

"I didn't know you were so anxious to leave us," Melanie says. She looks hurt and seems done with trying to change the subject.

Somehow both Jayce and Trisha are just continuing to eat their food as if we are having small talk.

"It actually has nothing to do with either of you. I just want to travel and see more. You both know this." I look at Owen, angry, "What is going on with you?"

"Nothing," Owen's smile is fake, "I'm doing great." Is he really this jealous of Mark? I can't help but wonder if the drinks were to blame. "I just find it funny that you guys are so close and yet claim to be 'just friends.' I've never seen a friendship like it, that's for sure."

"Aww, that is so cute!" Trisha smiles at me. The scary thing is, she is being genuine. Owen chugs the rest of his beer while staring at Mark. Mark stands up and places his plate on his chair.

"Can you help me with dessert in the kitchen quickly?" Mark asks me as his eyes send me mixed signals. I look around the room, flushed, then at Owen, who rolls his eyes at Mark.

"We haven't even finished dinner yet. Why don't you let her finish eating," he slurs.

"Alright, I'm trying to be nice, but back off." Mark's voice is getting edgy now.

I quickly get up and grab Mark's arm, "It's fine, we will just be a minute." I look around again. Everyone is staring at me. I smile awkwardly, "Just want to warm it up before serving."

I pull Mark with me to the kitchen, quickly turning up the music, hoping it will drown out our voices.

"What, Mark? Did you really have to make a scene?"

"Me? Are you kidding? I'm not the one who is acting like a jealous drunk!" His tone is harsh.

I sigh, not wanting to admit that he's right. I start fiddling around in the fridge to make it seem like we are doing something. I grab the whipping cream and shove it into Mark's chest, "Look busy so this doesn't seem so weird."

I search the cabinets for my whisks. We start working over each other but close enough so we can whisper.

"Look," Mark says, "I don't like the way he's treating you, okay? I want to put him in his place but I'm trying to respect your feelings."

"I promise he's not like this. I don't know what's gotten into him. Maybe just stop calling me Letta and acting like you live here. He's obviously feeling threatened by you . . ."

Mark's eyes laser focus on mine, "Are you listening to yourself?"

"What?"

"That is no excuse for him to act like that. If he's feeling threatened, he should talk to you like a normal adult."

I laugh bitterly at Mark. "Are you seriously giving me relationship advice? Wow, that is rich. Oh, so, totally unrelated question, how is it possible that your girlfriend over there doesn't even know what a Sous Chef is?" I glare at him.

"Trisha isn't technically my girlfriend, okay?"

"And there it is!" I smile sarcastically at Mark. "You never have an actual girlfriend, do you? It's always just a casual fling, and yet you think you're so much better than Owen." I shake my head, turning on the whisks to their loudest setting. I start whipping the cream, but Mark grabs my arm, trying to take the whisks from me.

"Give me those, you have no idea what you're doing." I oblige because he's not wrong. The noise from the whisks makes it so Mark has to lean down to whisper directly in my ear, "First of all, the girls I hang out with know what they are getting themselves into. I don't play with people's hearts and tease them constantly, giving off mixed signals."

I whip around to face Mark, completely thrown off by his statement. He doesn't look up, instead he clenches his jaw, staying completely focused on the whipping cream. I want to respond but I'm too stunned. His words make me feel attacked for some reason. I push my thoughts out of my brain and grab the store-bought blueberry pie from the fridge. I take it out of the package, putting it on a nice plate to give the homemade illusion.

Twenty-six

SOMEHOW, WE MADE IT through the rest of the dinner party without any major hiccups. Granted, calling it a dinner party is far too kind. Owen was on edge after Mark and I came back from getting the dessert ready, but thankfully he kept his mouth shut. Maybe his buzz wore off. Melanie didn't bring up my wanting to leave San Diego again, and Trisha provided entertainment with the things that came out of her mouth. Despite the lingering uneasiness from Mark's words, I was thankful I survived the night.

"Want me to stay and clean up with you?" Melanie asks as we bring our plates to the kitchen. "No, no. You go with Jayce. I got this."

"Okay, but you can't say I didn't offer." She smiles at me.

I hug her and Jayce goodbye. Right behind them is Mark with Trisha clinging to him. If she pushed her body any closer to his, they would literally be one person. Something about the sight makes my stomach turn.

"Thank you so, so much! I had such a blast!" Trisha exclaims. "That blueberry pie was delicious. You have to give me the recipe."

Mark lets out a laugh. We are both amused realizing she thinks I actually made that pie, but hey, I'll take the credit.

"It was no problem at all and sure, I'll send it right over," I smile at her. I have to admit she's kind of growing on me. I'm starting to see why Mark keeps her around. Trisha hugs me so tight that I can't breathe for a moment. I go to hug Mark, but he sidesteps me.

"I'll see you at work." He barely looks at me, he just walks past with Trisha clinging to him. Something feels almost broken between us. Maybe it's just a weird night.

"Bye, Mark," I whisper, and just like that they are gone. I turn around to see Owen cleaning up the dishes in the kitchen, his head down.

"You really don't have to do that."

He looks up at me, his face expressionless, "I want to."

At this point I don't know what to say to him. I'm upset and confused by his behavior. I remain quiet for a moment, checking the living room for any glasses left behind. I find a couple of beer bottles under Owen's chair. I pick them up and walk back into the kitchen.

I steady myself. "Owen, what was up with you tonight?"

"What do you mean?" His expression is not confused. He knows exactly what I mean.

"Look, I'm only going to ask you this once and we never have to talk about it again, but no matter what, I need you to be honest with me." I look at him waiting for his attention. "Do you have a problem with drinking?"

"No." He says it with complete certainty.

"Then what in the world was up with you tonight? I was raised by alcoholics. Once that fluid hits the bloodstream they completely change. Just like you did tonight." I cross my arms in an attempt to stand my ground, despite how uncomfortable this conversation is.

Owen sighs and puts both his hands on the counter, looking down. "I'm not proud of how I acted. Can we leave it at that?" I stare at him, keeping my arms crossed, no sign of backing down on this one.

Owen smirks, "You are cute when you're determined."

"This isn't the time for your sarcasm. Just tell me why you were being such a slurring jerk?" I say dryly, holding back my emotions.

"I was nervous for tonight. I wanted to get along with your friends, so I had a shot or two earlier just to calm down. I mean, your friends are so different from you and I was worried it would just be a lot of agonizing small talk about frivolous things." He shrugs as if he didn't just say something so insulting.

"You do realize how small-minded that makes you, not them, right?"

"I do," he says simply. "I was a pompous jerk. It's kind of my go-to attitude, but I'm working on it." He clears his throat. Is he actually nervous? "When I got here, I felt more relaxed until I saw Mark in the hallway." He looks up at me, keeping his body in place. "I wanted to come early to be with you and help you with whatever you needed, but Mark showed up ready to cook the whole dinner and everything. Then, when I saw how comfortable he was here, it made me feel sick. I mean, when I came by to ask you out for the first time, he was in the kitchen cooking you breakfast while you were in a towel."

My arms soften slightly, realizing how I would feel if the situation were reversed.

"I realized how close he and you are and . . . I'm trying to be the one to get close to you, Valletta." He shifts himself off the counter, staring at me now, "I'll admit I probably shouldn't have had so many drinks. I got uncomfortable and I drank more, which loosened me up too much because I couldn't hold those feelings in like I normally would. I hate to admit this, but I think I am a bit threatened by Mark."

I swallow, not sure how to handle his vulnerability. I do appreciate it. I know that isn't an easy thing to admit. What matters is that he is being honest with me.

"You have nothing to worry about when it comes to Mark," I say.

"Are you sure about that?"

"Completely."

"Does Mark know that?"

"What do you mean?"

Owen sighs, "Have you guys actually talked about this? I mean, I see the way he looks at you and how he treats you. He is completely under your spell."

Owen's words startle me. I'm used to Melanie teasing me about this but to hear it from someone else, never mind Owen, is unsettling, to say the least.

"Owen, Mark and I have been friends and only friends for five years. Trust me, there's nothing there but friendship."

He doesn't seem convinced, but he nods his head anyway, looking down again. He's acting so different right now, it's like seeing Superman without his cape. He lost his powers. Then I realize, all of this is a sign. A sign he's not untouchable, he really cares about me, and this is real. For the first time, I can see Owen's vulnerability. I can relate to him.

"I'm sorry for how I acted tonight. In hindsight, I should have tried harder to reign it in and control myself."

"It's okay. We all have those nights. Thank you for being honest with me." As I smile at him, his eyes have a small glimmer that's returning in the darkness.

Twenty-seven

"**Thanks for** staying to help clean up." I smile at Owen, grateful to have the person I liked back and not the monster from dinners past.

"Of course. Thank you for letting me." He walks over to me, placing his cold hand on my cheek. He guides my mouth to his and gently kisses me. I completely melt into his lips. The pressure of the first kiss behind me, this is what I have been waiting for, for things to start to feel natural between us. He pulls away just as gently as he pulled me towards him, his eyes full of glimmering stars.

"I should probably go," he says. He is searching my face. I swallow, realizing he's asking me more than telling me.

We both jump as my phone vibrates on the counter. I reach for it, wondering who could possibly be calling. I quickly press decline when I see the blocked number, praying Owen didn't see it.

"Who was that?"

"Just Melanie, I'll call her back." I pull away from Owen, avoiding eye contact. "You know, I am completely exhausted. I think I need to get to bed." I give an exaggerated yawn in an attempt to seem genuine.

"Who called you, Valletta?" Owen's tone is cutting, which throws me off for a second.

"I said, Melanie," I answer flatly.

"You're lying. I can tell." He breathes sharply. "Please, be honest with me, I was just honest with you."

I manage to make eye contact with him, "It was just a blocked number. I don't know who it was."

"Are you nervous it was your dad again?" We both know the answer to his question, It makes me angry that he has the nerve to ask.

Owen steps closer. "I wonder why he's calling again? Do you think it's to cancel or change the location?" He sounds worried.

"Honestly, I don't care. I feel like we should forget the whole thing, anyway."

"No, no, we are going. You agreed. This will be good for you." Owen pulls my chin up with his finger so I look at him. "I just wish you had answered that in case the location has changed, or something." He almost seems genuinely annoyed, which I can't help but feel angry at.

I look at him with confusion, "You know it is my decision if I want to talk to him or not, right?"

"Of course. I just want to be a support. I know how hard this can be, trust me." He smiles reassuringly.

He has no idea what happened last time. Since the first phone call in Catalina's, the memories of my graduation are threatening to resurface all of it, the good and the bad. I just want them to stop.

Even though I'm standing in my kitchen looking at Owen, I see Mark. I see us on my graduation day, right after opening the letter from my dad as the check fell to the floor.

"What do you need? Today is your day Valletta, your day. Don't let anything ruin that. We can talk about this and fully unpack it right

here and now. Or we can completely table it or bury it and carry on celebrating you, and what you have accomplished. Just say what you need." Mark is staring right into my eyes. He is talking in that way he only talks when he's really trying to figure something out. He's being so patient and kind as I stand completely frozen in my apartment.

We need to leave now to make it on time for graduation, so, I insisted on Melanie leaving ahead of us. I could tell it killed her to leave without me, but this was her day just as much as it was mine and I refused to ruin it for her. I told her that I just needed a few minutes to gather myself and I would be right behind her.

"Valletta?" Mark sounds desperate now. I think I'm scaring him. I want to talk but I just can't find the words. I close my eyes and focus on nothing at all. I need to put this out of my mind. Mark just rests his hand on my shoulder and gently rubs my back in circles, trying to soothe me.

When I open my eyes, I feel calm. A sense of clarity. Melanie and I have been through so much and worked so hard to get to this day. This wasn't my day. This was our day. How dare my family problems even try to disrupt that? I needed to be there not just for me but mostly for her. I take a deep breath and look at Mark with determination.

"Let's go. I want to be there with Melanie. I want to stick to the original plan. Let's celebrate and be young and twenty-one." I manage a full grin to show my sincerity. The funny thing is I'm really smiling. I don't think my brain is processing anything, which I am grateful for.

"Well, I'm twenty-two but I can totally act like I'm twenty-one." He winks at me.

"You act like you're eighteen, Mark, don't flatter yourself with false maturity."

"Ouch!" Mark exclaims but he's smiling. I can tell he's relieved.

"Valletta? Hey, are you okay?" Owen's arm is resting on my shoulder, his face full of worry. His voice sounds like it's a mile away, but it's becoming louder.

"I'm fine." I turn and flash a smile, not letting myself feel anything. I refuse to feel anything until he leaves. All I want is to find a sleeping pill and go to sleep, but Owen is here, so I grab the last item to wash. The dish soap is foaming around my hands. Owen reaches around me, turning the water off. I know what he's doing. He wants me to break down, he wants me to let him in. I stubbornly turn the water back on and say nothing.

"Valletta, you have got to deal with this. You can't run away." Owen's voice is filled with certainty which irritates me.

"You weren't there," I pause, taking a shallow breath but not exhaling.

"Where?" Owen asks softly.

"When I was ten, or when I was a teenager, or two years ago on my college graduation day . . . you weren't there." The water is starting to burn a little, but I don't shut it off. Then Owen shuts it off again. He takes the glass, placing it to the side while touching my shoulder, making me shudder.

"What happened two years ago?" I can tell by the way he's asking that he won't let me change the subject despite my desperation to run away.

"You want to know what happened?! I'll tell you!" I yell. "My dad is a drug dealer." I shrug, despite the anger building.

Owen is taken aback but moves a step closer to me.

"Yeah, that's right," I continue, "I was just a pawn in his dangerous business. Do you have any idea how it feels to learn that your father, your best friend in the whole world, is nothing but a liar?"

"Valletta, I'm so-"

"No, Owen. Save it, okay? That's it, that's the horrible truth you so desperately want to know . . . Happy?" I sneer, turning away from him.

I drop my neck over the sink, my dark waves providing a shield. My eyes are squeezed so tight together that they feel like they are being pushed further into my skull. I can feel each muscle in my chest as it tightens. Tears erupt like a volcano, a volcano that gave no warning until it was too late. I've been living under its shadow for two years, ignoring all the pressure building, the smoke pouring out the top. I spent each day in denial because I knew if I looked at the top of the volcano and acknowledged the steam, it would erupt.

My tears flow down like lava, hot and sticky, overtaking my face.

Owen grabs me and pulls me into him. "I'm so sorry, Valletta."

I push him back, forcing the lava to stop flowing, "I'm fine!" I realize yelling isn't the way to prove that I'm fine, but I lose control. "Owen, I really need you to leave. I just need to be alone.

"I can stay-"

"No! Please, just go." I can't tell if it's worry or stubbornness that fills his face, but either way, I want him out. "I promise I will be fine. I'm just extremely overtired and I'm starting my period like, any minute." That was a total lie, I was desperately grasping at straws, anything to get him out.

"Okay, if that's really what you want, I'll go."

"It is." I cross my arms and look around him to the door.

"Alright." He looks defeated. He leans in to kiss me on the cheek as he puts his coat on. "Call me if you need me, okay?"

I nod, trying to hold it together until I can get him out the door.

The second he leaves, the eruption starts, but this time it's overflowing. There's no stopping it. I sink to the floor and lay in the lava.

Twenty-eight

MAY 2021

Week following College graduation.

I was so anxious that my breakfast didn't stay in my stomach for long. The cold tiles on my bathroom floor soothed my trembling skin. I wish I could blame the food for being bad, but I knew it was the fact that I was going to the address today, the address from his letter.

I was going to see my dad.

I considered it all week, tossing and turning every night. But I wanted closure. I wanted to use the money for college so that I could help kids who needed me. That's what's important right? I refused to be one of those people who threw away an opportunity that was handed to them. When I'm old and wrinkly sitting in my rocking chair, I want to have no regrets.

So, I made up my mind. I was going to see the person who gave me life and then took it away. My mother could also fit into this category, but she only gave me life physically, nothing more, and for some reason that hurts less. I knew where I stood with her my entire life. Nothing had changed.

I recovered from being sick and managed to shower and get dressed without any problems. I rejected any thought that came into my mind outside of the next action. Put on a shirt. Put on pants. Brush hair. Dry hair. And so on.

Eventually, I was ready to go, ready to face the anxiety head-on. Mark wanted to come with me, but I said no, I needed to do this alone. I love Mark for even being willing to take on such a challenge. He said he would keep his phone on loud to make sure he wouldn't miss my call if I needed him. That's Mark, always there for me in any way I let him be.

I arrived at the address completely shocked. This was a house. Like, a legit house. Did my dad actually buy a house? There was no way. Unless he was truly doing that well. Maybe this was his redemption arc. As angry and hurt as I was, I was determined to be happy for him and try to move on. As soon as I started walking up the stone pathway, I panicked.

What am I doing here? I didn't even call. What am I going to say when I see him? My stomach starts clenching and I'm thankful I didn't eat anything else after breakfast. Before I know it, my finger is pushing the doorbell. It's like my body is on autopilot, sticking to the original plan, but my mind is trying to abort the plan and run away.

I hear footsteps. Someone is coming. Is there time to dash behind a bush until they go back inside, then make a run for it?

"Can I help you?" A big-boned gruff man who I have never seen before is standing in front of me.

"Oh, I'm so sorry, I think I have the wrong house. I'm looking for Derek Skye."

"Who are you?" His voice is all bass.

"I'm-" I pause, questioning if I should tell this guy anything, some scary-looking stranger I don't know. "I'm just an old friend, but clearly, I got the wrong house."

The man stares at me, his bushy eyebrows tilted downward looking at me. "An old friend, eh? What brings you here today?" He crosses his arms, and I realize . . . maybe I'm not at the wrong house. My stomach drops because if my dad does live here then something is wrong. Unless this is his roommate?

"Jennifer!" The grizzly man yells out behind him.

Oh, no. Please be a different Jennifer. Please. My heart is pounding as I hear someone else coming down. The smell hits me first, moldy flowers.

"Valletta? What on Earth are you doing here?"

"Mom."

"This is your daughter?" The bushy eyebrows go upwards.

"I had her very young." She looks ashamed for a moment. We both just stare at each other, not moving.

"So, Derek is your father." The man's voice is grave now. "That's useful to know if he doesn't do well on this trip." His words make my stomach sink.

"Vince, leave her alone. She has nothing to do with her parents, trust me." It almost feels like my mother is protecting me in the most unusual way possible. Of course, it's typical Jennifer Skye style. Her words stab me and protect me at the same time. She will probably expect a medal for that one sentence.

Vince stares at me, "Well, you can't ignore who your family is, sweetheart."

I turn away, not wanting him to study my face any more than he already has. Coming here was the biggest mistake. Why would my father give me this address? Something isn't adding up.

"*My daughter and I are going to chat for a couple of minutes. I'll be back in a few.*" My mother steps out of the house and closes the door right on Vince. She grabs my arm, and I instantly pull away. Instead, I follow her down the driveway. When we get far enough away, she spins around and glares at me. "*What on earth are you doing here?*"

"*Where's Dad?*"

"*He's not here, Valletta. How did you even know about this house?*"

"*Dad's letter.*"

"*His what?*"

"*Dad sent me a letter. It arrived on my graduation day.*"

My mother's eyes twitch. I know from my dad's letter that she knew about my graduation. She doesn't know what to say. I notice the red surrounding her eyes. She looks so much worse than how I remember her. I haven't seen her since I was eighteen. Four whole years have gone by.

"*What did his letter say?*" My mother's eyes soften for a moment, and it becomes clear that something has happened.

"*Who is that guy, Vince? Why is he here? Whose house is this?*" I ask anxiously.

"*Valletta, don't ask questions you don't want the answers to. Tell me what the letter said.*" She crosses her arms. She means business.

"*Just that he was sober and got a good job. Things seemed to be going well for him.*" This makes my mother burst out laughing.

"*Oh, is that what he said? Don't tell me he sent you some money, too?*"

I was silent. It's funny. Despite how disconnected we are, she can still see right through me sometimes . . . Just never when it matters.

"*How much did he send you?*" Her skin is getting tight, anger coming up. "*Valletta, you have to tell me. This is serious.*"

"*Twenty thousand.*"

"*Well, this explains everything.*" She shakes her head.

"Explains what?" A part of me doesn't want to know. I should just tear up the check and walk away.

"Let's just say your father gave you money that wasn't his and now he's paying the consequences. I always tell him not to get too excited with these payouts, but does he listen? Of course not, he is still your father after all." My mother says 'your father' as if it's a swear. She looks angry, her eyes searching the distance as if she would see him.

"Did Dad give me money he got from selling?" I contain my fear of the answer.

"You just graduated college which means you must be somewhat smart. Do you think your father got twenty thousand dollars from a 9-5?"

Leave it to my mother to burst the only tiny bubble of hope I'm holding onto. I hated my mother for that, but I hated her more for making me realize how naive I had been. I hated that her condescending words made me feel like the dumbest person in the world. Of course it's dirty money. Why would I even for a second believe otherwise? Why would I get my hopes up and think he had changed? I have no one but myself to blame. I trusted him for a moment, I let my guard down. I even went so far as to get excited about using this money for school. Now the anger was starting to build.

"I was going to use that money for school! What would've happened if they traced it? You're both so wrapped up in your messed up lives that you didn't even think about how this could've potentially wrecked everything, my reputation and my entire life! I can't believe I almost got roped into all of this!" I'm close to screaming at this point. It's setting in now, how stupid I was to come here.

"Only someone as selfish as you would turn someone giving you twenty thousand dollars into a bad thing. Honestly, Valletta, get off your high horse. You're no better than us. We are your family whether you like it

or not." She shakes her head in disappointment at me, as if I was twelve all over again, getting blamed for the fact that my father left us.

"Where is Dad?" I ask her slowly. I wanted her to answer that one question, I wanted to know why he suddenly sent me so much money and said he was sober. He's never done that before. I wish I could just not care. Just run away and never look back, why do I have to care?

"He's not too far. There's some business he's taking care of. Some high paying clients. So that he can fix the mess he made." She looks at me sharply, and exhales. It's then I smell the booze. I didn't notice it before, but now I see her face differently. The red overtaking the whites of her eyes. She hasn't been crying, she's been drinking. The one thing I begged her over and over not to do. I hated her when she drank, and she knew it. I always thought, if she cared enough, she would stop. Of course, now I'm old enough to know it's not that simple, but a child doesn't know that.

"Look I'll tell him you stopped by."

"Don't bother." I reach into my bag and hand my mother the check. The check that represented how even at twenty-one I was still so naive. The check that showed me good things just don't happen, always remain suspicious. Last of all, the check that showed me never to let my parents in again even for a second. When you let someone in that has that much power over your heart, the results are disastrous.

Twenty-nine

IT'S A MESS, A complete mess. I look around at my sink filled with the contents of my medicine cabinet. I've searched every corner of this bathroom.

Nothing. Not one pill. The only thing that stopped the flood of tears, getting me off my kitchen floor was the possibility of there being a pill. A way for me to just fall asleep and ignore the memories flooding me. Even the good ones hurt at this point. Then, I have an idea. I can check under my bed. Maybe one fell. It's very unlikely, but my desperation outweighs any logic. I run to the bedroom and look under the bed. Nothing.

I hear my phone vibrate on my bathroom counter. Who is texting me this late? As I stand up, my eye goes to the corner of the bed. I see something, something tiny, nestled right under my nightstand. A pill. What I've been desperately looking for. I grab it and hold it up to my face. As I examine the capsule, anger starts to build inside of me. Is this what my life has become? The threat of tears burns my throat, causing me to squeeze my pillow with my other hand. How can one freaking pill be my only source of relief? Just then, my phone buzzes again in the bathroom. Pushing down the rising anger, I place the pill on my nightstand, walking away to check my phone . . .

Mark

> Hey. Are you up?

I look at the time; it's one in the morning. Why in the world is he texting me this late?

> Hey, what's up? You ok?

I wait as I see the bubble indicating he's typing.

> What are the chances you can meet me outside?

> What?

> I'm outside your apartment building.

> Are you serious?!

> Yes.

> Coming.

I grab a sweater and head outside, rushing down the stairs. It's chillier than I thought. I fold my arms, shivering. Mark is pacing up and down the sidewalk like a crazy person. The scene makes my stomach drop.

"Mark? What's going on?" He turns towards me and stops. He looks completely disheveled. His dirty-blonde hair is all over the place, a frantic look in his bright green eyes.

"Hey. I'm sorry to ask you to come out here so late."

"It's okay, just tell me what's going on, you're scaring me."

Mark takes a long deep breath in and looks up at the sky. "How about we take a walk? Maybe go see the moonlight on the ocean?"

"Mark, it's 1am."

He bites his lip. "Can we please just go on a walk?" He looks desperate.

"Sure," I say softly. I can tell this is serious.

"I can drive us to the ocean. It will be quicker," Mark says, opening the passenger door for me.

I nod silently, getting into his car, full of nerves. He doesn't say one word on our short drive. I take a few glances at my best friend's face. The face that's so often filled with joy and humor is filled with either pain or anxiety. He takes us to the stairs looking out over Sunset Cliffs. It's too dark to see the actual cliffs but their silhouette feels haunted in the middle of the night. A booming sound echoes as the waves slam into the side of the cliffs. The ocean is angry, the intensity of the waves hitting us with a salty spray. He stops on the stairs where there's a little lookout. I reach over and place my hand on Mark's arm.

"Mark, what's going on? You're making me nervous."

He turns around to look at me, his face half lit up in the moonlight. It's the most serious I've ever seen him look.

"Valletta, what's going on here? Between us?"

"What do you mean?"

"Isn't it obvious? Lately, well, I guess especially tonight, something feels like it's shifting."

"What are you talking about?" I squint my eyes at him,

"Tonight, with Trisha, you acted jealous. You've never done that before. And, did I imagine it, or did you not want to kiss Owen in front of me? Not to mention Owen, he was a complete douchebag to you."

My face is full of confusion, completely taken aback. "Mark, I don't know what you're talking about."

"No, stop. Don't do that." He sputters, "After I saw Trish off, I walked around aimlessly for the last hour. I thought about us. Something has shifted. You can't possibly tell me you weren't acting jealous tonight. You even admitted you were upset I brought a date."

"I was upset you brought a date because I wanted this dinner to be about you and Owen getting to know each other. Not you and some clingy Barbie doll who's all over you but doesn't even know what you do for work. I mean, my goodness, Mark, could you care less about who you date?"

"There are so many things wrong with what you just said, Valletta, I don't even know where to start." Mark shakes his head angrily.

"What's wrong with me wanting you to date someone who actually cares about you and what is important to you? She should at least know your biggest passion! Just saying . . ." I cross my arms looking out over the dark ocean, trying to focus on the sparkling moonlight.

"So, let me get this straight. You want to dictate who I date?" Mark retorts.

"Isn't that what you're doing with Owen?" I snap. "You literally hated that I was seeing Owen, and I had to beg you to give him a chance. But instead of giving him a chance tonight, you are saying how awful he is!"

"He is awful, Valletta! He treated you like a total jerk! I don't trust him one bit, but you have on some rose-colored glasses right now."

"Okay, he was a little off tonight, I'll give you that, but you know what?" I scoff, "So are you. I mean, this?" I gesture at the space around us, "This right here is insane. It's 1 am and you're yelling at me about crazy stuff."

"I'm not trying to yell, Valletta, I just-"

"Also, why are you calling me Valletta now?"

"Wait, you're complaining about me calling you Valletta now, too?" Mark starts laughing, "You know, I might be acting crazy right now, but you are crazy. You always complain about me calling you Letta, but now I can't even call you the name you want to be called? I mean you are always back and forth with everything when it comes to me. You drive me insane!" Mark covers his face with his hands, frustrated.

"I don't know what you want from me, Mark, I really don't. I wasn't trying to act jealous with you and Trisha. I just wanted you and Owen to get along."

Mark uncovers his face and shakes his head. "I don't trust him, Valletta. I don't like the way he was treating you tonight and-"

"Mark, you worry way too much about me."

"Yeah, and why do you think that is?" Mark's eyes are the brightest green I've ever seen, staring directly into mine. There's something about the way he asked that question that makes me terrified to answer it.

"I don't know," I pause, my voice getting more and more quiet, "Because you care, just like I care about you, I guess."

"Of course I care, Valletta. That's the problem. I care too much. I care so much about you that I don't want to be with some girl who cares about me because honestly, there's no point. I already found the perfect girl." His words are charged with passion, but I know him well enough to hear the fear behind them. If he knows me just as well as I know him, he must sense that my fear is far greater.

I remain silent, frozen in place by his words.

"Look, can you just tell me if you were jealous tonight? Is this all in my head? I need to know." Mark looks desperately at me.

I take a shaky breath in, "It's not fully in your head, but that's just what happens with friendships like ours sometimes. They can be a bit complicated. I love you more than anything, Mark. But don't make things into more than what they are." He breaks our eye contact. I continue anyway, "We have something special as friends. Besides you waited until I was with Owen to say something. You're just not used to me dating someone."

"Valletta, I promise you, this has absolutely nothing to do with Owen." He groans. "Look, I love to run. I am completely terrified of committing to anyone and terrified of feeling trapped, and you're the only one to ever call me out for it. I realized something tonight, and it's probably the scariest thought I've ever had, but damn, is it true." He stops and looks at me, the intensity making me shift uncomfortably.

"What?" My voice is barely audible.

I realized . . ." He takes a sharp breath in, "Valletta, I am already completely, absolutely, and fully committed to you. I mean, every other girl feels like a placeholder. And you know I've always been comfortable with placeholders because they allow me to stay free. But this-" He gestures between us, moving closer to me, "This friendship is my compass, my true north. I mean, it's you and me against the world, right?" He strokes my arm, and I immediately shove his hand away.

"So, you choose now to tell me this? Now that I'm finally in a relationship? Come on, Mark, you're just jealous. That's all this is. Don't you dare ruin our friendship because you don't want me to be with someone else."

"Look at me." Mark's voice is commanding. He gently moves my chin so I have no choice but to look into the emerald ocean that is his eyes, an ocean so vibrant that I can see them in this moonlight, an ocean suddenly filled with clarity.

"Look me in the eyes as I say this." He stares right into me as another spray of ocean chills my skin. "This has absolutely nothing to do with Owen. This is about . . . Actually, I take that back. This is about you and Owen, but not for the reason you think. You needed time to deal with everything. I mean, heck, I needed time too. We both have grown so much. And don't even for a second fool yourself into thinking this is the first time I've wanted to tell you this. We both know there have been other times, but you've never been ready. And now you're finally ready to be with someone, and you pick a guy who is a complete know-it-all, an insensitive jerk to you and your friends. You deserve so much better, Valletta. So much better. Do you know how painful it is to see him treat you that way?" He pauses, searching my face.

"I've proven my loyalty. Five years, Valletta. Five years of me sticking by your side, being there for every disaster, every win, every complaint. It's you and me. It's always been you and me, from day one, when I literally fell for you. All the other girls were just me trying to find someone who could even hold a candle to you. But I never really tried to find someone because truthfully . . . I didn't want to. I wanted you. Only you. I still do."

My heart stops. I am completely frozen, staring directly into his eyes. They are so full of life, so full of truth. I want to look away, avoid eye contact and run. I can't. I'm stuck, like I am standing in glue.

"Mark-" My voice is a whisper, a faint pathetic noise. "I can't go there with you. I'm with Owen." I hate myself for saying it, for using Owen as an excuse. The truth is there in my heart. I know how I feel about Mark; and I know we wouldn't last. We are two well-meaning but completely broken people. I would lose the one person on this planet that I feel completely safe with. I refuse to risk that.

"That's your response?" Mark's voice is sharp, like razor blades. "You're with Owen?" Mark shakes his head, "I confess my love for you for the first time in five years and that's your response?" He pauses, "Wow." He puts his hands on his face in frustration and then runs them through his hair.

My heart is silently bleeding but I can't show it. He will get past this, and we will be Mark and Valletta again. I can save this friendship.

"Look me in the eyes and tell me you don't love me. That you're not just scared to give us a chance."

"Mark, stop. Please don't do this," I whisper.

He draws closer to me, his eyes filling with moisture. "I'm doing it because you need to know how I feel."

"No," I stammer. "You know I would do anything for you. You're my best friend." I manage to smile at him in hopes that he'll soften, "You're just getting confused now that I'm with Owen."

"I have never been less confused, Valletta. I have known from when we first met, when we talked all night in the hospital, that you are by far the most interesting, special person I have ever met. That hasn't changed. We just weren't ready, so I kept my mouth shut, but there have been so many times I would bet everything that you wanted this too."

"Don't you see, Mark? We've stayed close for five years because we are best friends." I attempt to smile.

"Well, I guess it's time you find someone who can look at you as a best friend because I can't anymore." Mark looks up, his eyes still glistening with moisture, like an emerald pond.

"You don't mean that." I stammer.

"I do." He sighs.

I try to hold back my tears. "Mark, please." I'm panicking, I have never seen this side of him, this pure determination. This is serious. For him to be here in the middle of the night, confessing something so vulnerable, I know there is only one thing I can do at this point.

Give him space.

I am willing to do anything to hold on to him. But maybe for a while, I need to let him go. I know for certain, one day he will be grateful that I didn't let us go there.

We can be Mark and Valletta again.

I can save this friendship.

Thirty

My breath is labored as I run upstairs, heading straight for the pill on my nightstand. I rush over to the kitchen sink, drinking straight from the faucet. Swallowing the pill creates another crying fit. At this point, I'm sore from all the crying I've done tonight. I just need to go to sleep. Maybe a shower will help. I quickly strip, letting the shower run until it gets hot.

As the water burns my skin in the best way, I immerse my head under the stream, trying to drown out Mark's voice, forcing my brain to blur out the image of his face. I've never seen his eyes like that before, filled with truth and desperation. And then it hits me . . . no one has ever looked at me the way he did. I will the water to drown it all out, but I can't wash away his emerald eyes as I repeat in desperation-

It would never work.

It could never work.

It won't ever work.

I can feel the sweat on the girl's arm as she passes me. I really need to get some space. The grad party is in full swing by now. Melanie and I proudly graduated college today. I couldn't help but beam with pride for both of us. Thankfully Mark and Melanie granted my wish and didn't mention the check or the letter. Somehow, today was perfect.

"Let's take a walk," Mark yells and gently takes my arm, leading me away from the crowd. The bass from the speakers vibrates my chest and the lights are making me dizzy, but I don't mind. This is the first party I've been to in college that I'm actually happy to be at. Maybe it's because I know this is the last one. This is it.

I give Mark a big grin because as much as I'm not hating this party, there's nothing that beats a walk on the beach at night. I follow Mark further through the back of the house, right into the squishy cold sand. Now that I'm walking away from the chaos, I realize how much I'm feeling those margaritas. I grab onto Mark's arm to steady myself. He always feels rock solid. I secretly love being able to hold on to him. It makes me feel safe.

"WOOHOO!" Startling me, he grabs my sides and lifts me into the air, spinning me around.

"No, please, no! I'm gonna be sick!" I scream in the air, my surroundings a blur flying by me.

Mark laughs, putting me down slowly, "Sorry, I'm just super-duper proud of you."

I burst out laughing. "Did you just say super-duper?" I stutter my words all over the place, feeling dizzy.

"Yup!" Mark exclaims proudly.

"You are the biggest nerd I've ever met and yet you look like-" I use my hand to show him off, not finding the word I need. "Well, you look like the complete opposite of a stereotype, is what I'm trying to say."

"I'm sorry, but it's 2021. Aren't stereotypes, like, dead?"

"Clearly." I wink at him to prove my point.

"So, what do I look like to you?" Mark asks sincerely.

My face scrunches a bit as I try to think of how I could possibly describe Mark. "You know, the first time I saw you, I thought you were the hottest guy at that party." I laugh at the memory, "But then I saw how much of an idiot you were, and your looks annoyed me." I grin playfully. The water covers my feet, creating the best feeling. We keep walking further away from the party. Mark is quiet for a moment. I can see a sliver of his smile, half of his face lit up by the moonlight.

"You thought I was the hottest guy at the party, huh?" he says teasingly.

"Don't act like that's such a surprise. You know you were blessed with some crazy good genes."

"Wow, I never knew you saw me like this, it's funny, actually." He laughs a little.

"Why is that funny?"

Mark stops walking and turns his face to me, his expression becoming more serious while his eyes remain full of warmth. I turn to look at him, waiting for his response. He reaches out his hand and slowly tucks some of my hair behind my ear.

Uneasiness fills my stomach, there's an intensity to this moment that makes me want to run back to the party. I feel exposed and there's no cover near me.

"It's funny because you were by far the prettiest girl at that party." Mark's eyes are dancing around my face. There's a sparkle in them that makes my knees weak.

He can't be meaning what I'm feeling right now. Could he? I shake the thought away. We are probably just feeling our drinks too much. It's Mark, my best friend.

"Prettiest woman, Mark, not girl," I smirk, trying to play it cool despite my insides screaming.

"Well, duh." He snickers as his eyes dance around until a soft expression settles over his face. *"Valletta, the past few years with you have been literally the best years of my life. I've never had a friendship like this. You are becoming my everything, honestly."* Even in the moonlight, I see his face flush; I've never heard him speak so earnestly.

His words make me feel sick. I can't be his everything. I can't let him be my everything. I need him as my friend. We are perfect as friends. No one could compare.

Mark is smiling, his eyes fixed on me. He starts to lean in closer and he uses one of his hands to graze my chin, his other hand gently touching my side, pulling me in close.

I can feel his breath. Its warmth gives me chills. He smells like his favorite peppermint gum. I swear he's addicted.

Before I know it, his lips are inches from mine. I'm torn between staying paralyzed in peppermint essence and emerald ocean eyes or being sensible.

I clear my throat and quickly pull away, *"You're my best friend, too. That's what makes us so great, right? We're best friends."* I smile and my words come out in a foreign high pitch.

Mark's face falls, his eyes close for a second. He looks disappointed. A part of me feels bad, but I know how much worse we would feel if we let a small moment of temptation and confusion ruin what we have. It's just a moment after all.

"Of course," Mark says softly, and then manages to look at me again nodding his head like he understands.

I smile at him, trying to cover my nerves. Perhaps this is all in my head, anyway. Knowing Mark, he just didn't have a date tonight and felt lonely, or something.

"You know, I think that margarita was stronger than I thought. I could use some water." My eyes look back at the party.

"Oh, are you feeling okay? I'll go grab you some water." Mark's tone is back, his typical concern and eagerness to help wash over him.

"I have a better idea." I look at Mark, a smile coming over my face. I know how to get us back to normal.

"I'll race you." I grin playfully.

Mark laughs a little too much, which I find slightly offensive, "You have no chance, Letta."

I roll my eyes, "Don't call me that!" Then I take off running, leaving Mark behind me.

"Hey, that's totally cheating!" I hear him yell from where I left him.

I laugh as I run, embracing the dizziness. I love this feeling, this playfulness.

This is us. Mark and Valletta as we should be.

Just then I feel Mark right behind me, grabbing me. I have no clue how he caught up this fast. He throws me over his shoulder and keeps running. I'm laughing so hard, tears are streaming down my face. I'm hitting his back trying to get let down, even though secretly I love this.

My face is drenched in tears, but I'm smiling. The memory was so real I could smell the ocean mixed with peppermint gum. I try to hold on to the memory, but it quickly gets replaced with the events of last night, which did not end in laughter.

We had never had a fight like that before. I check my phone, no messages. I can't help but wonder what Mark is doing right now.

Was he also lying in bed thinking about last night? Did he regret what he said? I hope more than anything that he did, that we could just put last night behind us and be friends again. Our friendship was rare, one that you only come across once in your life, if you're lucky. The thought of throwing it away over some complicated, messy feelings makes me want to cry all over again, but I don't think I could cry if I wanted to. My tears have all run dry. I take a deep breath in, closing my eyes. I do the breathing technique my therapist says will help, and after a minute I'm able to relax a little.

I know what I have to do.

I throw my blankets off me and get out of bed. I forgot how much of a mess my bathroom is. I still have everything pulled out of the shelves. I'm going to clean my apartment, call Owen, and go to work tonight as if nothing happened. I might even go to the grocery store. Tomorrow is the day I visit my father with Owen. That is the only thing I can focus on right now.

It hits me that Mark doesn't even know my father called, never mind the fact that I'm going to visit him. I can't help but feel guilty for not telling him. Maybe if he knew, he wouldn't have confessed his love last night and we could carry on like normal. I sigh, staring at my mess instead of taking action to clean it.

I need to get it together. It's the only way I will be able to handle tomorrow. I push the Mark drama out of my head. I can only slay one demon at a time. Mark will come around in time, anyway. Now I know that he was in fact trying to kiss me that night at the grad party, and by stopping it I got two more years of friendship. Two more years of cherished memories with him. If I had kissed him back, we probably would have been together for six months, tops, before one of us screwed it up.

It's time to focus on what I can control. Like my relationship with Owen and confronting my father. If I just stick with a plan, everything will work out in due time.

Thirty-one

THE RESTAURANT IS SWAMPED tonight. When I arrive for my shift, everyone seems to be in a panic. I go to the kitchen, preparing myself, my stomach completely overwhelmed with nerves. Everyone is bumping into each other and yelling.

"Hey, what's going on?" I ask Steph as she's rushing by me.

"Oh, we just found out about the new head chef. Everything's all crazy! They have Mark training two new people tonight."

"New head chef? What's happening to Clint?"

"I guess he's opening his own restaurant, in Boston of all places." Steph huffs and rolls her eyes, then continues past me carrying more plates than she has arms. I look around the kitchen and my stomach drops to the floor when I see Mark. He looks completely disheveled. His eyes are red, and his face is white. A girl and a guy are hovering near him, trying to listen to what he's saying. They must be the ones he's training.

"Get to work, Valletta! We're swamped!" Gregg rushes past me, pointing his finger to the plates ready to be served.

"Right, sorry."

Mark's eyes look up when Gregg says my name, but he looks away just as quickly. It's like he didn't even realize it was actually me . . . Or he did.

I get myself ready as fast as possible and hurry over to grab some plates to bring out. I try to catch Mark's eye again, but he doesn't look up. He just keeps explaining something to the new staff.

The first two hours of my shift fly by. There's not even a second to stop and think about anything, let alone Mark or what I'm doing with Owen tomorrow. I have never been more grateful for the chaos.

"It's madness!" Melanie exclaims as we rush to see if our orders are ready.

"Apparently, there's a new head chef coming." I reply, grabbing the order for table nine.

"Oh, so that means Clint is actually moving to Boston?"

"How do you know about this? I didn't even know Clint was moving."

"Girl, I know all the gossip," Melanie says proudly.

"Well, Gregg seems more stressed out than ever." As I drop off my dirty plates, I hear Mark yell so loud it makes me jump. His yell is followed by many cuss words.

"Is this your first time working in a kitchen?! What is wrong with you?! That oil is a million degrees you can't just-"

"Hey, hey! Mark!" Clive interrupts, "Relax! Just go run it under cold water."

Mark angrily storms right past me to the back of the kitchen.

I go to the break room, yelling out to Melanie to cover my tables, "Just five minutes!" I snatch the burn ointment out of the first aid kit, spinning around towards the door, and BAM! I collide directly with Mark.

"Geez, Valletta! What in the world?!"

"I'm sorry! I was just rushing so I could get you some burn cream." I hold up the tube as if to prove my story.

"Thanks, but I don't need you to get it for me. You're needed out there."

Seeing Mark, hearing Mark, breaks my heart a little. I can tell he's hurting. I was hoping that any minute he would say he was a little drunk last night, and he didn't mean any of it. I was hoping he would say, "Of course I will still be your best friend," and smile at me in the most earnest way anyone could ever smile. But instead, he grabs the tube of burn ointment and walks right past me.

My heart sinks. "Mark?"

"Yeah?" He doesn't turn around. He just tends to his burn with his back turned against me.

I steady myself and walk towards him, "Can we talk?"

He sucks in a deep breath and turns around to finally look me in the eyes. His eyes are dull. I've never seen them dull.

"I meant what I said, Valletta. I know you're hoping I'll take it all back, but I meant it. Every single word." His tone is firm.

"Why do you think I want you to take it back?" I walk closer to him, taking my chances.

He looks at me intensely then turns away, "Don't you?"

I inch closer, "Just the part about not being friends anymore." My voice is shaking now. I'm holding back so much.

Mark looks back at me, "I'm sorry, but that's just not possible for me right now." His face looks worn out. He walks to the first aid kit and grabs a bandage. "We are slammed tonight and there are a lot of changes and new people. You should be out there, Melanie can't handle both your sections." His tone makes my stomach turn. He's never spoken to me like this. So professional, so cold, like a stranger.

"Mark, I just-"

"Valletta, seriously, go back to work. I don't need your help here." I stand still trying to search his face for meaning, but he turns away.

Just like that, I go back to work. The pit in my stomach has grown so big tonight, nothing could fill it. Not even a good night's sleep.

Thirty-two

WHAT I'M ABOUT TO do is sinking in. I'm becoming more and more aware of my pounding heart and I'm trying not to let Owen see my shaky hands. Owen rests his hand on my leg and glances at me with concern. At first, I thought I knew where we were headed, but now I am completely lost. The sun set about an hour ago, the darkness adding to my uneasiness. For a minute, I wonder if my dad will even think it's a possibility we are coming. There was no way to contact him outside of this specific date and time. That's how I knew things were bad.

I sit stone faced, vowing over and over in my head not to get sucked in. My purpose in coming tonight is to face this demon head on, completely slay it.

"We're a minute away," Owen says as he glances at the GPS and takes one last turn down a poorly lit, cramped one-way. The sidewalk has trash sprinkled all around. To say there's a pit in my stomach would be like calling the Grand Canyon a small valley. There's a cluster of broken-down apartment buildings in this neighborhood and the GPS is pointing us to the last one on this street. The lights are on, which is a good sign, I guess. I expected all the lights to be off and broken-down steps for my feet to fall through.

"Are you ready for this? I'm right beside you." Owen gives me a reassuring smile. "Just remember, whatever happens, this is about you moving on."

Hearing Owen's words, I realize how lucky I am to have him here with me. Yet, I feel like my body is just going through the motions and my mind is far away. With Owen by my side, I manage to take a deep breath and knock. I haven't physically seen my father since I was in high school, and even then, he wasn't the father I remembered. It was like his body was being used by an alien whose only focus was getting high. To my surprise, the door immediately opens, and suddenly I'm bumped back to being ten years old . . .

My father is packing his bags. He's angry. He's never angry. My mother is screaming things that my brain is tuning out. I am focused on my father.

"Dad?"

He spins around, his face red, his eyes wet.

"Valletta." He says my name as if it's the last time he will ever say it. My stomach has a new feeling, something I haven't quite felt before, it's like a pit.

"Dad, where are you going?"

He sighs, then kneels down so he's eye to eye with me, "Valletta, you are the bluest sky I've ever been under. You and I have something special, don't we?"

I nod my head yes, scared. I go to him and hug him. He squeezes me so tight I feel his muscles flex.

"No matter what, always remember how special you are to me." Just like that, he's sobbing.

"Valletta? I can't believe you came." My dad's scruff is gray now. He looks tired and worn out, all his charm stolen from him. I notice a slight softness in his eyes that wasn't there when he would randomly show up in my teenage years.

"What do you want, Dad?" My voice is unstable. I'm reminded that Owen is beside me as my dad's eyes drift over to him.

"Hi, I'm Owen." Owen extends his hand to my father. For whatever reason I'm anxious, as if he needs my father's approval, which is the most ridiculous thought.

"Nice to meet you, I'm Derek." He returns his handshake. "Come inside, please."

I look back at Owen, hesitant to go in. He gives me a reassuring nod and puts his hand on the small of my back, almost propelling me forward.

"Okay, but we can't stay long." My tone is tight.

"Understood." My dad steps aside so we can walk in. It's a small, dimly lit apartment, one small lamp being the only source of light. I can tell he made an effort to clean up. There are piles of junk placed neatly on the small coffee table and his shoes are perfectly lined against the door. An organized mess surrounds us.

"Have a seat, please. I can make us some tea, coffee, or-"

"No, we are okay," I interrupt. "Just tell me what's going on. Why, all of a sudden, do you want to meet up?"

My father is quiet for a moment. He looks at Owen.

"Is this your boyfriend?" he asks.

"Just answer the question, Dad. Please."

He smiles softly and almost looks away. He seems either happy or embarrassed, "Wow, I can't believe how long it's been since I heard you call me Dad."

I say nothing. The silence is deafening, but I refuse to play along. This isn't a casual visit. This is a mission. Owen shifts uncomfortably near me.

"I'll wait outside for a couple of minutes, perhaps?" Owen looks at me, searching my face to see what I need.

Would being alone with my dad actually change anything? I guess for him it might. He probably won't talk if Owen is here. I nod my head yes to Owen, despite not wanting him to leave me alone. As soon as Owen steps outside, I spin around to face my dad.

"Look, I came all the way here because it sounded important. Please don't waste my time." I cross my arms, it takes all my strength to maintain eye contact. My father's eyes have a desperate look. He takes a deep breath before talking.

"I wanted to see you, Valletta. Listen, I know how much I've screwed up. Not only that, but I should have never given you that check prematurely. I feel ashamed of that every day. I just wanted to try and give you something that could possibly help you. I just wanted to try and help. As your father." He looks down. I can hear the emotions trying to surface.

"You put me in danger with that check, Dad. Whoever was after you could have come after me-"

"I would never put you in danger-"

"NO! That's the thing, you can't just say that you'll protect me! I mean what would you have done?! Kill them?" I stare at my father for the first time in years. His eyes are like honey. They always felt so sweet and warm when I was a child, but now they look dirty. He's stunned. I stunned my father for the first time in my life. He clears his throat slowly, probably trying to think of what to say. He was nowhere to be found two years ago. How convenient. He let Mom do the dirty work.

"I don't know what to say but I promise-"

I cut him off, "You know what, Dad, don't waste your breath on an apology. Just tell me why I'm here. I know it can't just be a nice day to try and see your daughter."

"I'm being framed."

I take a step back, "What do you mean?"

"For murder, Valletta. I'm being framed for murder." Now I'm stunned. He continues, "I'm getting things straightened out. I just had to try and see you as soon as possible because I didn't want to take a chance that the next time would be in jail. Not that I presumed you would visit me." He looks down at his feet.

I have no words. For a moment I question if this is a dream. I mean, who gets framed for murder except in the movies?

"Wait, what?" That's all I can manage.

"There's a girl who overdosed. Her drugs were laced. I swear I had absolutely nothing to do with it. I stopped selling right after I cleaned up my mess two years ago. I know you probably don't believe me, but it's the truth."

"Why would someone frame you?"

"I'm an easy target. Plus, once you try and get out of the business, there are a lot of very angry people who want to make a lesson out of you."

"I'm sorry, are you hearing yourself? This cannot be real! I mean 'out of the business', 'a girl overdosed'? This literally cannot be real!"

"I know this is a lot to take in. I'm sure you're struggling to believe that this is even possible, and honestly, for that, I am grateful. I know I did the right thing leaving when you were young and impressionable."

"You did not just say that." I shake my head. I'm suddenly shaking with anger, it's like having fiery hot coals in my throat.

"I was a mess back then, Valletta! I lost all control. There is no way I could have taken care of you. I regretted so much coming back when you were older. I never wanted you to see me like that. I-"

"STOP!" I cry out, trembling. "No, you don't get to do that! You don't get to come up with a silver lining for leaving me."

"That's not what I'm doing."

"That's exactly what you're doing."

"Do you think I wanted to leave you? You are my beautiful daughter . . . my best friend. Nothing on this earth could make me smile like you do. I know my actions have not shown it, but I would do anything to be us again. The hope that one day you can be my blue sky again is the only thing that kept me from giving up."

His words cut so deep. The tears have no way of holding back. I'm shattered.

"I worked so hard. So hard, to get that nasty addiction out of my life. I failed so many times. I almost gave everything up the third time I came home when you were eighteen. You were all grown up." My dad pauses, looking up at the ceiling, "I'll never forget seeing you and knowing I was too late. You were all grown up. I failed." His voice is barely holding on.

"Valletta!" I hear Owen call out from the front entrance. "The police just pulled up."

"What?" My dad's face washes out with fear. I turn away from him and walk to the entrance where Owen is. The flashing lights reflect on the door, their speed matching my heartbeat. Two officers get out of their cars and come straight for my dad's door.

"Did you call the cops?" My dad is staring right at Owen. His tone is frantic.

Owen looks at my dad, his eyes wide, "Of course not."

"Why would you ask him that?" I yell at my dad. There's a loud knock on the door.

"Police, open up!" Owen opens the door. "We are looking for Derek Skye." The officer is tall, his voice filled with intimidation.

"I'm right here." My dad's voice is soft behind me, defeated.

Thirty-three

A SHARP BUZZING IS radiating through me. Taking a breath is like breathing in cement. My eyes are open, but my vision is blurred.

"Valletta? Are you okay? Valletta?" Owen's voice is trying to reach me. I am squatting on the floor in my dad's hallway. Right where the cops just took him. This feeling is familiar but foreign. It's almost like I am reaching a new level of panic.

"Just breathe, in and out." I want to scream that I can't actually breathe. It's just not working. It feels like hours go by before I can calm down, before I can finally take a normal breath through my nose. Owen is rubbing my back, his voice coming in clear.

"Hey, you're okay," he whispers. He is sitting on the floor with me and holding me softly.

"I don't think he's guilty, Owen. I really don't. They just arrested an innocent man."

"How do you know that?" Owen's voice sounds sharp.

"I could tell by his eyes. He quit selling a while ago and he's clean."

"You can tell all that by his eyes?"

"Yes," I reply simply. I can't help but be slightly angry at how difficult it seems for Owen to believe me. It shouldn't make me angry. My dad is a criminal, after all.

"Well if you're so sure, then we should go visit him, get the whole story. My uncle is a lawyer, he might be able to help."

I wipe my eyes and sit up, trying to ignore the sudden dizzy spell. I repeat Owen's words in my head and realize, if I do that, I am doing the opposite of what I came here for. I came here to distance myself from my father, not get more involved. How did this happen?

"I'll have to think about it," I say as my head starts to clear.

"What do you need right now?"

"I need to go home."

"This will be our little secret." My dad's hand appears, gently stroking my hair. The sun is so bright I can't look at my father's face without squinting. I'm grinning from ear to ear at the thought of my dad and me sharing a secret together.

"Does mom know you picked me up from school?"

"Of course. But she doesn't know why or where we are going." He winks at me through the strands of sunlight between us.

I've begged and begged for my dad to teach me how to surf. My mother wouldn't let him, because she said there were more important things that needed to get done. She would say things like, "There just simply isn't enough time for the two of you to go galivanting around, ignoring the needs of our family." Her face was so serious, it made me angry. Angry that she thinks she has the right to stop me and my dad from spending time together. So, I am overjoyed when I walk out of school and see my dad waiting there with surfboards on the roof.

"Now, just remember, the waves are your friend. Use them; don't be afraid." My dad smiles as he takes the surfboards down.

Even now, in Owen's car, at nighttime, I can almost feel the warmth of the sun from that day. There wasn't a single cloud in the sky.

"Can you take me somewhere?" I ask Owen. He nods, and I direct him to the same beach where my father took me surfing that day.

When we arrive, I get out of the car and it's as if I can see myself and my dad standing there in the parking lot. I was trying to carry my own board, but I was struggling so much. I laugh at nine-year-old me, not caring about how crazy I must have looked, as I stand here seeing the past.

"Why did you want to come here?"

I don't respond to Owen. I just start walking, anxious for my feet to feel the chill of the moonlit sand.

"Whatever happens, I'll be right here," My dad is saying. I am the happiest kid on earth at that moment, surrounded by Pacific Ocean waves.

"Ok get ready! A wave is coming. Are you ready?" My dad's face is filled with warmth. He is enjoying this as much as I am.

"Yes." I say it confidently, even though the closer the wave gets, the more I start to panic. It's like a skyscraper is coming towards me. My heart accelerates, and now, I truly do feel panicked. I don't say anything. I want my father to be proud of me. I want to conquer the wave, just like he taught me.

SLAM.

I am suddenly rolling around under the water. Water fills my nostrils. I feel pressure building in my ears. My arms and legs are moving aggressively, trying to get to the surface. I can't find my dad. I frantically reach out in all directions, trying to grab onto him. I raise my arm above me and feel the surfboard. I grasp it, pulling myself to the surface. When I come up for air, I hold on to the surfboard for dear life. Upset, I look at my father. why didn't he help me up? He's just swimming calmly in place, a foot away, not a care in the world. A big grin appears on his scruffy face.

"You did it! You survived your first slam dunk!" His honey eyes are almost buzzing with electricity. He seems so proud of me. Proud of what? I didn't understand.

"Dad, I didn't like that."

"No one likes being hurled down by a wave, sweetie. But you came back up all on your own!"

"But you said you were gonna help me." I was trying not to cry. I didn't want to seem weak to him.

"I did. I helped you be independent. That's the kind of stuff that makes you fearless! That's the stuff a good surfer is made of." My dad pulls the surfboard towards him while I cling to it, still in shock.

"Let's catch another wave!" He yells at the top of his lungs in excitement.

"Why are you laughing? Did I miss something?" Owen asks, bringing me back to the present.

I look at him, my ankles covered by seawater, as my feet sink further and further into the sand. I am laughing and crying at the same time. I don't know which emotion to choose.

"You know," I say, "I never knew if he did the right thing. I still don't know."

"Who did what?" Owen's tone gives away his concern over my weird behavior.

"I mean, do you let your nine-year-old figure things out the hard way, or do you make her feel safe and protected? People would argue both sides, no doubt." I pause, breathing in the salty air. "That's the thing about my dad, Owen. You can never decide how to feel about him. Oh, and it's never on your terms. I mean, you have no choice but to be carried away by his every whim and desire. You can't choose when you want to see him or what you need from him. He decides all of that for you. The funny part is, I can't help but feel like he really was my best friend. I mean, for the first ten years of my life, he was. He was my best friend. Then he was my nightmare . . . Still is."

I start laughing at the thought. I look at Owen, expecting him to look at me like I'm the craziest person in the world, but instead, he looks like he might actually understand. There's not one ounce of judgment in his eyes. I continue, "You yourself said I needed to come here tonight to get closure. Yet, just the opposite has happened. I was DONE!" I can't help but yell, "I was DONE with this pit in my stomach at the mention of my dad. I wanted to get away from the drama. Instead, I'm deeper in it. I mean, how do I just close the door on him now? I know he's not guilty, Owen. I know he's clean." I shake my head, trying to ignore the pressure building behind my eyes. "I can't let my father rot in jail." My voice is trembling. Owen's hand is on my shoulder now.

"Hey. We will figure this out. We will get him out of jail."

"What could we possibly do?"

"Trust me." He smiles, pulling me towards him, kissing me. As I sink deeper into Owen's kiss, I'm amazed by the power he has to melt away my thoughts. He pulls away, looking at me with intensity, as if he's trying to read my mind. Then a smile overtakes his face, a smile full of . . . mischief? He grabs my hand and pulls us back to the dry sand, then without another word he's taking off his shirt, then his pants, leaving only his briefs on.

"What in the world are you doing?" I scream over the wind.

"We are going swimming." He says it with such certainty, like it's a decision we both already agreed to.

"Oh, absolutely not. It's freezing! And dark!" I gasp.

"Valletta, we live in San Diego, how can it be freezing? You sound like a wuss." He smirks at me. "Come on!"

"Owen, this is crazy."

"The cold water is good for you, it will push all that anxiety out of your brain. Trust me, I used to go swimming all the time after my mom died. It's the best medicine." I bite my lip, trying to think of a way out of this.

"Okay, you have ten seconds to undress or else I will throw you in with your clothes on." Owen crosses his arms. He must be the pushiest person I know.

"Fine!" I quiver as I take off my clothes, the cool night breeze sliding over my skin, giving me chills. The moonlight dances off half of Owen, the other half of him blending in with the night sky. I focus on the sound of the waves, still seeing the flashbacks of me and my dad in the sunlight. When I'm down to my bra and panties, Owen grabs my hand and faces the water, like a runner at the starting line.

"Ready?" he says, turning to me.

I shake my head no as Owen counts down from three, and then, just like that, we're off. When my legs hit the water, I almost don't feel anything. It's as if my senses are dulled. Before I know it, I'm being lifted into the air, a scream escapes my mouth just in time for Owen to throw me into the ocean. My body hits the water with a smack. When I open my eyes under the surface, I see nothing but darkness, which causes panic to rise in my chest. When I surface, Owen is smiling at me.

"So, how does it feel?" He grins. I don't know how to respond. I feel terrified but completely alive.

"You could have warned me before throwing me in like that," I say bitterly.

"Life doesn't give you a warning before throwing you around, does it?"

"You know, you're always trying to prove a point or teach me a lesson," I snap back.

"I'm sorry. I can get carried away. I'm just trying to help. I can tell you were having a hard time back there." He swims over to me, pulling me towards him.

"It's okay," I whisper. He's so close to me now, it's hard to stay mad at him. His hair is glistening in the moonlight. I give in to my desire and reach out to stroke his jet-black curls which are drenched in salt water.

"Close your eyes," Owen whispers. "You hear the waves? It's almost like each wave is contributing to a symphony of sounds . . . Listen." When I tune my ears into the sounds of the water, the waves slap at the hard sand and then retreat.

"Keep your eyes closed. Relax." Owen slowly lifts my body until I'm horizontal. I float on the surface of the waves. A sense of calm comes over me, nothing in my brain but the ocean sounds. I lose track of time as I open my eyes and look up at the moon. I've always had an affinity with the moon. Maybe it was the fact that it lit up the darkness, making it so I wasn't so afraid of what was out there.

I get so lost in the moment, it takes a few seconds to realize Owen isn't holding me anymore. I snap upright in the water, searching for him. His head pops up on the surface and he begins to swim. He swims silently, completely lost in the moment as his head comes up out of the water in a perfect rhythm. A tranquility falls over me that I didn't know was possible.

Owen was right. I needed this. I needed to let go.

Thirty-four

I'VE ALWAYS BEEN A master at procrastination. It's almost like the more I need to do something, the further I run away. It's why I still work as a waitress after graduating college. Melanie was the reason I even went to college in the first place. She always knows what she wants, she always has a plan. The only reason she still works as a waitress is to help her get through grad school. Mark works there because he wants to be a chef. I still work there because honestly, I just don't want to make a decision about what's next.

My procrastination has also led me here. Sitting on a bench outside, staring at my phone, wondering if I should call my father. Wondering if I should just go see him. It's been two days since he was arrested, and I haven't said or done anything about it. A part of me wants to run to him and tell him I will help him get out of this mess, but to say those words to him implies forgiveness. Forgiveness that I don't feel capable of. So here I sit, staring at my phone at a bus station, wondering if I should take this bus to him. Maybe if someone else is driving, I won't have a way to turn back as easily.

An elderly woman with bright white hair and pink-framed glasses sits down beside me, using her cane as leverage. She turns to look at me. I'm embarrassed to be caught staring at her, so I smile and quickly turn away.

"Hello, dear," she says, as I turn away from her.

I turn back and manage a smile. "Hi."

"Where is such a pretty young girl as yourself off to?" Her voice is shaky, yet sweet and inviting.

"I don't know, actually." I tell her the truth.

"Are you lost, sweetheart?"

I smile at her, trying to hold back tears. "Kind of, but I'll find my way."

"Can I help? I know this city very well. I've lived here for fifty years." She smiles at me with reassurance.

"Wow, I can't imagine living here for fifty years."

"Well, what's not to love? There's nothing better than being near the ocean, is there?"

I smile and nod my head in agreement.

"Although, I do wish I had traveled more. That's my only regret. So, get out there and see the world while you still can, my dear. Trust me." She emphasizes her words by pointing outwards with her cane.

"That's good advice." For some reason, my emotions are so close to the surface and this woman seems to pull them out of me. I turn away as my eyes fill with water.

"You sure you're okay, dear?"

I look back at her. "I'll be fine."

"I have to say it's nice to have someone to talk to." She sighs, "The only thing about living in a city like this is the loneliness. People are always so busy."

"Do you have any family nearby?"

"Not anymore, my only daughter moved to the East Coast years ago. She used to visit more, but I think it gets harder for her as time goes on."

"I'm sorry." I try to give her a sympathetic smile. She waves her hand back and forth in dismissal of my words.

"Oh, no, I'd rather she be happy. She has a big job out there in a hospital. Can't complain about a daughter who is saving lives, now can I?" She smiles softly at me. "What about you, hon? Do you get to see your family often?" I take a deep breath and look across the street at the palm trees framing the row of houses.

"My situation is a bit complicated."

"How so?" she inquires. I hate that the conversation has turned in this direction. I'm tempted for the first time to open up to this sweet woman. She's a stranger, after all. She'll never meet my family. Plus, maybe all her years of wisdom could help me.

"I'm actually sitting here debating whether or not to visit someone."

"Is this someone important to you?" The breeze seems to carry her words away into the air, away from me. I follow the breeze as it rustles through the palm trees, digesting her words. I repeat them in my mind . . . Is that someone important to me? I look over at the kind woman, noticing her shaky hands resting on her floral cane.

"Yes." I'm amazed at my response, it just comes out, almost against my will.

"Well then, my dear . . ." She pauses, leaning in closer to me. "Don't hesitate. Just go. You'll never regret visiting someone who is important to you. No matter how complicated it is." She pulls away from me, following my gaze across the street, but her eyes are fixed on the blue sky, a few seagulls flying by. "But you know what you will regret?" The squeak from the bus pulling up pierces the air, as it stops right in front of us, blocking the palm trees.

"What?" I say in desperation.

She smiles softly as she stands up slowly, putting all her weight on her cane. "Well, this is me." I hurry up to help her.

"What will I regret?" I stammer.

"What was your name, dear?"

"Valletta," I say a bit too quickly, frustrated that she's not finishing her thought.

"Valletta, dear, take it from an old woman who needs help getting onto a bus. Life is too short not to be with the ones we love. Don't regret not trying."

Time is almost still as we walk forward until I pause only a couple of feet from the stairs. I'm paralyzed.

"So, are you coming?" she asks sweetly, almost knowingly.

"I, uh, I forgot something. I think I'm gonna have to catch the next one." I swallow.

When she's at the top she looks back at me. "You take care now, Valletta, dear."

"I will. Thank you; you take care as well." I back away from the doors as the bus driver closes them. I keep my eyes on her bright white hair as the bus drives away. When it's out of sight, I pull out my phone and send a text to Mark.

> Hey, I know we are technically not talking still but I just wanted to say hi. I think this may be the longest we've ever gone without talking which is insane. I can't help but miss being annoyed by you lol. Hope you're well…

A moment later my phone dings and I look down in excitement. My excitement falls when I realize it's not Mark.

It's from Owen.

I let my phone screen go dark without replying. Honestly, I didn't want to be whisked away tomorrow. I wanted to make things right with Mark and figure out what to do about the situation with my dad. But the more I thought about it, the more I realized that running is better than staying right now. After all, I can't fix these things overnight. Maybe being with Owen for the day, away from my problems, will give me the clarity I need.

Thirty-five

ROCKY **MOUNTAINSIDE** WITH CAR-SIZED boulders carves out the road ahead. Two hawks circle the desert terrain below where small yellow flowers sprinkle over the thirsty vegetation. It seems like we are heading inland as we go away from Del Mar and into the mountains. Owen picked me up at noon and hasn't said much of anything on our drive. He insists on keeping our destination a surprise. His silence lacks the usual comfort and instead feels like a placeholder for something he doesn't want to talk about.

"Hope what I'm wearing is suitable for whatever we're doing," I say, as I hold my gold pendant. I'm looking down at my sage linen jumpsuit, one of the only things in my closet that is both casual and dressy. I had thrown on a pair of thrifted Birkenstocks to round out the comfy-yet-classy look. I just wish my mental state would match the carefree yet put-together vibe I'm going for.

"You look perfect." Owen flashes a tight smile. He's wearing a casual cotton top and bottom button-down look. As always, he looks like he has money but doesn't want to announce it.

"Thanks," I sigh, "How much longer till we're there?"

"Not long." Something about Owen's tone makes me uneasy, especially since these are his surprise plans. The further inland we head, the curvier the roads are getting. We seem to be heading deep into the mountains. I sit back and try to enjoy the scenery.

"Okay, we are just about there," Owen says as we round a switchback I would not want to be driving on at night. Every driveway we have passed since we came into town is like an entrance to Narnia. The gates alone look like they could cost half a million. There's no way to even glimpse the villa it's leading to. Owen puts his blinker on before taking a right into the next driveway, which seems swallowed by dense tropical plants.

"Wait, this is where we are going?" I sit up straight to get a full view out of the windshield.

"Welcome to La Casa de Belmont," Owen says, almost under his breath, as he reaches out to type a code into the gate-bell- or whatever you call it. The mystical iron gate towers over us.

"What?" My eyes practically plunge out of their sockets at Owen. "No, no, no, do not even tell me this is where your uncle and aunt live!"

"It's also the home I grew up in and I figured it was time you see it." Owen clutches the steering wheel as he talks, and my mouth goes dry.

"Oh my gosh, Owen. Okay, I'm trying not to flip out on you but-"

"Wait- this is you trying?" I get my first smirk of the day from him as he goes deeper into the dark driveway.

"I can't believe you're doing this to me! I'm not even slightly prepared to meet your family! Oh my gosh . . . Oh my gosh!" I'm practically hyperventilating.

"Valletta, relax! My aunt Cecilia will absolutely love you, and I figured you could use the day away from your usual stomping grounds to help clear your head. Plus, Cecilia has been hounding me to bring you here for dinner. She won't shut up about it."

My response is overridden because my eyes are in complete awe at the structure we are driving up to. The Narnia-themed driveway is cut off by a perfectly structured cactus garden with a stone spiral walkway, which leads up to a blood-red door, so big that a giant could walk through it. The door, however, is like a small button on the enormous villa. A wide-brimmed sun hat pops out from the side of the house. It's a woman tending to what looks like a small patch of flowers. When she stands up, she wipes her brow with the back of her hand, smiling at us. She's wearing gardening gloves and holding a pair of scissors. There's a small basket with flowers she's picked beside her. She takes off her gloves and places them gently in the basket before rushing toward us. My heart rate accelerates more and more the closer she gets. There's no time to yell at Owen or figure out who she is, because, before I know it, Owen is opening my car door for me, and she collides right into him.

"If it isn't my precious Owie Bear!" The woman with the wide-brimmed sun hat exclaims as they hug. Owen seems happy to see her too. He has a big smile on his face as they untangle, and then her eyes drift to me.

"Is this the beautiful Valletta you've been telling us about?" Her voice is sweet like a honeycomb.

"I don't know about beautiful, but I am Valletta." I smile, standing up out of the car.

"What a lovely name! Oh, and you are just the cutest little thing. I can see why Owen is so enthralled." I can feel my cheeks redden. I glance over at Owen, but he is just staring at the house. He is clearly lost in thought, which does not help my nerves as I try to respond.

"Would it be safe to assume you're Aunt Cecilia?"

"Yes, dear." She smiles wide before hugging me tight.

"Oh, today is just going to be wonderful! I want you to treat this place as if it's yours. Come on, now!" Cecilia grabs my hand and leads me towards the door. I look behind and Owen is silently following. As we walk, Cecilia continues talking to me.

"So, Valletta, dear, please feel free to use the pool of course, or you kids could play some tennis. There's even a nice trail Owen could take you on. Oh, he would go up that trail almost every day as a boy. There are swimsuits and towels in the guest bedroom, and whatever else you may need!" She opens the blood-red door while my head is spinning from trying to follow her torrent of words.

"Jessica, dear!" Cecilia's call echoes out into her vaulted ceilings and within a matter of seconds, a small young Mexican woman appears with a shiny black bun wearing an actual housekeeper's uniform. Did I just step onto the set of a reality TV show? I've never experienced anything like this before.

"Yes, Mrs. Belmont?"

"Jessica, could you please help Valletta here with whatever she needs. She can settle into the second guest room." She turns to me, "There's a washroom for-"

"Aunt Cecilia, it's okay"- Owen interrupts. "I can help Valletta. Maybe give her a second to breathe." Owen touches Cecilia's arm as if to calm her excitement.

"Oh, silly me, of course. I know you hate being fussed over. I guess I should assume the same for your guest." She smiles warmly at me before continuing, "Well, okay then, how about you two get settled in and then I can give Valletta a garden tour. How does that sound?"

"Yes, definitely, that sounds amazing," I reply, in a daze.

Owen takes my hand and guides me through the stunning interior. The entryway is a bit dark with wooden beams above and a dimly lit chandelier that looks like something you'd find in an antique store. The kind of antique store I couldn't afford to even walk into. There's a half-spiral staircase that Owen leads me up, and a unique mosaic tile accents the front of each wooden stair. My hand drifts onto the iron railing that's beautifully curved with the spiral design. My eyes are trying to take in every detail, but it's impossible. I catch a quick glimpse of the outside through the small arched windows. Did I see an oasis or a backyard?

"Here's your room to use for the day. Despite all the activities my aunt listed, there's no pressure. We can even just take a nap until dinner." Owen releases my hand as I stand in a room that might be as big as my entire apartment. There's a bronze chandelier in the middle of the ceiling throwing off soft yellow light as if the room were lit by candles. The vanity is neatly covered with makeup and jewelry. A rose gold oval mirror hangs above it, surrounded by a spiral decal. Owen is rifling through the wooden dresser.

"Owen, why didn't you tell me we were coming here?" I say softly as I look for somewhere to sit. I'm torn between the sofa and the bed. "A sofa in a guest bedroom," I mumble under my breath as I choose the sofa. As soon as I sit down, I notice the artwork above the vanity. It has an almost haunted feeling to it. It's a portrait of a young woman with swirling jet-black curls framing her ghost-white face. But her eyes are what really draw me in. It's like looking into two pieces of coal. They feel almost soulless, yet something about her is captivatingly beautiful. I'm so engrossed in the portrait that Owen's presence startles me.

"She's beautiful, isn't she?" His voice is a whisper. When I turn to look at him, his eyes are locked onto the painting. He pulls away and settles his eyes on me, our faces just inches apart. I could get lost in him. He opens his mouth to speak while I sit captivated.

"I didn't tell you because you tend to overthink everything and worry. You have enough on your plate this week. I just wanted to sweep you away for a day." He leans in and presses his lips into mine, a feeling I'm slowly becoming addicted to. The way his ice-cold lips press gently against mine causes my mind to blur and makes it impossible to focus on anything else. When we come up for air, I reach out and touch his soft curls. He smiles and asks, "So, do you forgive me?"

I sigh, still lost in our kiss. I back away from him to get my mind clear again.

"I guess you're forgiven. Just don't let me come off as a lowly loser to your aunt and uncle," I plead, and he chuckles.

"Not possible." He gently kisses the back of my hand, causing my head to swirl all over again. "Now, put this on," he says, handing me a bathing suit, "We're going swimming." His eyes twinkle.

"No way am I wearing this! Only a model could pull this off. What is this, vintage?" My mouth falls open as I hold up the cream-white one-piece. It has a rose for the halter neck with a perfectly shaped cut-out below. Not that I know what high-quality feels like, but this has to be high quality.

"Owen, it says handmade in Italy!" I gasp.

"There's a whole bunch in the dresser, but I think that one will look amazing on you, trust me." Owen winks as he stands up. "I'll give you some privacy. The washroom is right through that door. Meet me at the pool when you're done." Owen's smile is wide as he leaves me in this fairytale room, holding a designer bathing suit. I sigh, slouching back on the sofa, wondering if this is a dream I'm about to wake up from.

I cover myself with the big white bathrobe I found in the washroom, a washroom I could spend the day in, I might add. Everything was marble. The white bathtub was gorgeous, with a gold faucet attached to it and hanging plants above. There was a view of the pool through the bathroom window, so I had an idea which direction to go.

Owen is already swimming when I get there. He's doing laps like he's a professional. I think I'm learning he really loves to swim. Stones outline the pool in an irregular shape, with tropical plants filling every space in between the scattered lounge chairs. It's far from a standard design. Instead, it's like swimming in a jungle.

"You found me." Owen smiles as he bobs up and down in the deep end, "What are you waiting for? Come on in!"

I bite my lip as I dip a toe into the cool water. When I remove my bathrobe, a wave of self-consciousness comes over me. I feel like a fraud in this swimsuit, it's too beautiful for me. I reach up self-consciously to double-check that I tied the halter straps in a secure bow, not wanting any surprises if it were to come undone. Once I'm sure it's tight enough, I let the ends of the straps hang down over the cut-out in the back.

"Wow, I was right, you look absolutely stunning," Owen says as he swims over to me. I can't help but blush. I'd be lying if I didn't say I stared at myself in the mirror when I tried it on, but it's the vintage suit that's beautiful, not me.

"Just jump in, the water's perfect."

I take a deep breath before I plunge under the water. Once I'm beneath the surface, I spin around like I'm a kid again. When I come up for air, Owen is hanging onto the side of the pool near the small waterfall, staring at me with a big grin on his face.

"You look great in the water," he says.

"So do you." I smile, treading in one place. "How did you learn how to swim so well?"

Owen shrugs and looks up at the palm above him. "The water is my happy place. I could swim all day if it didn't turn me into a raisin."

I laugh at the image he painted. I can tell he's telling the truth. There's something about him and water. It just works.

"I guess I can relate," I reply. "The ocean is my happy place. I especially love being underwater."

"Why is that?"

"It's hard to put into words. I guess I love the way it drowns out everything on the surface."

Owen doesn't reply, he just looks at me thoughtfully, as if he's processing what I said.

We spend a while swimming together. I try to race him, but he beats me each time. Cecilia brings out some lemonade and coffee cake, letting us know the garden tour would be starting soon, as if it were a scheduled event for which she was a tour guide.

Owen shakes his head laughing as he pulls me close to him under the water. "She really takes her gardens seriously." He kisses me. I pull away quickly, anxious Cecilia is watching, but Owen doesn't seem to care. I could stay in this oasis all day with Owen holding me, our skin cool and refreshed from the water. It's perfect, but it's not just us here. I need to make a good impression with his family.

"I don't want to keep your aunt waiting. We should go get ready." I swim away underwater, taking a few minutes to savor the sensation of all sound being blocked out.

Owen and I rinse off using the outside showers in the oasis, and I head back to the guestroom to change for the garden tour. Now that my hair is wet, I look way too sloppy to tour this villa. The sage jumpsuit is not cutting it. I decide to take up Cecilia's offer and head over to the vanity. My finger grazes the abundance of powders and lipsticks until my hand settles on a shade of apple red, wondering if it would make my freckles pop. The contrast is striking against my olive skin. I never feel bold enough for a color like this, but something about this place makes me want to try and stand out. I carefully outline my lips with vibrant red and fill in the rest, like a coloring book coming to life. I finish off with some mascara and fill in my eyebrows a little, then I scrunch my hair with a towel to give my waves some shape. I take a deep breath in as I study myself in the rose gold mirror. My eyes drift back up to the portrait and I tilt my head to the side as it captivates me again. There's something so . . . familiar about her.

I shake myself free and meet Cecilia and Owen beside the pool. I assume we are just going to go back out front to the cactus garden with her small patches of flowers along the way. The place she actually leads us to is far beyond anything I could have imagined. Two large wooden doors with iron stripes and handles tower above us, ivy curving around them. Cecilia opens one of the large wooden doors, and when I walk through, I have no clue where to look first.

"Oh my goodness, this is unreal!" I exclaim.

Cecilia's grin takes up her entire face at my enthusiasm. "Isn't it beautiful? It's my secret garden. I've cared for these plants for over fifty years, ever since I was a little girl. Each one is like a special friend. I've added quite a few since you've seen it last, Owen."

"I can tell," Owen says as he looks around. Each corner of the garden has arches and pergolas, all showcasing a different plant. I notice grapes on one, lemons under another, roses, and even a gorgeous purple wisteria. It's like stepping into a dreamland. Cecilia's knowledge blows me away. She knows everything about these plants. It's like her entire world. We walk around for a while before Owen stops.

"This is my favorite section. All these plants here," Owen motions with his hands, "They are all poisonous. Just a few snips of some of these and BAM, you're dead."

"He's quite morbid, isn't he?" Cecilia shakes her head at Owen, then looks at me. "He wasn't that way as a little boy. He just woke up one day with a dark side." Although she's laughing, there's a sense of seriousness in her tone.

Owen keeps his eyes on the poisonous plants. "Hey, just wait, one day you'll be tempted to snip a few of these and put them in Lance's breakfast."

"Oh, Owen, you're horrible!" Cecilia smacks his arm in disbelief. "What is Valletta going to think? She hasn't even met your uncle yet. Don't put bad ideas in her head."

"Right." Owen takes a deep breath while putting his hands in his pockets. "You know I'm just messing with you, Aunt CeCe." Owen leans down and kisses his aunt's cheek, causing her to smile and put her arms around him.

Oh right, the uncle. I completely forgot. I haven't even met him yet. I remember Owen's reaction when the cops brought him up. He seemed cold at the mention of him. Is there bad blood between him and his uncle? I assume not. Otherwise, why would we be here?

"Alright, now, I've been saving the best for last." Cecilia leads us to the very back of the garden, an almost hidden slot as you walk through Rhododendrons, like a secret entrance. Asian lanterns are placed around a variety of Bosnia's. There's a stone in the middle with "The Sister of the Secret Garden" carved into it and a weeping Bonsai is placed above.

"She was especially fond of the Weeping Willow," Cecilia whispers. Owen's face is stone cold. He looks angry suddenly. She continues, "I want you to come here anytime and visit her secret garden." Cecilia's face is filled with emotion. I am completely lost as to what is going on. I'm afraid to ask because of the tension filling the air.

"Does Lance know you built this?" Owen asks angrily.

"Oh, Owen, please don't ruin a good moment. This is for you and me. What do you think, Valletta? It's a beautiful spot, isn't it?" I look over at Owen, unsure how to react.

"Yes, it's stunning. Is it in remembrance of someone?" I ask, and right away Owen turns around quickly, grabbing my hand.

"We need to get ready for dinner. Let's go," he says sharply, pulling me away from the secret garden. I look at Cecilia with wide eyes, not knowing what to do. I stumble along the pathway out of the wonderland of Cecilia's decades of care, trying to keep up with Owen. He's ignoring all my requests to stop. When we pass the two wooden doors, I yank back on Owen's grip, forcing him to stand still.

"Owen, stop!" He looks at me and I'm completely taken aback by his dark expression. "I don't know what that was all about, but we can't just leave your aunt back there like that. Please, just tell me what's going on."

He closes his eyes for a moment, not saying anything. "I'll tell you more, just not here. We can go for a walk after dinner." He glares at the villa. "Let's just get through dinner, okay?" he pleads.

I swallow. Get through dinner? Suddenly I want nothing more than to leave. I have a bad feeling about this evening. The one solace I have is that this is not my family, not my drama. I finally have a chance to support someone else, to support Owen. I reach out and squeeze his hand, and then for the first time, I'm the one who initiates a kiss.

I step towards him slowly and kiss him tenderly, trying to wipe away his anger.

Thirty-six

A DEEP BLUE DRESS is laid out on the bed in the guestroom. I gently lift the chiffon fabric with the short lace sleeves. There's a shoebox next to it containing a pair of gold sandals. My stomach drops. Did Cecilia think I was underdressed?

I hear footsteps in the hallway and turn to see Jessica looking at me with a soft smile on her face. "That's for you to wear to dinner if you would like, Miss Skye." I smile at Jessica, feeling very uncomfortable with this whole housekeeper experience. She adds, "Of course, you don't have to wear it if you don't want to."

"Thank you, Jessica."

She nods and dismisses herself, disappearing into the hallway. I walk over to the door and close it, desperate for a little privacy.

A nagging sensation is slowly overtaking me. Something feels off. The secret garden alone was enough to fill my brain with a million questions. I'm dying for some answers. The question is how do I get them? I know snooping is wrong, but my curiosity about Owen's family is at an all-time high. I can't get rid of that nagging feeling that something is off. Besides, is snooping around really that harmful if no one knows you're doing it? Granted, there's probably nothing in this guestroom to snoop through.

I search the nightstand drawers and the vanity, finding nothing. I look in the closet and through the wooden dresser with the bathing suits, shirts, and pajamas, pretty much anything a person might need to wear but forget to pack. There was nothing out of the ordinary. I gave up on my snooping and sat on the bed, picking up the dress again. I can't decide if it's more uncomfortable to wear this dress or not to wear it. I lay back on the mattress letting out a heavy sigh. This day is crazy. Pangs of guilt start to come up when I think of how at this very moment, my father is sitting in jail, and I'm here in a multi-million-dollar villa. Probably the craziest part of it all is that Mark doesn't even know I'm here, or that my father is in jail, never mind the fact that I went to see him. This is the longest I've ever gone without talking to him. I close my eyes, trying to prevent them from welling up, firmly pushing down any emotions from surfacing. Now is not the time to dwell on any of that. It all feels out of my control anyway.

When I sit up, I bounce on the mattress a little, a thought popping into my head. It's unlikely that there's anything, but I get off the bed and kneel on the carpet. I spot what looks like a photo album placed directly in the middle underneath the bed. I reach out and grab it, resting my back against the bed frame as I sit on the floor, opening up the album.

There are pictures of two young girls. Sisters, perhaps? They are smiling, holding hands, with flowers in their hair. Several photos are of them planting little plants in the dirt, big grins on their faces. One of the girls has a small resemblance to Cecilia, the other one has jet-black curls and pale skin. I wonder if they are related. Then it clicks, The Sister of the Secret Garden. A sadness rises within me as I flip through the album. The sister with the jet-black curls is holding a young boy with exactly the same hair. He's standing on what looks to be the back patio and holding a daisy up to the woman. You can't see either of them head-on, just their side profiles. That's all I need to know. That boy is Owen.

I stop. Is Cecilia's sister Owen's mom? I assumed for whatever reason that Lance was Owen's blood uncle, because the photos of him in the entryway look more like Owen than Cecilia does. It's funny how that works sometimes.

The last photo in the album is of what looks to be an older version of the woman I'm assuming is Owen's mom. She's stunning. she has prominent features with swirling jet-black hair, full lips and ghostly yet pristine skin. But her eyes are what draw me in. If I just saw those eyes alone, I would swear it was Owen. I mean they are pure onyx. Except there was one thing absent. Perhaps it's the fact that it's a photograph and the camera can't pick up on what Owen's eyes so often show. The glimmer in the onyx, the sparkle of life, the sense of determination. They are just stone. Then it clicks. I stand up and carry the photograph over to the portrait above the vanity.

It's her. She is the haunted portrait that is so captivating. It's almost like whoever painted it was trying to disguise the fact that it was her. But once you see it, it can't be unseen . . .

"Hey, Valletta, can I come in?" Owen's voice comes through the door. I rush over to the bed, putting the album back where I found it.

"Uh, yeah, come in." I sit on the mattress, trying to cover the fact that I'm out of breath. Owen opens the door slowly, peeping through with a smile on his face, almost gliding over toward me on the bed.

"I was wondering what kind of dress Cecilia would pick out for you to wear to dinner." He smiles as he picks up the dress, his anger gone from just a little while ago. "She has great taste." I shift uncomfortably.

"Honestly, I wasn't sure whether I should wear it or not."

Owen turns his head to me inquisitively. "Why wouldn't you? You don't like it?"

"I love it; it's beautiful. It just all feels so . . . weird, I guess."

"In what way?"

I shrug, "I don't know... I guess in the way that this is absolutely surreal. I mean, I've never experienced all this before. This is a completely different world for me." I swallow. "I feel like a cheap Cinderella who went to the ball."

"You really don't think much of yourself, and yet you are the only person I've ever wanted to bring here. It's rare that I trust someone so soon. You're special, Valletta. As cliche as it sounds, you are truly special." He grazes my face, tucking my hair behind my ear. "Now please, put on this beautiful dress and meet me downstairs. I have someplace special to show you after dinner, just in time for sunset." I smile in agreement, deciding against asking the burning questions on my mind. I'm sure he will tell me when he's ready.

I catch Jessica's eye as I walk down the spiral staircase. I can't help but feel embarrassed that I'm wearing a dress that's not mine.

"You look lovely Miss Skye," Jessica says warmly. She gives me a little wink as if she can tell I'm totally out of my element, and she gets it.

The dining table is on the patio under a grape vine pergola with lanterns hanging down from the top. The table has a cream lace runner, with bouquets of peach roses in tall, red glass vases. Each place setting includes multiple plates of different sizes stacked on top of each other and a beautifully rolled napkin, held together by a pearl napkin ring. I'm panicking, realizing I have no idea which piece of silverware to use for each course.

"I just picked the roses as I was leaving the garden." Cecilia's voice comes from behind me. I turn to see her in a flattering white two-piece pant suit, the kind you would see a proper lady wear at a horse race. Her hair is neatly tucked into a French twist. "Oh, Valletta, dear, that dress is absolutely stunning on you! I'm so glad you wore it." She gleams.

"Thank you, Cecilia, I wasn't expecting you to lend me a dress."

"Oh, no, I'm not lending it to you, it's yours!" She hugs me, planting a kiss on my cheek.

"Oh, I couldn't . . ."

"Yes, you can. Outside of gardening, gifts are my second greatest joy, so don't take away my joy." Her honeycomb voice is so soothing.

"Thank you . . . Also, I have to say, your house feels like I'm inside an enchanted villa. I mean, it's all so magical."

"That's because she is magic," Owen says, appearing through the French double doors that lead outside. He walks over to me, lifting my arm towards him so he can gently kiss my hand. "Wow! Again, that dress is just perfect." I shake my head and look away towards the pool, ready to move on from talking about how I look.

"You have decorated this table as if there's a special occasion," I say to Cecilia.

"Anytime we get a visit from Owen, it is a special occasion," she gleams.

"For you, perhaps." Owen's voice is soft, as if he didn't mean to say that out loud. His eyes drift to the double doors. Cecilia either didn't hear him or is choosing to ignore his words.

"Your uncle should be home any moment now... Jessica!"

Jessica appears within a matter of seconds. "Yes, Mrs. Belmont?"

"Can you please let Chef Gregory know that we will be ready for dinner as soon as Mr. Belmont arrives?"

"Of course."

"Thank you, dear." Jessica nods and walks off. "Why don't you two have a seat," Cecilia says, gesturing to Owen and me. "And I will be right back."

She glides away as Owen moves the chair out in front of me, motioning for me to sit down. I oblige, sitting very carefully so as not to knock over any crystal. I'm feeling like the very definition of out of your element.

Owen showed me which silverware was proper to use for each course. I'm grateful we had a few moments alone before the actual dinner. A man's voice comes from the villa. Owen's hands turn to fists in response, and he straightens up. His body language is making me nervous.

When Lance walks into the room, his presence is unmistakable. If power has a feeling, he sends waves of it rushing into the room. I would be lying if I were to say my heartbeat didn't double in anticipation of meeting him.

"Lance, sweetie, this is Valletta, Owen's friend." The look on Cecilia's face makes me wonder if she's trying to send him signals to behave.

"Hi, Mr. Belmont." I greet him as I awkwardly try to get up from my chair. "I'm Valletta." I give him a firm handshake which I'm told is what you do with important people.

"Lance is fine . . . It's nice meeting you. It's not often Owen brings a girl home." He looks me up and down while talking which makes me uneasy. He turns his attention to Owen, who is still silent. "The car doesn't look like it's been in any accidents. I'm surprised."

Owen's face is stone cold, completely expressionless.

"What? Don't I get a greeting?" Lance prods, glaring at Owen.

"I was just waiting until you were done talking. Long day at the office?" Owen sounds robotic.

"Hell, that place would fall apart without me." Lance shakes his head in annoyance while pulling out a chair. "So, Valletta, are you in school or have you graduated?"

"I've graduated." I swallow, hating that the attention is on me. Leave it to a wealthy man to act like there's no option outside of college. I wish I could roll my eyes.

"What do you do now?" Lance asks the question I was dreading.

"I'm waitressing at the moment."

"So, I'm assuming you're not using your degree at all?" The way Lance asks the question makes my skin crawl. Thankfully, Owen feels my panic.

"I don't think Valletta wants to be interrogated right now."

"Well, I suppose we could talk about your journalism. Is that still considered a job?" Lance chuckles, his belly bouncing a bit as he grabs his whiskey on ice. Owen seems to ignore his comment, but I catch a glimpse of his hand tightening around his napkin.

I was not prepared for the four-course meal that followed. The soup and salad alone tasted better than what I have most nights for dinner. Cecilia made sure the conversation stayed light while we ate. It seemed like something she was used to doing. I couldn't help but watch her. Something about her worried me. It was as if she was holding herself together, but at any moment, she could fall apart. She seemed like a completely different person than the plant enthusiast who was show-ing us her garden. Maybe that was all in my head, though.

Owen threw subtle jabs at his uncle in retaliation for his judgmental comments. He was all over Owen's case, questioning everything he was doing in life. It started sinking in how lost Owen really was in life. I hoped to find out more about what he was trying to do next for work, but he remained tight-lipped. After dessert, Lance excused himself to send out a few work emails, but he insisted on having a nightcap with Owen privately before we left. I thought Owen would be more hesitant, but he almost seemed eager to talk to him one-on-one.

"Why don't you show Valletta the trail out back, your hiding spot as a boy." Cecilia's expression seems filled with nostalgia.

"Thanks, Aunt Cece. We will be back after." Owen hugs his aunt and then reaches out for my hand, and I follow him to his special spot.

Thirty-seven

Suddenly I'm surrounded by incredible beauty, the kind of beauty that knocks the air out of your lungs. "Wow," is all I can manage.

"I had a feeling you would love it. It's where I used to come to think, sometimes run away. One time I ran away for an entire weekend here when I was nine." Owen smiles.

"What were you running from?" I look out over the desert valley with the sea of green mountains behind, a view that can provide comfort in the most poetic way.

"Does it really matter?" His eyes sharpen. I can tell I've hit a nerve. I reach out and touch his soft curls, smiling at him, and his expression slowly softens.

"Huh, so, nine-year-old Owen. I'm picturing a brooding kid dressed in all black, who charms his teachers out of any homework assignment . . ."

Owen laughs at my description, "Not bad. But you're missing my accessories, specifically a journal and a camera. I was always taking pictures and journaling the world around me. I was especially suspicious of people who were up to no good. I guess you could say I was quite the little investigator."

"I have a feeling that hasn't changed . . . Is that what's in that special journal of yours?"

Owen's head jerks at me as if taken a little by surprise. "You're a sharp one, Valletta Skye." He smiles. "I guess the major thing that's changed is, I'm a lot less naive."

Now, when I look at his eyes, his mother's face comes to mind, almost haunting me.

"So . . ." I start, choosing my words carefully, "You never really talk about your mom. I don't know if that's on purpose, but I just hope you know that if you ever want to tell me about her, I would be more than happy to listen." I am trying to keep my tone casual and low-key. Owen is quiet, almost as if he's reflecting. I continue, "You know, that portrait above the vanity really looks like someone related to you . . ."

"The eyes?" He says softly.

"Yeah, they drew me in like yours do . . . It's just a gut feeling . . ."

"When I couldn't sleep, I used to sneak into that room, move the sofa near the wall, and just stare at her picture. Her eyes weren't always like that when she was alive. At times they were, but other times they had the most magnificent light. She would get so excited about things." He pauses. "'Stay curious.' That's what she used to tell me." He smiles, getting lost in a memory. His memory seems to change as the expression on his face grows dark.

"I'm the one who found her. The bath water was still warm . . ."

Owen's words leave me stunned for a moment. I can see the pain wash over him. It's like he's being flooded by some sort of gloom.

"Owen," I rest my hand on his shoulder. "I am so sorry." The words come out slow and intense, a simple phrase that's carrying so much meaning.

"Everyone seemed to misunderstand her, everyone but me. I knew she just needed help, but people thought she was lazy, that she was a bad mother. They didn't get how great of a mother she really was. No one, and I mean, no one, got me like she did." The sadness in his eyes seems to turn to rage, rage towards something or someone, perhaps? His expression feels so familiar to me, mostly because I have that rage in me.

"I wish I could have met her." I decide not to ask any more questions about his family or try and figure out what the anger in his eyes is. It won't help. The only thing that would help is to bring his mother back, the one thing I definitely can't do. But I can allow him to talk about her.

Owen stands up and walks towards the edge of the valley. He seems to come out of his darkness. "I'm going to help you get your father out of jail. You deserve a chance for a better ending."

I am completely thrown off by Owen's transition. I've been trying to put my father out of my brain. Granted, it hasn't been going so well. I don't know how to respond. I get up and walk to him, reaching out to hold his hand as we stand facing the sea of mountains.

Thirty-eight

I HOPE OWEN ISN'T leaving you here all by yourself!" Cecilia's voice came from behind me as she walked into the courtyard. It's the perfect star-gazing spot. The stars above are vibrant specks of light.

"Oh, no, it's okay, Lance wanted to have a quick nightcap with him. Besides, I'm happy sitting under the stars." I smile, despite the anxiety I can't seem to shake. Owen had squeezed my hand before walking off with Lance. For whatever reason, that squeeze almost felt like a warning.

"Good, good." Cecilia seems so tired all of a sudden. No doubt hosting took a lot out of her. I couldn't help but see a subtle shake in her hands that wasn't there at dinner.

"I'm glad Owen has you," she says. "He was always a very lost and angry child. I feared for his future. That boy has a lot of demons." Her eyes are glazed now as she's looking past me.

"Well, I wouldn't worry too much about him. He's very passionate and driven. In fact, I can say for certain that I've never met anyone like him." I look at her and it's as if she snaps out of her daze.

"You're strong, though. You can handle him." It was like she didn't hear what I said, as if she was having a conversation with herself. All of her perkiness and grace were gone.

Suddenly, I hear yelling coming from the house. My eyes jump over to Cecilia. Her face is calm, as if she didn't hear it. The yelling sounds closer but I can't make out the words.

"I haven't asked you for ANYTHING!" Owen's voice booms. Within a matter of seconds, Owen is standing in the courtyard; he looks filled with anger.

"We're leaving." He stops and looks at Cecilia for a moment in hesitation, then swings around to look at Lance. "You know, you're completely right, uncle." He spits out "uncle" as if it's a dirty word. "My mother wanted more for me. She wanted me to have a father, but instead I got a hot-tempered, angry uncle." He walks away leaving me standing there with his ghost-like aunt.

I turn to Cecilia. "Are you going to be okay?"

"You should go, dear." Her voice is a whisper.

There's a part of me that doesn't feel right leaving her here. Then I hear the engine start in Owen's car and I panic. Without another word I hurry away, leaving a woman standing in her own courtyard looking like she wants to be one of the statues surrounding her.

Before I even have a chance to close the door, Owen is speeding off down the long dark driveway. My heart is racing. His eyes are fixed on the road, his jaw tight. I've never seen this side of him, this anger. I don't know what to say. I feel like anything will set him off. for the first time being with him . . . I feel afraid.

Rows of trees become blurs. We are flying down a winding road. I have to say something, otherwise, we might crash.

"Can you please slow down?" I manage.

Owen doesn't listen, he just keeps staring at the road.

"Look, I don't know what happened in there, but your driving is scaring me."

"You don't trust me?" He breaks his silence with a cutting tone. It's like being stabbed with words. He picks up speed. I swear we are doing 60mph around switchbacks.

"Owen, this isn't funny. You're scaring me." My heart rate has skyrocketed. I put my hand on the door rest, but it slips because of my sweaty palms. "Just, please, pull over and we can talk this out," I plead.

"There's nothing to talk about," he sneers. He takes the next corner like we are in a race. We're going to crash. I close my eyes, and tears stream down them. I'm terrified. There have been so many times in my life that I wanted to be in this position, to just drift away accidentally, away from my problems, away from my memories.

An escape. A way out.

But here I am, in this moment, and I would do anything to live.

I have two options. I can let Owen control this or I can try and fight.

"YOU'RE GOING TO KILL US!" I scream. "PULL THE CAR OVER NOW, OWEN!"

Then I say in the most even tone I can manage, "If you care about me at all, you will stop."

His onyx eyes flash towards me and his jaw softens. He slowly eases off the gas, but it's too late. If he had done it only three seconds earlier, he wouldn't have hit the deer. He probably could have slowed down in time. They say the worst thing you can do is swerve out of the way.

Owen swerved.

Thirty-nine

AT FIRST, I THOUGHT I was imagining the beeping. It sounded distant, like it was in another room. My eyes flashed open for a second, but the light was so bright, they closed just as fast as they opened. I heard chatter. Then I felt someone squeeze my hand.

"Valletta?" It was Mark's voice.

I tried turning my head to the side. "Mark? What's going on?" My voice was hoarse and foreign.

"You're okay. You were in an accident. Owen was-" Mark's voice fell, and he cleared his throat, clearly trying to maintain composure. "You're okay."

"Owen was what?" A flash of a memory hits me and I remember Owen was driving. "Wait, is he ok?" I ask Mark in desperation.

Mark quickly turns away from me, then returns his gaze. "I'm sure if it was anything serious, we would have heard by now. Besides he's the reason-" Mark stop, his nostrils flare as he breathes in his anger. "Look, can we just focus on you? He's being taken care of."

I swallow, respecting his wishes. I'll find out as soon as I can talk to the doctor in private. I feel Mark come close, trying to get into my line of vision. His arm grazes mine and I can feel warmth radiating off of him.

"How did you know I was here?" I manage, trying to get my normal voice back.

"I'm your emergency contact, remember?"

"Right," I whisper.

I never went to the doctor, which drove Mark nuts, and when he insisted that I finally get a primary care, he went with me to the first appointment for emotional support. When I was filling out the papers, I got to the emergency contact and stopped writing. Mark saw that I was staring blankly at the papers, and without a word, he gently grabbed the clipboard and listed his own information. That gesture meant more to me than he would ever know. Now, he's here. Despite everything, he took that responsibility seriously.

The passage of time felt like molasses slowly dripping off a tree. I couldn't tell if I was in a dream. It could have been hours or days for all I knew. Mark never left my side. I heard him on the phone with Melanie. It was like he was talking a mile away, but I think he was still in the same room. Before I knew it, Melanie was at my side with a fancy fluffy pillow and a make-up bag, insisting I would get better faster if I felt good about myself. The last thing I wanted was my makeup done while sitting in a hospital bed, but I knew it would make Melanie happy.

They both stayed in the room as the doctor gave me my assessment. I was finally feeling less drowsy. I could hear clearly. As the doctor talked, I looked over at Mark. He was listening attentively to the doctor. Turns out, I had a concussion, a fractured wrist, and some bad whiplash. It could have been so much worse. I felt so much worse. I was anxious to hear about what happened to Owen, but I didn't dare ask when Mark was around. I think just hearing his name from my mouth would cause Mark to become homicidal.

When the doctor left, Mark yawned and stretched, then went over to the chair as if he was going back to his post. Melanie was close to me, and I looked at her hoping if telepathy was real it would work at this moment. She tilted her head to the side. I think it was actually working. I looked out of the room, then back at her, trying to hint at what I needed. Then I mouthed 'Owen' slowly. She took a deep breath in, almost looking annoyed at my request for an update on him, but instead of being typical Melanie and opening her mouth loudly to share her thoughts, she just nodded her head, looking defeated. She squeezed my hand and gave me a sad smile.

As she turned around, she looked at Mark. "Hey, I'm gonna grab a coffee. I'll be back."

Mark nods, then rests his head back on his chair. I can tell he's exhausted. I try sitting up a little, the drugs make me feel heavy.

"Mark?" I try to clear my hoarse voice.

He pops his head up and looks over at me, concerned. "What's wrong? Do you need something?" I bite my lip, thinking how best to approach this. I know if he could do something for me first, it will soften him. That's just how he works.

"Do you know if there's like, a cough drop, or something I can use to help my throat a little?"

"Of course." He's back in the room within a couple of minutes with a handful of cough drops. "I had to give the nurse my number for these." He smiles as he brings them over. Even though he sounds like he's joking, there's no doubt in my mind he flirted to get these. I mean, few guys could pull off this horrific hospital lighting and no sleep. His eyes alone probably hypnotized her. I wonder if she will be back sooner now to check on me. I smile a little at the thought.

"Thank you." Despite the cough drop being an excuse to ease the tension, as soon as I swallow it, a soothing comfort coats my throat.

"Would you maybe bring your chair a little closer? I could use the company. I think I'm done sleeping for now."

His body language gives me the feeling that he isn't as thrilled about this request. I wonder if it's because he still can't handle talking to me after his night of confession? But he obliges. Of course he does. It's Mark, after all.

Now that he's close, and I manage to look into his eyes, I get a sharp pain in my heart, realizing how much I missed him. I missed us just being us.

"So, how are you?" I manage.

"I'm fine. Just worried about you." He looks me over in concern.

"I will be fine. You heard the doctor." I reach over and try grabbing his hand that's resting on the edge of my bed. I graze his skin, but he pulls away and clears his throat.

"Valletta, no." He sits back in his chair.

"Sorry, I didn't mean-"

"It's okay. Just forget it." He looks pained, his eyes drift towards the window.

"How was your last couple of weeks? I haven't seen you at work."

"I, uhm, I ended up visiting my mom."

"You went to Boston?"

He nods his head yes. I was shocked. Was it because of me? Did he take an emergency trip home to get away from me?

"Wow, I didn't know you were planning on going to Boston. You never said anything." He shrugs in reply, avoiding eye contact. "Well, that's great. How's your mom?"

"She's okay. She's having a hard time right now, so I'm glad I got to visit."

Mark has a very special relationship with his mom. I am amazed that someone could be that close to a parent. It was just him and her mostly. His older brother seemed like he left as soon as he could. Mark always felt it was his responsibility to take care of her, which I felt was a bit unfair. But who was I to say anything about a normal parent-child relationship? I wonder if that's why he's so big on just having fun and enjoying life, to make up for not being granted that as a kid. I admire his philosophy, to just let go and soak in the rays whenever you can.

"I'm sure she was thrilled to see you." I smile softly at him, trying to get his eye contact back. There's a deafening silence between us.

"I miss you, Mark." I can barely get the words out without crying.

His head falls, making his dirty blonde hair fall over his face a little, shielding him from me. "Even after all this, are you staying with Owen?" His words are tight.

"It was an accident," I whisper.

Mark doesn't say anything in reply. Instead, he raises his head towards me. I get the most unsettling feeling as he looks at me. The expression on his face is so serious. Like there's something he wants to say that's too painful for me to hear. I swallow, tasting the honey from my cough drop.

"I'm going to go find Melanie." Mark stands up, looking around the room. "Take care of yourself, Valletta. It seems like you will be okay, thankfully."

And just like that, he's walking out of the room before I have a chance to think of what to say to get him to stay.

I wake up from another nap to see Melanie sitting beside me, scrolling Instagram.

"Is Owen okay?" My throat is dry, barely able to let out any words.

"He's okay." Melanie's words are sharp.

"Have you seen him?" I can tell she doesn't want to say more, which is driving me nuts.

"No, but I saw Mark as he was leaving and he seemed upset. What is going on with you guys, Valletta?"

"He left?" My heart sinks.

"Yeah, he was looking for me on his way out, wanted to make sure I was going to take care of you. The nerve of him sometimes, I swear." She laughs a little. Their weird competition over me exists even while I'm lying in a hospital bed.

"I can't believe he left," I say softly, even though I could totally believe it. I just didn't want to.

"I mean, he was here the whole night with barely any sleep, he came straight from his flight from Boston. He stayed by your side the whole time."

"I know."

"So, like, what in the world happened with you guys? I can tell it's something big. Especially for him to leave like that and not even tell me he was coming back to check on you."

"I will tell you some time but just not now." I sigh. "Can you please tell me about Owen?

"Why are you worried about the person who put you in this situation in the first place?"

"Mel, it was an accident. he didn't crash on purpose."

"Well, the cops said the car was going double the speed limit when it crashed."

"Wait, what? The cops were here?"

"Uhm, yeah." Melanie looks at me confused. "Damn, those drugs really were strong."

Crap. No wonder Mark asked me about why I was staying with Owen. He was in the room when the cops were here too. This is a mess.

"Look, he had a bad moment, but Owen isn't a bad person. It was a really crazy night for him. We were visiting his family. Emotions were high."

"Okay, I know you are not excusing him for driving recklessly with you in the car." Melanie crosses her arms and shoots daggers at me.

I close my eyes, not having the energy to argue with her. "I just need to know what happened to him."

"He was released," she snaps.

"What?

"He was released, Valletta. Gone. Totally fine. Oh, and where the hell is he?" She looks around angrily.

I was trying to act calm, but I couldn't think of a reason why he wouldn't check on me. I am starting to burn with anger at the thought of him just leaving the hospital. I hide my emotions from Melanie, who doesn't need any more encouragement to hate him right now.

"He's swallowing you up." Melanie looks at me, her eyes filled with sincerity. She always says things with a sparkle of humor in her eyes, but there's not even a faint shimmer.

"What on earth are you talking about?"

"Owen is swallowing you whole! I mean, can't you see it? You have been so enveloped in his presence that you are disappearing. Your best friend Mark who cares about you more than anyone on earth is in pain, and you don't even seem to care. All you're worried about is Owen! This guy, who comes out of nowhere, stresses you out and makes you feel self-conscious about where you stand with him. Then, he acts like a total jerk at a dinner party with your friends. Now you're telling me he brought you to his family's house of drama, when you guys have only been dating for like a minute. Oh, and uh, yeah; he drives like a maniac and crashes into a tree, leaving you in the hospital." She stops, out of breath.

I've never in over a decade of friendship heard Melanie talk to me like this, taking things so... seriously.

"You know what, Melanie? Do you want to know how Owen and I actually met?" I return her glare. "We met at a meeting for people with alcoholic relatives."

Her face falls in silence.

"I didn't tell you because I can't talk about those things with you. It's always been too much for you to handle my family drama. Owen gets it, Mel. He understands what it's like to deal with the kind of crap I've dealt with for my whole life. Things that you just could never understand, and you know, Mark just can't understand either. You guys want me to just move on and keep it in the past. Owen has helped me to face my crap head-on. He may not be perfect, but you know what? He gets me. He has his own demons that he has had to face, and I don't feel shame when I talk to him." My voice is cracking now. "Oh, and Mark. You don't think I care about Mark? What the hell is wrong with you? I care about him so much that I had to lose him, Melanie! Okay?! He wanted more, and because I didn't, I lost him! He can't handle being my friend anymore. So, stop making Owen the bad guy. Just stop!" It takes everything I have not to scream.

Melanie is almost ghost white. Her face is twisted. She looks like I took a bat and smacked her head. Then she steadies herself. "I was there before Mark, Valletta, and way before Owen. I was there since we were in freaking middle school! Don't you dare treat me like some stranger who can't handle your drama. I care about you more than anyone in my life. I was there for your first panic attack after your dad came home randomly when you were sixteen, remember? When he was high as a kite, and you completely fell apart after. I was there when your mother was yelling at you from the car as we walked to my house, that if you didn't do your chores, she wasn't buying the groceries that week because she shouldn't have to do her responsibilities if you didn't do yours." Now Melanie's voice is cracking. "The only reason why you think I can't handle your problems is because honestly, Valletta, talking about them isn't going to help you anymore! Your parents are totally screwed up! I hate seeing you so wrapped up in problems you can't actually solve. You need to move on. Enjoy life for goodness' sake! You can't control what they do. You can only control what you can do." She takes a deep breath. "Maybe I'm totally wrong, but I think Owen being able to relate to you isn't as romantic as it sounds."

Her words hit me like a ton of bricks. I am completely speechless. I want to shove her to the ground and scream at her for what she just said. All I can do is glare at her. Glare at my friend who just tore my already broken heart out.

"Just get out of my room." I sneer at her.

"No." She folds her arms stubbornly.

"GET OUT!" I scream, tears welling up behind my eyes. Shock washes over her.

A nurse pops her head into the room. "Is everything okay in here?"

Melanie wipes her face as if tears have fallen, and takes a deep breath. She turns to the nurse and smiles. "Everything is fine. I was just leaving." Melanie grabs her purse from the chair and walks out of the room without turning around.

Leaving me completely alone.

Forty

I STROKE THE CAST on my hand. I've never had one of these before. It reminds me of Mark's cast when he hurt his wrist. Somehow, that thought gives me comfort.

My arm is being compressed, a feeling I always hate when getting my blood pressure checked. The nurse is trying to make small talk, little jokes here and there when she can. I think she feels bad that I'm completely alone here. Maybe she even overheard the argument I had with Melanie.

"Excuse me, but is there any way you can tell me about the person I came in here with? His name is Owen Belmont."

The nurse looks over at me with a little confusion. "Oh, I'm so sorry, I didn't realize someone else was with you? I wasn't told of anyone. But I can certainly check for you."

"There was definitely someone with me. Owen was the one driving."

"Okay, I will check as soon as I can. The doctor should be in soon to finalize everything with you. We'll get you out of here as soon as we can."

I watch the nurse leave, joining the choreographed cast of doctors and nurses, some dodging out of the way of one another, and some flagging the others down. Sitting here all alone makes my mind spin. I'm doing everything in my power to not think about the accident.

The doctor finally steps into the room. "Okay, Valletta, it looks like you're going to be getting out of here very soon. Also, the nurse, Haley, said you were asking about the person who was with you in the car. He's okay. He insisted on checking out last night. The car hit the passenger side of the front. He didn't experience nearly as much impact."

"Wait, I'm sorry, he checked out?"

"Yes, last night." He says casually while looking over his clipboard. "So, do you have any questions for me before I review everything with you?"

My heart is in my stomach. Why in the world would Owen just check out without saying anything? It's like he just abandoned me here.

"Valletta? Any questions?" The doctor is making direct eye contact with me now. I stare at him for a moment, trying to process everything.

Yes, I have questions! Where the heck is Owen?

I clear my throat. "Uhm, no. No questions."

The sun hits my eyes like a bullet. The air feels so fresh despite all the cars and emergency vehicles surrounding the parking lot. The doctor recommended someone pick me up and stay with me tonight because of the concussion. The thought of calling Melanie or Mark just fills me with anxiety. I've never had a fight with Melanie like that before. Mark would probably answer but not because he wants to. I'm the last person he wants to be around. As angry as I am at Owen for abandoning me, I know there must be a good reason. Maybe he saw Mark in my room and decided against it, or maybe he was too ashamed to face me. I could tell visiting his family took a lot out of him. I put away my hurt and pride and call him. It goes straight to voicemail, and I hang up frustrated.

The Uber driver drops me off at my apartment. When I get out of the car, I realize it's the last place I want to be.

"You okay, Ma'am?" The Uber driver was still there, his window rolled down. Normally they would just speed off, but maybe my appearance and the fact that he picked me up from a hospital made him wait.

"Yes, I'm all good, thank you. Just waiting for my friend to meet me outside." I manage a smile at him to appear like everything is under control.

"Okay, just making sure." He nods his head before rolling up the window and driving away. I stay paralyzed on the sidewalk, just staring at my bedroom window above. I don't care how disgusting I feel, I can't go up there.

So instead, I start walking.

There's probably nothing I need more right now than a shower. Thankfully, Melanie brought me my favorite black Passenger T-shirt and my comfy high-waisted jeans. They are my oldest and most worn-in pair. She knew what I would want. Before leaving the hospital, I put the blood-stained chiffon dress Cecilia gave me in a plastic bag with the gold sandals. Every swing of the bag in my hand, a reminder of the accident.

The smell of dark roasted coffee beans calms me as I walk into Catalina's. My internal GPS took me here on instinct. I order my latte and avoid eye contact as much as I possibly can, not wanting to know if people are judging me for the post-hospital state that I'm in.

When my latte is finally in hand, I look around for a seat. The sofa is open, the same sofa Owen and I sat on together when my father called, right before our first kiss. I swallow down the memory and decide that today, I'm going to sit outside in the fresh air.

Sitting outside Catalina's is like being at a completely different cafe. Cactus plants surround the stucco exterior, and tall, industrial-sized windows show the chaos inside. There's a small olive tree right in the middle of the seating area, and I decide to sit underneath it at a table for one. I sip my latte, letting the familiar comfort bring me calm. Time for my favorite activity when I'm stressed; people-watching. Something about seeing other people live their lives instead of focusing on mine gives me a bit of an escape.

After some time, my latte is gone and so is my patience. My frustration and worry about Owen is starting to turn to anger. Why the hell hasn't he called me? I anxiously tap my fingers on my phone, going back and forth in my mind about what to do. I try calling him one more time, and again, it goes straight to voicemail.

"Damn it!" I mutter a little too loud, causing a head to turn at the next table. I hit the table in anger as I stand up to leave. I feel like I'm starting to go crazy. I grab the plastic bag with the dress in it and start walking back out to the main road. I pace back and forth in front of a bus stop, my heart racing faster by the second. I can feel a panic attack coming on.

"No, please, no!" I cry under my breath. "PLEASE, NO!" I cry out loud now. My veins fill with stress. I seize up. Desperate for air. I squeeze my eyes shut, doing everything I can to block out the noise around me.

Go underwater, Valletta! Go! Please! I'm chanting in my head, my chest tightening. I lose my grip on my phone, letting it fall to the ground as I push my good hand against my chest. STOP! I will myself, but it doesn't work. I yank on my hair and pull so hard my scalp is on fire.

"One . . ." Breathe. "Two . . ." Breathe. "Three . . ." Breathe.

I gasp, finally coming up for air. My eyes open, but the tears blur out my vision. After a few moments of stillness, my heart rate finally starts to calm. I blink away the remaining tears that haven't fallen and look around. There are so many crazy people in San Diego that I don't even think anyone took a second look. For all they knew, I just got high and was having a bad trip. I pick up my phone, now with a fresh crack in the screen and walk over to the trash bin, shoving the plastic bag with the dress and sandals inside, not wanting it in my possession for a second longer. I walk over to the posted bus schedule, running my finger along the routes and times and then checking the time on my phone.

Twenty minutes. There's a bus in twenty minutes and it's time I do this.

Forty-one

THERE HAVE BEEN MOMENTS in my life when it's as if I have suddenly awoken from a dream, right in the middle of the day. Like completely spacing out while driving. This was one of those moments. I am standing in front of the San Diego Correctional Facility, and I can barely remember how I got here. One minute, I'm at Catalina's and the next I'm stepping off a bus downtown. Everything before that feels like a blur of color and movement rushing around me in circles. I touch my cast, a motion I keep repeating today to prove to myself that I'm not dreaming. This is real. My dad is inside.

I close my eyes, gaining the courage to open the door, to step inside. There's something about being here that makes me feel guilty, like at any moment I'm going to get arrested for something I forgot I did.

"Hi, I'm here to visit Derek Skye."

The person behind the desk examines me, his eyes drifting over to my cast.

"Just a moment." He takes his eyes off mine and types something into his computer. "Have you visited him before?"

"No." My voice is a whisper. How could I have waited a week to see him? The guilt starts to pull upward into my throat. I remind myself I don't owe him anything. I don't need to be here.

"Fill this out please, then I'll go over the procedure with you."

The metal chair feels like ice, cold and hard. The walls are the color of vomit. My nostrils fill with the acrid smell of bleach, a feeling of uncertainty running through me. Inside I'm screaming, but on the outside, my face is like stone. He's walking towards me, his hands behind his back. The person who created me and destroyed me. It takes everything I have to maintain eye contact. When I look into his eyes, I'm blasted with regret. Those eyes were my comfort for the first decade of my life. When they were gone, I saw them every night when I closed my own, for what felt like years.

"My Blue Sky." His words are trembling.

"Hi, dad." I manage.

He smiles softly at me, his eyes brimming with sadness. "I wasn't sure if you'd visit. It means so much that you're here." I shift uncomfortably in my chair, the hard metal pushing through to my tailbone. I'm careful to keep my arm with the cast under the table. A part of me wants him to see it. Will he react like a dad reacts, or will he just ignore it? Either reaction could kill me.

"How are you? Have you been treated okay?" I ask.

"Oh, I'm okay." I feel a strong emotion radiating off him. It's pulling me in. "Valletta, I-" He stops, his neck dropping down. I can see the top of his head. His hair is thinning. He always had thick, brown, wavy hair, carefree and messy. It hurts to see signs of him aging. I feel angry that I didn't get to see him age slowly. I'm forced to suddenly see this older, broken version of him.

"I know my promises are worth pennies to you, but if there's any way you could possibly trust me ever again in your life, this is the time to do so. I have done so many unforgivable things in my life, to you and many others." He stops, taking a breath of air before continuing. "I have been out of the business for almost two years now. I just really need you to know that. Whatever happens, I can handle it, but I can't handle my daughter thinking I was the reason this girl died."

"I believe you," I say with confidence, which seems to take us both by surprise.

"I . . . just assumed you turned me in that day and I-"

"Wait, what? Why would you assume that?"

"Your friend, Owen, came here and implied that you asked him to call the cops that day. He wants to help me in exchange for my help with something. I have to say, Valletta, as your father. I don't trust him."

I'm in shock. Total and complete shock. There is no way Owen came here.

"What are you talking about?" I sneer my words without meaning to, anger and frustration building.

"You didn't know he came here, did you?" He shakes his head as if he's not surprised. "I figured you didn't know."

"What are you saying? Are you losing your mind?" I sit back in my chair, putting as much distance as possible between me and my father. Accidentally exposing my cast.

His eyes immediately land on it. My heart rate accelerates.

"What on earth happened to your arm?"

"It's nothing. I'm fine."

"Did he hurt you?" His voice starts to sound panicked, like he's desperate to know what happened. He is acting like a father. I can't help but notice. In a way I can't explain, it breaks my heart. I'm getting a glimpse of what I missed out on for so many years.

"Why would you assume that?"

"I guess in the world that I live in, that's a common concern, un-fortunately." His voice breaks.

"Well, you're wrong." I swallow, not wanting to admit he's half right. But I need to know why my dad is accusing Owen of bribing him. I know there's been some sort of misunderstanding.

"I don't know what happened exactly, but there's no way Owen was here. Or if he was, there's no way he was like, bribing you, or whatever."

"Valletta, I'm in prison; I'm stone-cold sober. I didn't imagine this. He was here two days after I was arrested. Dark, curly hair, black eyes. It was the same person that came with you when you visited me. His voice was deep and intense. He seemed angry and . . . desperate." My father sounds completely sure of himself, which makes me even more angry. What right does he have to be sure of such an outrageous accusation?

"Why are you doing this to me?"

My dad shifts in his chair, uneasy. "Valletta, I'm sorry. I don't know what to tell you. It was definitely him." His voice is lower, as if he is trying to be gentle. Pity is overtaking his face. Something grips my stomach, making it turn. Nothing disgusts me more than the look on his face, the look that I get from someone when they pity me. The fact that it's my father out of all people, the one person in my life who has caused me more pain than anyone . . .

Does he even know that? Does he realize how broken I am because of him? And now, he accuses Owen of betraying me.

I lean forward, closing the distance between us. "You expect me to believe anything you say?" I growl.

"I know how much I've screwed up, but I am still your father, and as a father, I care about you more than anyone on this earth. The fact that you are having this reaction about this person. I mean, who is this

Owen, anyway? Do you know his past? Why would he want me to set up his uncle?"

There's a raging fire inside of me. I can barely see straight. I can't control myself anymore.

"As. A. Father?" The words barely come out of my mouth. "A father would never leave their ten-year-old at home with a neglectful, narcissistic mother. A father would never deal drugs to make a living. You are not a father." The words come out so slow and so angry. A fire could combust with each syllable. "I waited and waited for you to come home, until finally, I gave up. Oh, and then you did come home, completely wasted and a mess. You were gone, my father was gone." I try so hard to remain like stone, but I can't anymore. The tears pour out. "You were... you were my best friend." I cry, "It was us against everyone else."

"Valletta, please, you have to know you were the only reason I didn't give up, you-"

"NO, STOP! You don't get to do that. Can't you see I'm a broken person because of you?" I stare into his eyes, searching them for understanding. "I'm terrified of ever losing anyone like I lost you. I'm so terrified, I don't even try. I pause. "Except with the one person you are accusing of coming here behind my back." I glare at him. "I don't know what sick game this is, but I won't let you ruin what I have with Owen over your faulty accusations. You're probably getting high in there somehow. You don't know what you're seeing or saying, just like old times."

I can tell I'm cutting him deep, but I don't care. I won't let him ruin me again. I won't let him put doubts in my mind. I stand up and stare right into his broken eyes. Shame washes over my father's face as he looks down at his lap, down at his hands that are cuffed, giving a visual confirmation of my words. The sight gives me a pang of guilt. I swallow it away as quickly as it comes.

"I can't do this." I stand up to walk away, waiting for him to look up. To tell me to wait. That it was all a misunderstanding.

There's nothing but a crushing, heavy silence. I turn around, running away from the biggest hole of all before it swallows me.

Forty-two

I WRAP MY CAST in a plastic bag before getting into the shower and washing away the filth covering me. Filth from the accident, filth from the hospital and most of all, filth from visiting my dad. The fact that Owen hasn't tried to contact me in any way is making me insane. My dad's accusations would be easier to shove aside and ignore if he had actually contacted me. The more I think about it, the angrier I get. I trusted Owen. I let myself open up to him. The nerve he has to cut me off after I've been in the hospital is almost incomprehensible. I need to find him. I'm done running and hiding from things. I'm done drowning in doubt and uncertainty. I want answers.

As I wipe off the steam on the mirror, a sense of determination comes over me. Determination so strong, I couldn't ignore it if I tried.

There's one place where I know I can check. His happy place.

I take a deep breath and start my car. As I drive uphill, I force the flashbacks out of my head. My mind is trying to transport me back to that night, to the accident. Back to being in the passenger seat, completely helpless, as Owen takes that switchback. A layer of sweat covers my pores. I shake my head back and forth as I breathe out as if to shake away the memory. Just focus, Valletta. Stop thinking. Just focus.

I decide to start counting, not stopping until the docks are in sight.

I run down the pathway near the water, my eyes scanning every boat I pass. The sea breeze is blowing my hair into my face. I pull the small strands off of me, keeping my eyes peeled on my surroundings. Most of the boats seem to be docked by now. It's getting close to sunset. I walk the ramp that leads to the launch point. Seagulls are in single-file lines on both sides of the railing, their unblinking eyes staring at me as I walk past.

I get to the end of the ramp and sit down, completely exhausted. As the ramp rocks up and down, the sound of the water starts to calm my nerves a little, allowing me to think of a plan. Do I wait here until he comes back to shore? Or, do I go and find him? I have never felt this bold, this ready to confront someone. If he did actually put my father in jail and then bribe him, I have never been more betrayed by anyone in my entire life. I don't even think my mother is that level of evil. The only way to know the truth is to look into his eyes. They are the portal to both his darkness and his light. Eyes never lie.

I stand up after a while and look behind me, shivering in disgust as I glance down at the layers of bird poop caked onto the dock that I was just sitting on. I look back at the shore and realize all I can do is wait for him there. The other option is trying to somehow get a boat and go searching for his sailboat in the dark, which seems like a recipe for disaster.

A group of friends on camp chairs are sitting around a beach fire. Their laughter is drowned out by a helicopter going by. I settle in, not too far from them, resting my head against a palm tree. I'm not leaving until Owen's boat comes back, and the fact that it's not docked here means chances are very high that he's out there somewhere, possibly anchored at his favorite spot.

Sunset creates soft and gentle brushstrokes of pale yellow over an icy blue sky, merging with darkness in the distance. Silhouettes of California palms are scattered along the shoreline, a beautiful contrast against the ever-changing, colorful sky. How can a moment feel so calm and yet dire at the same time? My body sinks further into the sand. I ignore my hunger pains, deciding to just focus on the sky as the night takes away the day.

I wake up to the sound of water gently moving rocks. My neck is the first thing I notice, a spasm preventing me from moving my head. The rest of my body slowly wakes up. My arm is throbbing. I'm surrounded by darkness. I look ahead and see the city lights across the bay, the outline of the sailboats pointing up, above the water. The first thing I see when I check my phone is a low-battery notification. I quickly dismiss it, then I see the time.

It's 4am. How could it possibly be 4am? How did I fall asleep so quickly? I slowly sit up, wiping the sand off my cheek with my good arm. My mind starts to catch up with my body and I realize why I'm here. This isn't a dream.

Wait. I didn't dream. I just fell asleep and woke up, the one task that felt completely impossible to do for over a year. I guess all it took was a major car accident, a fight with my two best friends and visiting my father in jail only to realize Owen is possibly a lying psychopath. I'll have to remember those things for next time, far more effective than sleeping pills, after all. I shake my head in annoyance at my dark humorous thoughts as I walk toward the water.

Everything around me feels eerie. The moon is bright, reflecting beautifully on the water. There's a slight fog in the sky, giving the moon a bit of a nightshade at moments. I anxiously scan the water, searching for Owen's boat. From what I can see, it's still not here. There's a good chance he never came back to shore. Did he just go on his boat to escape it all? He escaped it all and left me to pick up all the pieces with no assurance of his safety or care for how I'm doing. The thought makes me boil.

I guess that leaves me with only one option. I'll just have to get to him. Force him to face his mistakes, force him to be honest. Starting today, I'm done with liars. I need a plan. I need to figure out how I can find him. I could check his favorite spot, the spot he took me on our first date. Of course, maybe he lied about that as well. Maybe he hates that spot. Either way, I have to try. I'm not going to just sit around until he comes to me.

I stand up and pace back and forth on the cold sand, my wrist throbbing as I look around. My eyes narrow in on the cluster of dinghies piled around each other. There are several with motors . . . Could I do it? Would borrowing a dinghy without permission make me a criminal? Even if I manage to take one, could I navigate to that same spot he took me to on our first date? I walk over to one of the small boats that looks the easiest to pull with one arm. I follow the rope attached to it to see if there's a lock. When I get to the end of the rope it's attached by a knot to a weight. There's no lock . . . I could actually pull this off. Is this what it feels like to lose your mind? If it is, I happily embrace the feeling. For the first time in a long time, I feel I have clarity. It's time I trusted myself.

I unwrap the rope with my good arm, while I hold it in between my legs. I glance around to make sure nobody is watching before pulling the boat with all my strength to get it into the water. The sound of the motor makes my heart race. Holy crap. I'm actually doing this. I laugh to myself as I direct the dinghy into the ocean.

Owen has no idea what's about to hit him.

Forty-three

As I GET DEEPER into the Pacific Ocean, my small dinghy feels more and more unsafe. I try to push my constant anxious thoughts out of my mind and just focus on getting to the cove. I use satellite mode in Google Maps to keep checking on my location, which is working better than I thought it would. Adrenaline courses through me. There's something about being all alone on a small boat in the Pacific. I keep watching the stars disappear as the sunrise begins, helicopters and planes constantly overhead. I wonder if anyone in a window seat above is looking at me.

Wait . . . I stop for a moment, narrowing my eyes on a small white sailboat in the distance. I panic, sitting upright and looking at my GPS to see if it's in the direction of the cove I'm headed for. Sure enough, it is. I pick up speed again and keep my eyes fixed on that sailboat, desperately trying to get a clear view to verify that it's Owen's. The closer I get, the stronger the feeling gets that it is. It looks familiar.

Finally, I see the gold calligraphy along the side. It says, Frisson Merveilles.

I manage to climb the ladder with one arm, using my adrenaline to push me. There's an eeriness on board that makes my skin crawl. The cockpit has beer bottles scattered everywhere.

"Owen? Are you here?" I walk toward the cabin door. The sea breeze gives me a shiver. All that adrenaline is seeping away as I take in where I am and how I got here, never mind the fact that I have no idea what I'm walking into.

"Owen!" I scream it louder now, banging on the cabin door. I stand still, trying to listen to any small noise or movement.

My heart stops. I'm automatically holding my breath. Someone is coming. I slowly back away from the door, my eyes wide. I'm greeted by someone who has all the presence of Owen and yet none at all. It's like Owen was body-snatched and replaced by this disheveled mess before me. His hair is unkempt, his shirt unbuttoned. Like a lost, broken poet who is writing his goodbye letter before jumping overboard. As soon as he puts his head up and looks at me, I'm paralyzed. A darker onyx doesn't exist on this planet. They are completely hollow, soulless.

I'm used to being paralyzed by his eyes but never for this reason. This combination of pure terror and... pity. I know why I hate pity so much now. No one should ever look at another person like this.

"Valletta?" From his sandpaper voice, it's clear he hasn't spoken to anyone in a while. "How on earth . . .?" Owen looks around me, clearly trying to figure out how I'm here, standing in front of him on his boat surrounded by water. Seeing him in front of me has brought all the adrenaline back into my veins.

"Are you the reason the cops came that day?" I glare at him, knowing his eyes could tell me the truth before his mouth would.

"I really can't do this right now." Owen pinches his eyes together, sighing.

"Tell me the truth. Was this entire relationship a set-up?" The question pours out without thought. It's only when I say it out loud, I realize it was burning in the back of my mind.

"I need coffee before I can have this conversation." Owen stumbles past me, the smell of alcohol pouring off of him. His reaction is all I need to know that what my dad said was true. Heat rushes into my chest, the kind of heat that makes me think I might be capable of murder.

"HOW COULD YOU DO THAT? YOU PUT MY FATHER IN JAIL!" I'm screaming at the top of my lungs.

He turns around to look at me, his expression callous. "I have the worst hangover of my entire life. I would appreciate it if you didn't yell." His hands move to his temples, pressing on them to try and relieve the pressure.

Somehow, I'm speechless. I am standing here, stunned. Out of all the reactions I had envisioned, this one definitely never crossed my mind. He's not admitting or denying anything. He's like a brick wall. I could ram into him at full speed, and I don't think he would even flinch. He's making me feel crazy.

He reaches down to pick up a pair of Ray-Bans that were lying on the floor. He puts them on and then reaches into his pocket, pulling out a pack of cigarettes and a lighter.

My stomach clenches. I think I could actually throw him overboard with a smile on my face, not a second of regret.

He lights the cigarette, looking casually out over the ocean. "So what, did you steal a dinghy or something?" I can tell he's trying to hide his curiosity. He always wants to hide anything that makes him slightly vulnerable.

I realize my fist is completely clenched. "I swear to god, Owen, if you don't start answering my questions, I will drive this boat into the biggest rock I can find."

"It may be hard to drive a sailboat when this is only your second time on one." He smirks at the sky.

My eyes narrow. Did he really just smirk? At a time like this? He freaking smirked?! I rush over to him, everything around me blurred out by my rage. Despite not seeing his eyes through his Ray-Bans, I can still sense his concern as I rush towards him. He must see that I'm a loose cannon. A cannon that he ignited. I grab the cigarette out of his mouth and throw it overboard. I get within an inch of his face.

"Did. You. Call. The. Cops. Yes, or no?" I growl, practically spitting in his face.

"Your father will be released, okay?"

"Why won't you answer the damn question?" All I want is a yes or no and he refuses to give it to me.

"You know he isn't innocent in all of this, right?" He snaps back at me, looking away sharply. He's trying to put distance between us.

"Coward."

"What?" He looks back at me, clearly irritated by that word.

"You. You are a coward. You can't even admit what you did," I sneer.

That was all it took. With that one word I ignited his cannon now. He jumps up onto his feet. "Fine. I called the cops." He looks at me with the cruellest expression I have ever seen. "Is that what you want to hear? I was the reason your father got put in jail. And you know what? I would do it again in a second."

I can't move. I can't even breathe. I want to run but I'm captured. For the first time since knowing Owen I don't want to be captured. I want to be free. I want back the trust I squandered on him. The one thing in life I don't have anymore, as of this moment. I gave him the little that I had gathered.

"You used me." Those words came out before I wanted them to.

"Why am I the bad guy? Selling drugs is illegal. It kills people. Your father deserves to serve his time. People can't just get away with things, Valletta. Don't be biased just because he's your father." He runs his hands through his hair in frustration. "Plus, I have a plan to get him out. I just need him to cooperate, which he is failing to do."

"My father is innocent! You psychopath!" I scream. "He hasn't sold anything in two years!" You put an innocent man in jail. For what? So that you can use him as a pawn in a sick game you're playing with your family?"

Owen lets out a cruel laugh. "Are you listening to yourself? Your father is innocent because he hasn't sold in two years? Did he ever go to jail for his years when he was selling? No. He got away with it." He shakes his head. "Just because he wasn't responsible for this incident doesn't mean he's not a criminal."

His words are tearing through me. I stay quiet. My anger is mixed with an abundance of confusion, leaving me paralyzed. I can feel his eyes on me. He's examining me for the first time since he saw me on his boat.

"Is your arm okay?" Owen's voice is almost soft suddenly.

I glare at him. "You have no right to ask me about my arm." I look away from him, trying to focus on the calm waves lapping around us. "You just left me in the hospital. Who the hell does that?"

"I knew Mark and Melanie were with you." My anger is slowly taking over my confusion. Is that his excuse? Does he actually believe his actions are justified? "Just tell me why. Why did you do this to me? Why even start a relationship with me?"

"I know you're upset, but I do care about you." His words carry so much coldness despite their meaning.

"Don't you dare say you care about me. I defended you to the two people in my life who actually do care about me, and I completely pushed them away!"

"I may have done a lot of things, but you can't blame me for all of it. You were already a broken person to begin with. I tried to help you find your voice."

"You did nothing but give me more scars." I spit the words into his face. I'm done with him. I narrow my eyes, knowing his eyes are burning black behind his sunglasses. I may have wanted answers, but not this bad. Now, I just want revenge.

"Forget it, Owen. Two can play at your sick, manipulative game. You take away what matters to me? Just wait." I storm away from him, equally confident and afraid.

I'm going to crash his boat.

Forty-four

EVERYTHING OWEN TAUGHT ME on our first day sailing is buzzing through my mind. I just wish I remembered it better. It's like a bunch of particles that dispersed through the air and didn't come back together properly. I know there's at least three things I have to do. Get the mainsail up. Bring in the anchor. Face the boat into the direction of the wind.

I also know that the ropes are called sheets, and I have to pull them around the winch to tighten them, so they go in the right direction. The problem is, there is so much else I don't know or remember. The other problem is, a sailboat is probably the worst boat to try and hijack, especially with the experienced owner on board with you.

But hey, at least this sailboat has an engine. Is it the mature thing to do? Of course not. Do I care about doing the mature thing at this moment? The moment I've found out I'm dating a cold-hearted, manipulative liar who's trying to ruin my life?

Absolutely not.

I run over to unzip the main sail, releasing it from the big pole thing. I think it's called the boom. I unzip it so fast then rush over to pull the rope, pulling as hard as I can with my one good arm.

"What on earth are you doing?" Owen's voice is filled with confusion. I smile, because I can almost hear a little uncertainty in his voice.

There's nothing scarier than a loose cannon. Even if that loose cannon is a 125lb woman with one good arm.

The last time I did this, Owen was helping me bring up the mainsail. It's amazing how hard this is. But determination mixed with adrenaline is also amazing, and I have both of those things on my side.

"Are you actually trying to sail this boat?" There it is, the confidence and amusement are back in his voice. I don't say anything, I just keep trying to get the mainsail up.

I use all my anger for every pull of the rope. I would do anything to have both arms working at this moment. That way, at least it wouldn't feel so pathetic, and I could seem like a real threat. After a few moments of awkward tension, I somehow manage it. I get the mainsail up. I don't take a moment to gloat. Instead, I race to the front of the boat to get the anchor in. I grab the remote at the front of the boat and press the button to raise the anchor. I rush over to the steering wheel. I remember to put the boat on autopilot. And then I realize the boat is actually moving...

It's not until I put my hand on the big round silver steering wheel that I realize, I am trembling.

What am I doing?

It feels like vines are moving over every inch of my chest. Grabbing me, holding me in place. Unable to take in a single breath, I'm gripping the steering wheel so hard that my hand feels like I'm losing all of the blood in my fingers.

Focus, Valletta. Come on. Focus, dammit.

I'm sucking in air. This is the worst possible time for a panic attack.

"Okay, okay. You have proved your point. Now, can you please stop before you hurt yourself?" Owen's words are getting chopped up by the wind that's starting to come in stronger. I look back at him to see if he's coming towards me. He hasn't moved at all. His hand is on his stomach, he's about to lose it.

I need to get into the wind.

He runs over to the edge of the boat lurching his head over the side, waiting to be sick. I'm about to ask him if he's okay, but I snap out of my sympathy. This is it. This is the moment to take advantage of. His weakness. I can hijack this boat. I use my good arm and aggressively move the steering wheel into the wind.

"Valletta, NO!" Owen's scream is cut off by a BANG. I turn around in a panic.

He's gone.

The boom is swinging slightly back and forth after the impact. What just happened? Oh my god. What just happened?! My heart is completely in my throat.

Abandoning the wheel, I rush over to the edge. I don't see him anywhere.

"Owen!" I'm screaming frantically as the sailboat slowly moves away from the spot where it was anchored, gradually gaining momentum.

Think, Valletta. Think.

I scramble over to the orange life ring, throwing it into the water. I get up on the edge of the boat and scan the ocean in desperation. There's nothing. I know what I need to do...

Before I realize what's happening I'm hitting the cold Pacific Ocean headfirst.

I surface, choking on salty water. I use my good arm with my legs to swim to the life preserver. Every millisecond that passes feels like an hour. I might have actually killed him. I kick my legs aggressively toward the spot where Owen fell in.

"HELP! SOMEBODY, HELP!" I'm trying to scream but I can barely breathe.

Just then, Owen's head appears a short distance in front of me. I'm hit with relief. He's not dead. I didn't kill anyone.

"Owen!" I scream over to him while holding onto the life preserver. He looks over at me for a moment. It looks like he's still processing what happened. He replies, but I can't make out what he's saying over the sound of the wind and the water in my ears. From the look on his face, it's no doubt a string of curse words. He's realizing that his sailboat is quickly sailing away from us. There's no possible way we could catch up with it at this point.

It's going to happen. I'm going to destroy his happy place. The thought is no longer bringing me joy. Instead, it's filling me with fear. A fear that has come on just as suddenly as my anger. We are floating in the Pacific Ocean, with one life preserver. I have one good arm, and Owen is hungover.

His eyes are fixated on his boat. It's almost like I'm not even here. He looks so sick, his skin as pale as toothpaste, his eyes bloodshot.

"Owen? Are you okay?" I say it louder, worried he has sudden brain damage from hitting his head, or something. Although, I don't think it works like that.

"I need to get to my boat."

I can barely make out his words. His tone is stale and quiet for such chaos. He swims past me, his stride focused with a surprising amount of speed for someone in his position.

I stay buoyant, hanging onto the life preserver. Lost at sea.

As time passes, Owen fades away into the marine layer, its fog settling on top of the gentle waves. He doesn't even glance back.

I turn my head to the side, tracking the sound of a motor approaching. I see people on the boat waving at me as it nears my position.

"HEY! Are you okay? We are coming to help!" Their screams carry over the distance. The only thing here right now is my body. My mind is miles away. The fog is slowly lifting, leaving me completely uncertain about how much time has passed.

I look back over to the rescue boat, the roar of its motor piercing my ears now. A man and woman are on board. Their eyes are filled with worry as they look at me bobbing about, waiting to be rescued. How far had I drifted?

"Oh, you poor thing!" The woman with the worried eyes is trying to help me on board. "Oh my gosh, hunny, she has a cast on her arm!" she yells over to the man on board as he steers the boat.

"I'm okay, really." I try to smile unsuccessfully. The woman helps me on board, and it's not until I sit down that I notice how tight my whole body is. I was clenching from stress for who knows how long. I'm shaking uncontrollably as a soft blanket gets draped around me.

"Everything is going to be okay."

"Thanks," I say softly. Little does she know things are far from okay.

"What's your name, sweetie?" she asks with a bright smile. I can tell she's a mom. The kind of mom I was always yearning for, the kind of mom who worries about her kids.

"Valletta."

"Wow! What a beautiful name! So poetic." She beams at me, clearly trying to cheer me up. "It's such a pleasure to meet you, Valletta. I'm Charlotte. My husband is the one driving the boat."

"Nice to meet you too." I smile back, slightly more successfully.

"Was anyone else with you? How did you end up in the ocean alone?"

"There's someone else. He swam off to catch his sailboat. I think we should be able to find him in that direction." I swallow, wanting nothing more than to just leave him alone in the Pacific. He clearly had no problem leaving me.

"Don't worry, Valletta. We will find him."

That's what I'm afraid of, I think to myself.

"I'm sure the Coast Guard has already found him. This fog is a pain. I bet he's right up ahead," Charlotte's husband says as we head in the direction Owen had swam.

Seconds feel like hours as we travel through the marine layer. For whatever reason, it hits me over the head that I never asked why. I sit up, panicked. How did I not ask why? I'm left with nothing but a million questions and a broken heart. A heart broken into a million pieces for a million reasons.

My deepest scar yet.

"Is that him up ahead?" Charlotte asks.

My heartbeat increases. There's an emergency boat next to Owen's sailboat, and Owen is on board, leaning over the edge with an emergency blanket draped over him and a man standing next to him.

"Looks like he's okay!" Charlotte says as she squeezes me, hugging me close. My eyes fill with moisture as we get closer, panic completely taking over.

"Can you please just take me back to shore?" I tremble, managing to look at Charlotte. Her eyes peer into mine and her entire expression changes, almost like she knows. She turns to her husband.

"Why don't we get Valletta back to the docks."

"Doesn't she want to-"

"Hunny," she interrupts him, "Let's get her back to shore." Her voice commands obedience, not a hint of uncertainty in her tone.

And just like that, this stranger rescues me. If she does have kids, they are the luckiest kids in the world.

As we change directions, Owen looks up. I try to look away, but I can't. It's too far to fully make out his face, but I know he sees me. The question that's burning in my mind is if he even cares that I was rescued. And the question that will haunt me is, why?

Why did he do this to me?

Forty-five

As soon as I get back to shore, I take off running. I run for what feels like hours, pins and needles exploding all over my legs. I don't stop despite the lightheaded feeling threatening to take over. My body knows the destination more than my mind does. I pass the perfectly planted gardens in the small, fenced yards. Apartment buildings gradually make way for big, beautiful houses as I get closer to the water. The smell of salt tickles my nostrils.

I stop short at the drop, on the edge of the cliff. My favorite spot to escape the world.

The roar of the ocean at Sunset Cliffs provides me with exactly the background noise I need, the merciful rumbling of the waves drowning out the world around me. I can barely hear my own thoughts. That's what I love about it.

The wind whips my hair around my face, strands sticking to the sticky hot tears. Somehow, I didn't realize I was crying.

I made it in time for sunset. As I touch my soggy cast it feels like this has been the longest day I've ever lived.

I look out over the cliffs, blinking away the tears that blur the deep orange hazy sunset. A line of pelicans passes me overhead, their wings flapping casually. I keep my eyes fixed on them, wondering how magical it would be to join the line. When I can't see them anymore, I take a deep breath and make my way down the cliffs to my spot. The spot where I can be hidden from the world. I nestle myself towards the bottom of the cliffs, but still high enough not to get drenched by the waves. Right below me is a small cave that creates the most haunting echo. It's as if the ocean is whispering creepily at me, a harsh whisper that carries a warning.

I look at the waves ahead of me, dark and overpowering just like Owen's eyes. Just like my mother's force. Just like the dark hole I've been falling down for the last thirteen years. Just like the feeling the sleeping pills give me as I embrace the darkness they provide.

The waves are more powerful than I could ever be. Why fight them?

I close my eyes, letting the tears come again. As they stream down my face, I see flashes of my dad and me building castles on the beach. The hole in my stomach is becoming unbearably large. The image of my father's face alone opens it so wide. I feel like it will never close again.

The haunting echo of the waves hitting the cliffs grounds me, keeps me from letting the large dark hole completely swallow me up.

It hits me. I haven't told my father that I love him since I was ten years old. I've let my anger dominate. He could have worked with Owen, but instead, he told me the truth. The first thing he did when he sobered up and came into money was send me a check to support me. As horribly misplaced as his actions were, he still cares about me. I've been running from this big gaping hole for so many years and it's only getting bigger.

It's gotten so big that I embrace any contributors. It's become my safety blanket. But instead of keeping me safe, it's suffocating me, choking me so I can't move.

I open my eyes and I am stunned by the sudden vibrancy of orange and red that has overtaken the sky. I let my feet dangle over the edge.

I inch forward.

I'm holding my breath as I look down to the waves below. The color of them makes me dizzy. They are as dark as onyx. The darkness that has completely pushed me over the edge.

I don't want to be knocked over by the dark waves anymore. I take a deep breath in, my body now trembling. A part of me just wants to be swallowed up by the swirling mess of water below. I shove away the thought.

I refuse to let the waves drown me fully. They've kept me under long enough. I'm at the bottom of the ocean now, sinking into the sand. I look above me as the oxygen is leaving my body. I see the light. I use all my energy to calm myself, bringing myself to the light. Bringing myself to freedom, to oxygen.

As I swim to the surface in my mind, I escape my vision for a moment, grounded by the sandstone I'm sitting on, the sunset now reflecting on the water. The onyx ocean is providing a mirror for the beautiful colors swirling around me. I let myself scream into the hollow cave below.

"I'M DONE!" I cry out.

"I'M DONE!" I scream so loud my voice becomes hoarse.

An explosion of tears follows. I see Owen in Catalina's. He's walking in slow motion, this time towards me, his eyes captivating. I feel his hands graze my cheek, his lips press slowly onto mine. I touch my lips as I feel the phantom touch from his kiss.

"I'm done." I cry out softly this time. I squeeze my eyes shut, letting go of him. Letting go of his hold.

As I slowly open my eyes, it's as if I reached the surface. I can take my first breath on my own. Filling my lungs with oxygen.

And then it happens.

My mind clears, my heart calms, and my breath is steady and strong.

The ocean calms. Instead of dark overpowering waves crashing into me, I'm floating. Floating on calm waves the color of emerald.

The color of Mark's eyes.

Forty-six

I HAND MELANIE THE steaming macchiato, her face slowly lighting up as she sees it coming. "It's made just how you like it. Extra foam." I smile warmly when her eyes meet mine. "Thanks for meeting me here. The weather is perfect today."

I cringe at my effort to make small talk with someone who can see right through me. Granted, that means she understands how hard I'm trying.

"Yeah, it's so nice. I don't want to have to go to work. Just wanna bathe in the sun." She looks up at the blue sky as she sips her macchiato, closing her eyes.

"So, how are you, anyway? I feel like I don't know anything right now. How's Jayce?"

"Do you actually want to know?" She slides herself upright, opening her eyes but keeping her gaze upwards.

"Of course I do." I reach my hand over to hers and give it a gentle squeeze.

Melanie sighs, pinching her eyes closed. "Gosh, I hate it when we fight." The breeze floats by us, rustling the California palm as the birds of paradise swing gently around the trunk. The sounds in the park are muffled by the wind.

"Melanie, I am so, so sorry for everything I said. I should never have yelled at you." My voice is soft and reassuring.

"Do you actually feel that way, though? That I don't understand you like Owen does?" Her voice catches, showing how much those words affected her.

I take a deep breath in, carefully proceeding. "You want the honest truth?"

"Always." She's looking at me in a way where I can't figure out whether she's bracing herself or not.

"Well, for one thing, you were right about Owen. He doesn't get me like I thought he did. Not at all." Her eyes widen at this news. I put my hand up before she has a chance to ask what I know she's dying to ask. "I don't want to talk about it, not yet." Somehow, she seems to respect that because she stays quiet, her face full of curiosity.

I bite my lip, unable to keep a teaser from her. "But just a slight story preview, I may have hijacked his sailboat."

"WHAT?!" Melanie gasps.

I shake my hand away at the thought, not wanting to go into it any more than that. "I promise to tell you all the gory details, but not yet. This is more important."

She sighs heavily. "You can't do that to me!" She groans at the sky, but I can tell she's anxious to hear what I want to talk about.

I continue, "I'm no good at this; this, expressing myself thing. But I'm going to try." I take a deep breath before continuing. "I will admit, I always feel like a weird, malignant tumor that you and Mark walk around with. I carry so much inside of me, so much shame, that it feels like you guys could never understand me. I mean, your parents are these incredibly strong immigrants who have sacrificed everything for you and your siblings. You have never questioned whether they love you. You're goal-oriented and you let things just roll off your shoulders. You have no idea how much I look up to you and your family. And Mark is just, well, he's Mark. He's the life of every party. He's always down for anything and everything. He views life like a rollercoaster and embraces all the ups and downs. But me, I am an anxious mess of a person with a family who I honestly don't know if they love me and that-- well--I mean, I just don't know what it feels like to be loved by someone else. How could I know if you really love me or if I'm just someone who is wearing a mask that allows you to tolerate me?" I swallow, my chest pounding as I admit how I feel. "That's the complete honest truth."

Melanie's face is twisted for a moment and slowly, understanding seems to overcome her. "Valletta, you've never said that. You never told me that's how you felt."

"I think I was too afraid to admit that's how I felt even to myself, never mind say it out loud." My hand starts to tremble, and I make a fist, forcing it to stop. I'm suddenly enveloped in Melanie's embrace. I can smell her coconut conditioner as strands of her hair tickle my cheek.

"Valletta, I love you so much. You are far more powerful than you think. You are a consistent piece of joy in my life, the most loyal friend I could ask for. Do you know how much that means to me?" She pulls back her hand, grazing my cheek gently as she slides a strand of my wavy hair behind my ear. "You are the glue that makes me feel secure."

Her words pierce through my heart, but instead of pain, I feel an explosion of warmth.

The park is filled with laughter, and for the first time in a long time, I was contributing to that laughter. Melanie and I walk around Liberty Station, something we haven't done in forever. She tells me all about Jayce and their whirlwind romance. I still didn't understand their relationship, but I smiled in support. We walk by the Barracks filled with local art, food and boutiques. I take in the tall Italian Cypress trees outlining the park. We eventually make our way down by the river to my favorite spot, across from the San Diego airport. I love to imagine all the places the planes are coming from and going to.

As we sit together on the bench, I do my best to act out my day of insanity, explaining how I hijacked Owen's sailboat. I don't think I have ever captivated Melanie more than at this moment. I do my best to follow her instructions and not leave out a single detail. I can't help but laugh at certain moments. Unable to believe that it really had happened.

"Oh my gosh! Between Owen's rich family, him calling the cops on your father, the car accident, you hijacking his sailboat and almost drowning, you could write a book about this relationship." She laughs, still in shock.

"That's for sure."

"Wow," she says simply, slowly coming down from the emotional rollercoaster. Then she pivots to the side, looking at me directly. She's getting ready to say something serious.

My heart drops in anticipation, knowing where this is probably going.

"I have to ask . . ." She twists her lip to the side. I can tell she's tip-toeing.

"Just say it, Mel." I squeeze my fist tight.

"Mark," she says simply.

"What about Mark?"

"Well, like, what in the world is going on between you two? Things are different, and he's kind of disappeared."

"I dunno." I shrug. "We aren't exactly speaking currently." I try to swallow away the lump that's forming.

"I mean, come on, Valletta. For Mark to disappear like this and for you guys to not be talking, like, every single day . . . This is kinda legit."

"What do you mean, 'kinda legit'?"

"I mean, he loves you, Valletta, and I know you love him. You guys have been doing this dance for five years! This was going to happen eventually." She sips her macchiato.

"It's not a dance, Melanie. It's called friendship."

"You're right, it's probably the best friendship I have ever seen between two people who are also completely attracted to each other. I don't know how you both have managed to avoid it this long, honestly."

I sigh. "I don't know either."

"WHAT? VALLETTA!" Melanie slaps my arms, her mouth hanging open from shock. "I actually cannot believe you just said that!" she squeals. "I mean, for you to admit that is major!"

I laugh, honestly just as shocked as she is that I allowed those words to surface.

"Hijacking that sailboat has really changed you." She gleams playfully.

"I guess I just have some clarity." I take a deep breath in as the wind picks up, taking in the smell of freshly cut grass.

"So, what are you gonna do?" she asks excitedly. I slouch against the bench and bring my latte to my lips. I have no idea how to answer her. I sigh and turn to look at my beautiful friend who has been there through it all.

"Honestly, Mel, all I know right now is, I just need to see him."

"Well, I would say that's a pretty good start." She smiles.

Forty-seven

I TAKE A DEEP breath in before knocking on the door, the sounds of music blasting through. I bang as hard as I can until finally the music lowers and the door swings open.

My heart sinks.

"Hey, Valletta! What's up?" Mark's roommate, Sam, is standing in front of me, his messy brown hair sticking up in all different directions. He's wearing a torn-up Ron Jon tee-shirt and red boxers, his bare feet adorned with the rope ankle bracelet he never takes off.

"Sam, hey." I twist my head around to try and see into the apartment.

"Come on in!" Sam steps to the side.

The apartment is filled with the smell of takeaway pizza and beer. As soon as I walk in, something feels different. It feels empty.

"I'm surprised you're here! What can I do for ya?" Sam's expression is pure chill.

"Oh, I'm just here to see Mark." I flash a smile then head to Mark's room.

"Oh, uh, you know he's not here, right?"

I turn to look at Sam, confused. "His car's out front . . ."

Sam's head tilts to the side. For a moment he looks uncomfortable. "Uh, this is kinda awkward." He scratches his head. "He's not here."

"What are you talking about?" My chest starts to feel tight. The apartment feels emptier by the minute.

"I really thought he would have told you of all people."

"Told me what, Sam?" My patience is wearing thin.

"He well . . . He kind of moved out."

My mouth falls open in disbelief. I rush over to Mark's door and swing it open.

My eyes are punched with the sight of his room. His double bed remains in the middle of the room, completely bare. Everything is gone.

It's all just gone.

I hold on to the doorknob, letting it hold up my entire body weight. The air feels thin, causing me to struggle to get a good breath.

"Are you okay, Valletta? Do you want me to call Mark or something for you? I'm sure he can explain-"

"No!" I whip around to look at Sam. "Please don't call him. In fact, don't even mention that I was here." I slam the door shut to his room and rush to get out of there. A place that once felt like a safe space is literally sucking all the air out of my lungs.

"Sorry about barging in like this," I say, trying to hold it together.

"No worries at all." Sam clears his throat. "Do you want a beer or something?"

"No, I should be going." My voice breaks at the end. I keep walking forward, finally getting outside.

I rush down the stairs, the ocean breeze making me feel sticky.

Then I notice it.

A 'for sale' sign on the front windshield of Mark's car.

Forty-eight

"You're probably wondering why I'm here." I go to tug the hair at the nape of my neck, then refrain.

"I'm honestly just delighted to see you, Blue Sky." My dad smiles softly at me. "I've been worried about you."

I breathe in deeply, but not out of anxiety. It's more to ground me, to make me realize that I'm actually sitting in front of my dad, and this time, it's because I'm thankful for him. I'm thankful that he stuck up for me. He put me first.

"I guess you were right about Owen. I'm sorry I didn't believe you." I look into his eyes, almost comforted by them for the first time in a long time.

"Valletta, you have absolutely nothing to be sorry for. I hate the fact that you were put through that. You deserve so much better. You deserve the world."

I smile and shake my head, unable to fully agree with his words. I look down at my nails. They are a total mess. Uneven, brittle, and jagged.

"I know you have to say that because you're my dad but-"

"Woah," he cuts in. "Stop." His voice is suddenly serious. "I may be a lot of things, a horrible father, a criminal, an addict, not to mention my irresponsible way of handling money." A sad chuckle escapes his mouth. "But my biggest accomplishment that I will always stand proud of is the fact that I helped bring you into this world, Valletta Skye. You are a witty, talented, loyal, hard-working, beautiful woman. The kind of woman very few men are worthy of." Moisture fills his dark brown eyes. I see a hint of life in them as he talks, the life I couldn't find the last couple of times I saw him. That spark of life makes his words sink in so deeply that I almost can't handle them.

"You haven't been around for the last decade. How can you know I'm any of those things?" I clear my throat to try and hide the fact that my voice is cracking.

"Because, you were all of those things as a young girl. You haven't lost those qualities, they just ooze out of you. They have only matured." He smiles confidently at me. "Granted, I know your mother and I have messed you up in ways we can never fix. I hope you can continue to move past all the ugliness and darkness. I know I was never able to." He shakes his head regretfully.

I swallow, my throat burning with the threat of a waterfall of emotions trying to escape. "I'm trying to."

"It shows, Blue Sky. It definitely shows. You are a fighter, and I am so proud."

I look at my father, and then around at the dull cinder block walls, and the metal bars. There's a feeling of dread surrounding us, a feeling of being trapped with yourself, with no way to freedom. Despite everything, I want to give my dad hope. It takes all I have to look directly into his eyes. I say the only thing I can think of that will give him hope.

"I know you're a good person."

My words hit him like a tidal wave. A tear escapes the ocean of emotion inside of him.

"I just need to know one thing." I begin to shake, terrified for both of us after I speak the words that are on the tip of my tongue.

"Go ahead." He breathes in like he's ready. Like he knows something difficult is coming.

"Why wasn't I enough to stay and fight for a little harder? I mean, I just thought we were each other's support, and then you just left." My palms are now covered in sweat.

"Valletta . . ." My dad is boiling over with an emotion I'm trying to recognize. "There is not one day that goes by that I didn't and don't regret leaving. I needed help so badly, and I just didn't want to put you through living with all my demons. But I know leaving was almost as bad in a way. I just think it was the lesser of the two evils." He chokes, "Valletta, I am so, so sorry." His hands quickly gravitate over his face, cuffed together.

He left to protect me from himself. It sinks in. He does care. He loves me.

In the matter of forgiveness, they always say the option to forgive is the best option for yourself. A way to not be weighed down by the poison that is anger.

At this moment, it makes sense now. That weight was tied so tightly around me, it became part of me. I didn't even know I was still carrying it.

I reach across towards my father's hands. I slowly pull them down, off of his face, revealing his pained expression, revealing his regret.

For the first time since being a little girl, I hold onto his hands. The gesture turns his expression soft again, gratitude filling his eyes. We both know how hard this is.

"I'm going to help get you out of here, Dad. I know you're innocent. We will figure this out."

"No." My dad shakes his head, pulling away from me, his hands leaving mine. "I don't want you mixed up in this. This is my battle, not yours."

"I think it's a little late for you to tell me what to do, Dad."

"Valletta, I'm serious. You need to live your life. I've held you back long enough. If you really want to help me, I want you to enjoy your life. Okay?" His eyes are stern, almost like a father's. He means this, I can tell.

"Fine," I lie. "I won't get involved." I know I can't keep my word with this one. But that's for me to know, not him.

"Thank you." He smiles gently at me. "You have grown into such a beautiful young woman. I just can't believe it." He shakes his head in disbelief. "Would it be too much to ask you to visit me every so often?" It's a weird feeling to see my father express vulnerability, a vulnerability that only I can soften.

I swallow. My immediate instinct is to hold in the tear threatening to escape. But as I suppress my emotion, I realize for the first time in a long time that I don't want to hold it back. I take in a deep breath, releasing the build-up.

"I will, Dad, I promise." A singular hot tear runs down my cheek. I don't wipe it away. I just let it linger, leaving me exposed.

"Could you do something for me before you leave?"

I nod my head yes.

"Will you tell me a little something about your life?" His voice is filled with sincerity. "It can be anything at all. Your friends, your work . . . anything." He smiles.

I chuckle. "Trust me, there's nothing interesting to tell right now. Just a bunch of drama."

"Anything you have to say is interesting to me, Blue Sky."

I look down at my nails, giving in to the urge and pick at the jagged one, trying to make it straight. I lower my voice. My turn to be vulnerable. "I think I lost a best friend." The lump expands.

"Why do you think that?" he asks gently.

"I really messed up, Dad," I choke. "I had this friend that I could be myself around in every way. He was there through it all over the last five years. He's seen every side of me, and I was a total idiot. I just pushed him away. I miss him so much, my heart literally aches."

"He sounds special."

"He is." I smile, realizing how true that statement is.

"Well, if he has any sense, he won't walk away from you forever. You guys have been friends for five years, no?"

"Yeah."

"Then he knows how special you are. He knows that walking away from you would be the biggest mistake he could make." He grins at me, confident in his words. "I'm going to tell you something I have learned the hard way. Don't ever give up on someone you feel safe enough to be yourself around. If he provides happiness in your life, then you fight for that happiness, Valletta. No matter what happens, fight for those people you have, the ones who make your life better. Don't be afraid of letting people who care about you help you. I really wish I could go back and do that." He shakes his head. "I was so determined to get things right on my own, to prove myself to everyone. I turned away anyone that wanted to help me. Please, don't make that mistake."

I'm suddenly hit by the fact that my father is sitting across from me, giving me advice that makes sense. As surreal as this moment is, I can't help but feel comforted.

I'm sitting in a correctional facility, with the man who abandoned me when I was ten years old, with cuffs around his hands, and he's giving me comfort.

Epilogue: Autumn

I HAVE NEVER UNDERSTOOD why my mother, who loves the sun so much that she has permanent freckles from stubbornly tanning all her life, would pick Boston, of all places, to settle down. Whenever I've visited her in the past, the city seemed nice enough, but I couldn't justify the winters. Now that I've lived here for two months, I'm starting to get it. Of course, it's not winter yet, and people do say fall is the best time to be in New England. So, maybe all the pumpkin spice is going to my head. I think it's the crisp air. There's something about it that makes you feel . . . ready for anything, perhaps?

"You have to go apple picking in New Hampshire. You will love it!" Gracie says as she sips her Starbucks pumpkin spice latte. Her burgundy scarf casually hangs over one shoulder as silky black ribbon curls poke out. I smile over at her, unable to deny how fast I'm becoming addicted to her wide grin. I was determined to just start fresh in Boston and not get involved with anyone for as long as I could manage. My heart needed a rest.

I needed time to recover from the effort it took to show so much vulnerability. I didn't realize until after I told Valletta how I felt, that those feelings were haunting me almost every day. I guess I was just focused on the good times we had together, I didn't even have time to bring in those messy complicated feelings. A part of me knew we felt the same way about each other, anyway, I was sure of it. But being sure of something doesn't make it hurt any less. And now, the fun and electricity that embodied our entire relationship is gone. Vanished as soon as she said that she didn't feel for me what I felt so deeply for her.

Of course, did I want to commit to anyone? Honestly, no, not at all. I loved my bachelor life, I loved my freedom. But unfortunately, I loved Valletta more. Still do, but I'm working on getting over that.

"New Hampshire, huh? I hear there's some great hiking up there too." I wink at Gracie, then instantly regret it, trying not to come off too flirty. I mean, I'm just a flirt with everyone, but I'm realizing that may be a problem if I don't want to date for a while. I met Gracie when I was taking my mom to her MRI at Brigham and Women's. She was the nurse technician who had been helping my mom this whole time. The whole time my mother had kept it from me that she had cancer.

I found out my mom had cancer the same week I told Valletta I loved her. How's that for a bad week? As soon as my mom told me, I got on the next flight to Boston. Only to go back to San Diego to sort out, well, everything, I guess. I knew it was meant to be that I move up here because Clint offered me the job as Head Chef at his restaurant, the thing I've been working my butt off for since getting my culinary degree. I was back in San Diego with just enough time to be at the hospital for Valletta's accident. I wanted to tell her everything the second her hand squeezed mine. I wanted to blurt out, "My mom has cancer and I'm moving to Boston to stay by her side. Come with me, please, just come with me." But as soon as she looked at me, I could see it . . . I could see that she was worried about him. About the person who put her in the hospital bed in the first place. That's when I knew I needed to get out of San Diego ASAP.

I know running like that, without any explanation, wasn't the mature thing to do. But that's what I do. I run. I like freedom. I don't like to feel stuck in place. It's probably better she rejected me, anyway. I've never been able to commit to any girl long enough to even meet her parents. And Valletta is too afraid to ever trust someone with her heart. That's not going to change anytime soon. Between the two of us, we are not cut out to be in a relationship.

So, anyway; Gracie. I'd be lying if I didn't admit she's been the best part of Boston. My mother insisted she show me the ropes, and Gracie has kept her word to my mother. She's been by my side through this entire move.

"We should go up in two weeks. That will be peak foliage in the White Mountains." Gracie grins wide and slides her arm into mine. I tighten, not knowing how to handle her random display of affection. I hope she's not catching feelings. Crap. I hope I'm not catching feelings.

"That sounds amazing, but weekends are swamped at the restaurant." I shrug, taking a sip of my coffee.

"Oh, right." Gracie bites her lip then tilts her head to the side as we round the brownstones with my favorite maple tree in front, its leaves turning yellow. I can't help but want to snap a pic and send it to Valletta. I know how much she'd love to see the leaves changing.

"Well, maybe we can go up on a Monday, and just stay until Tuesday. Those are your slow days, yeah?" she asks sweetly.

"Yeah, maybe." I smile, not ready to commit to a trip to New Hampshire with a girl I'm trying not to fall for. As soon as I hear myself think girl, I can hear Valletta yelling at me, "She's a woman, Mark! Not a girl." Her face is covered in that sarcastic smirk I love so much.

Gracie nudges her elbow into my side. "Hey, there's somebody on your steps. She looks lost."

My heart skips a beat as I take in the sight of the girl. Her sandy brown waves sway as she turns her head back and forth and looks up at the brownstone apartments above. She keeps looking at her phone, then examining the intercoms, as she glides her fingers down them again and again. I see her shiver in her short-sleeved black T-shirt.

"Valletta," I whisper to myself.

Epilogue: Summer

IT'S BEEN TWO WEEKS since, well, everything. Since the accident, since I hijacked Owen's sailboat and since Mark left. Two weeks without talking to my best friend. I never knew my heart could ache every moment of every day for someone. Even with my constant effort to not let anyone get too close, and the painful decision to not go there with Mark, I still end up broken. The biggest thing this summer has taught me is, trust is not the enemy.

Trust is something I need. I just need to trust the right people. The scariest part is you never truly know who those people are, but I would be lying if there wasn't that small part of my gut that knows. I guess I'm still working on trusting that part of myself.

So, here I am, working on trusting myself, working on listening to my inner voice, instead of screaming at it to shut up. Right now, that inner voice has me on my phone looking at flights to Boston.

I need to see him. A phone call isn't enough.

Of course, the first thing I'm going to do when I see him is wring his neck for leaving like that, without even so much as a text message. I'm going to pummel him to the ground and mess up that stupid, beautiful, dirty blonde hair. Hair that somehow falls perfectly into place when all he does is shampoo and rough dry it with a beach towel lying around in his bathroom. I can't help but smile at the image of him in my head, his messy yet gorgeous self.

As I scroll through the budget airline prices, the thing holding me back is, when do I go? My biggest hesitation is my dad. I've been visiting him every day now, and surprisingly, it's been what's been getting me up in the morning. I never imagined this could happen. I don't want to leave him without at least having a plan. I even have a strategy notebook I picked up to figure out how to prove his innocence. Unfortunately, the pages are still blank. But my determination keeps me thinking, always thinking.

There's one thought that I have been forcing out of my head every time it creeps back in. It's a thought that my body is almost protecting me from. There is one person who could come up with the money for a plan, or rather the money for the lawyers. The one person whose presence might cause me an actual nervous breakdown.

I put down my phone with the flights still on the screen and pick up the strategy notebook and pen. I hold it open and stare at the blank pages and tap the pen on my forehead as if it can stimulate my thinking. After a few moments, I sigh and lay back down in my bed, covering my face with my comforter. What's the use of any of this? There's no way I can pull either of these things off. I'm not the type to follow through, instead, I remain paralyzed in endless indecision.

I'm startled by a knock on the door. I shove the comforter off of me and quickly sit up. My heart starts to race, no doubt a form of PTSD resulting from the abundance of unwanted surprises my life has been lately. I wait a moment in silence until there's another knock, a louder more desperate sound. I get up and head over to the peephole.

As soon as I see the jet-black curls and chilling side-profile of what could be a statue, my body boils with rage.

I swing open the door, ready to forcibly attack him, shove him off the railing, if I can manage it. But before I have a second to think, he stops all my thoughts with his words.

"Look, I know you want to kill me." He holds up his hands as if I'm about to arrest him. "Valletta, I know you need me." He says the words so confidently. "Before you freak out, just give me five minutes to explain. Just five minutes," he pleads, as I remain frozen.

Again, I'm a master at turning paralyzed.

"I'm here to help you. I have the resources to get your father out of jail. I know at the end of the day, helping him is what matters to you. I just need your help in return."

Everything around me is invisible. I remain focused on his eyes, steadying myself, calming my burning rage with determination. After all, this might be the only way.

"What do you need my help with?"

To Be Continued . . .

Thank you for reading!

Want the sequel? Please visit leahjoannewriter.com to grab a copy of **"Breaking Beneath Emerald Waves."**

It would mean the world to me if you would take a moment to leave a review. Reviews are the lifeblood to an Author and provide a way for other readers to find this book. Two of the most helpful platforms to leave a review are Goodreads and Amazon.

To keep up to date on future releases join my newsletter! You can sign up right on the home page of my website. leahjoannewriter.com

Acknowledgments

TO EACH AND EVERY reader: There is no one more vital to a writer than a reader. You not only took a journey with me through my mind, but you allowed these amazing characters a place in your heart. I can't wait to continue this adventure with you all. Thank you for lending your mind and heart to me.

To Beth, Cara, and Monika: You three paved the way for me to no longer be afraid of sharing this story with the world. Your enthusiasm and feedback made my heart fill with gratitude. Thank you for being the best Beta readers a girl could ask for. Beth, thank you for being an editor who believed in my story so much so that you gave it heartfelt time and attention. Love you all.

To my husband: I don't think I could ask for a more supportive husband. It's just not possible. You believe in me so genuinely. You came twice to San Diego just so I could do research for my book and you were fully present in every moment, brainstorming creative ideas the entire time. You push me with your advice, and you make sure that I am doing whatever I need to do so that I can be a successful author. But what I find the most comforting is how strongly you believe in this book. You fell in love with these characters, and the plot. That means more to me than anything else could as we travel this journey together.

To my mom: Mom, words could never be enough to express how I feel about your contributions with regards this book. You are the only one who was there from the very beginning, I mean all the way back to when I was a teenager and we used to sit in the back yard together as I read to you what I had written. You met Valletta before she was even Valletta, back when my story was a total mess, but you saw something in the run-on sentences and poorly developed characters. You saw the potential. You worked tirelessly with me in the re-writing process and you were the first person to read anything I wrote. At times your advice made me want to pull every strand of hair out of my head, and I listened screaming and kicking, determined to prove you wrong. But you were always right in the end, your suggestions took my story from a messy first draft, to what it is today. No ones gives me more time, attention, praise, and love than you. I owe you all the gratitude in the world.

About the author

Leah Joanne has many passions, but two of them have now become a necessary part of her life; writing and traveling. Fiction has always been Leah's coping mechanism of choice when life tastes sour. Traveling has opened her mind and heart. She combines those two passions to create a world for readers to escape to when they need to jump into a new life for an hour or two. Leah loves to entertain her readers while sneaking in powerful messages about complex human emotions. She writes with all heart and no fluff. Leah Joanne is currently working on her next novel, continuing to create worlds with compelling and additive characters. She takes her craft seriously, traveling with intention to the locations where her books take place, but sometimes she binges on of her favorite character dramas (as an excuse for more research and inspiration of course). You can't get more complex than Gilmore Girls after all.